Carole Morden is a wonderful new voice in fiction. Her debut novel is sure to please mystery fans everywhere. Don't miss it!

—best-selling author Norma Beishir

Carole Morden offers a well-paced, intriguing tale of brutal murder, hidden motives, and lingering mystery. From the opening prologue, her crisp, compact style pulls you in. Morden is a sharp-eyed observer who exposes the quirks of human nature and weaves subtle humor throughout her story of an "ordinary" pastor's wife drawn into extraordinary circumstances surrounding the death of a former high school classmate.

—Sam Collins, editor for Warner Press

An intriguing integration of a current murder and a thirty-year-old cold case. *Dry Bones'* twists and turns had me captivated from the beginning. It kept me guessing until the climactic ending.

—St. Louis' Images Agency

Carole Morden's debut novel is a page-turning mystery from beginning to end. Great heroine! Complex plot! Hopefully, Morden has a series on her hands.

—Jessica Ferguson, author of *The Last Daughter;*
staff writer for *Southern Writers Magazine*

Dry Bones will keep you guessing, as a pastor's-wife-turned-detective tries to solve a murder case in which she is the prime suspect. Carole Morden's debut novel will garner her lots of devoted fans—myself included!

—Kent Crockett, author of *The Sure Cure for Worry*
and *Slaying Your Giants*

An intriguing, fun read. Carole Morden gets the important things right. She deals with the difficult, dark realities of today while pointing to the way God works and heals. In addition to poking fun at traditional Christianity in a good natured way, she ministers to believer and non-believer alike.

—Karen Alexander, reading teacher, Kansas

Dry BONES

A Jamie Storm Novel

CAROLE MORDEN

*He led me back and forth among them, and I saw a great
many bones on the floor of the valley, bones that were very dry.
He asked me, "Son of man, can these bones live?"*

—Ezekiel 37:2–3

Dry Bones

© 2015 Carole Morden

Scripture taken from the HOLY BIBLE, NEW INTERNATIONAL VERSION,

Copyright © 1973, 1984 by International Bible Society. Used by permission of Zondervan Publishing House.

This is a work of fiction. Names, characters, businesses, places, events, and incidents are either the products of the author's imagination or used in a fictitious manner. Any resemblance to actual persons, living or dead, or actual events is purely coincidental.

Published by
Deep River Books
Sisters, Oregon
www.deepriverbooks.com

ISBN: 9781940269351
Library of Congress: 2015930305

Printed in the USA
Cover design by Jason Enterline

For John,
Muncher, Ethon, Levi
I couldn't breathe without you.

And in Loving Memory
Of my Dad
Fred Marjerrison

CONTENTS

PROLOGUE

Tuesday, thirty years ago

Dacia Stewart veered off the path winding through Mounds Park. Her fingers raked through cropped, black hair. Sweat beaded her forehead, and dark-brown eyes snapped in anger. When a wave of revulsion gripped her insides, she deposited the contents of her stomach behind a huge, maple tree. Wiping her mouth on her shirtsleeve, she eyed each park visitor with suspicion. Backing farther into the woods, she hoped no one had seen her get sick. It wasn't likely. Most people milled around the playground, watching their kids, enjoying the not yet humid May, and taking no thought of the drama unfolding around them. With shaking hands, she twisted the cap off the telephoto lens and focused sharply on the striking young blonde who had just arrived in the park.

Dacia let her mind wander for a moment. One more week of student teaching and she would be a full-fledged, high school, English teacher. Her applications had already gone to at least fifty townships in Indiana. Bloomington would be her first choice. It was home after all. She missed the rolling hills, fishing on Griffy Lake—her dad patiently teaching her how not to tip over the canoe—but mostly, she

9

missed her fiancé. Craig taught at Edgewood Middle School while taking classes for his masters at IU. He thought he would prefer being a principal to teaching. And he was willing to put off the wedding until she found a teaching position in Bloomington. Dacia objected. She wanted to get married now. The semester of student teaching in Anderson made her an enemy of distance, and she wasn't prepared to go another year without Craig. How she wished he were here now.

She turned her attention back to the teen she'd followed from Highland High. Still alone, the girl folded her arms across her chest, her fear palpable. Dacia's stomach cramped, but she swallowed hard. No time to get sick again. She needed every bit of courage she could muster to take the pictures that would give credence to the ugly story she had to tell. *Funny. If it weren't for Mom, I wouldn't be here.*

Dottie Stewart was deaf. Dacia grew up learning sign language, lip-reading, and body movements like most kids learn to speak. It was her second language, and she was fluent in it. She could interpret a raised eyebrow as easily as some people interpret their own spoken language. She could watch television with the sound turned down and understand the entire content of the show. And, as was the case this afternoon, she could stumble onto something that demanded stepping out of her teacher role to become both protector and whistle-blower. Could it have been just an hour ago?

It had been 3:30 and the final bell had rung. Glad chatter filled the halls—another day finished. Dacia maneuvered down the busy walkway toward the teachers' lounge in search of advice on a matter regarding a parent's criticism of her teaching methods. All classroom doors had windows in the upper half, a change demanded by the task force to prevent student violence. Ms. Perdue straightened music stands, Mr. B. stuffed papers into his briefcase, and Ms. Alexander hurried out the door.

At one classroom, Dacia stopped short. A teacher and student were engaged in what looked like a nasty confrontation. Dacia watched the teacher's lips move: threatening, demanding, and then insistent. He gripped the girl's thin arm and squeezed, his other hand tracing its way down her frightened face. Shame, revulsion, and panic passed through the young eyes—and finally, submission. Stunned, Dacia raced back to her own classroom to pick up her camera, thankful she was wearing flat shoes and slacks. She dug in her purse for the Anderson map and found the quickest route to Mounds Park—the forced rendezvous spot.

Dacia jolted back to the present. *Concentrate. He'll be in the park any minute now. Stay alert. Stop shaking.* The mantra continued in her head even as she scoured the park for any trace of the man.

Broadening the focus to include the area surrounding the young woman, Dacia was ready for the teacher to show up. Her camera wobbled. *Take slow, deep breaths.* If she didn't settle down, the photos would be of little value. It was the only way to prove what she had "overheard" this afternoon. Accusing a teacher of molesting a student was a serious charge, and she hoped the photos would protect the girl, her own job, and make sure nothing like this would ever happen again. Looking at her watch, she frowned. He should have been here already. Had she misread the time? Where was he?

A twig snapped behind her. She turned just as a thick, black crowbar swung toward her head. Dacia crumpled to the ground, murdered without uttering a sound.

CHAPTER ONE

Tuesday—Present Day

I feel compelled to tell you that you never suspect when your life will take a one-hundred-eighty-degree turn. You busy yourself with the mundane routine of living and then wham—right in the kisser, as Ralph Kramden would have said.

Today my routine consisted of baking pies for the annual church bake sale. I opened the oven door to check on the third set of pies. Five more minutes should do it. Gooey sugar sauce oozed out of the wheat-shaped cuts I'd sliced into the crusts. The aging, three-bedroom parsonage smelled of cinnamon and apples. Six pies already steamed on the table, and three more unbaked pies nestled on the flour-covered counter waiting their turn.

My name is Jamie Storm. I'm the pastor's wife of a small congregation in Great Falls, Montana, which is one hundred and twenty miles south of the Canadian border. It is the third largest city in Montana and still has only sixty thousand people.

Being a pastor's wife doesn't net me much coin, but it's a full-time job none the less. You can bet I'll be fodder for the gossip mill if I arrive with a paltry offering of baked goods. Not that the church women are mean. They just go all out for this annual sale.

It has quite a community following and at least fifteen tables would be full of cookies, cakes, breads, rolls, and candies. For a small church, we always outdo ourselves. The sales from this event generate enough income to provide the support for two overseas missionaries. I didn't want to disappoint the constituency, and twelve pies should keep tongues from wagging. No tarnished pastor's wife halo for me.

The phone's shrill ring interrupted my train of thought. Swiping flour-coated hands off on my faded Wranglers, I snatched the receiver off the hook by the fourth ring. With hardly a chance to say hello, the caller cut in, talking a mile a minute.

"The last pastor's wife only brought three dozen cookies to our bake sale. Three dozen cookies! Can you imagine? You can't send a missionary to Africa on three dozen cookies," snapped Abigail Thornbush, the nearly deaf and self-appointed conveyor of useful information. I could almost see her shaking her little, gray-bunned head in despair at the thoughtlessness of pastors' wives.

"Hello, Sister Thornbush. How are you today?" I forced a cheerfulness into my voice I didn't feel. I love the people in the church, including Abigail, but she has a knack for setting my teeth on edge. She's eighty-two, opinionated, and involved in everything that goes on in the church. My take? This woman could get on God's nerves.

Ignoring my attempt at small talk, Abigail continued in a conspiratorial whisper. "I'm not even sure they weren't store-bought. Store-bought! Can you imagine that?"

Sigh. "No, no, I really can't."

Clutching the phone between my left shoulder and chin, I pulled one of three bubbling pies out of the oven. Time to cut the conversation short.

"I'm baking pies so you needn't worry. No store-bought

cookies for me. But the timer just dinged so I need to let you go before I slop apple goop all over the oven. Bye, bye."

Without waiting for an answer, I dropped the receiver in its cradle. "I love you though," I muttered. That was my "Christian" way of saying, "You annoy me to no end."

I removed the baked pies from the oven, positioned the remaining three on the lower rack, and reset the timer for fifty-five minutes. Once again I wiped my hands on the multi-purpose jeans, thankful for washing machines.

Scraping the countertop with a dishcloth, I pushed bits of raw crust and flour into a pile. I cupped my left hand into a makeshift dustpan and slid the unused crumbs into it. Struggling with my sweet tooth, I tossed the makings of an excellent cinnamon-sugar snack into the garbage. Unfortunately, my thighs were already trying to split the seams of my size twelve jeans. I'd like to blame my weight gain on the numerous meals I ate in parishioners' homes—one of the many perks of being married to the preacher—but truth be told, restraint was not my strong suit. Nor was boring exercise.

The doorbell rang, saving me from further self-recriminations. I gave the countertop one more quick swipe and hoped it wasn't Abigail popping over to inspect the pies. She couldn't have gotten here that fast, could she? My T-shirt left a Hansel and Gretel trail of flour through the kitchen and living room as I brushed myself off, hurrying to open the front door.

Two Great Falls police officers stood on the porch steps. It took a minute to register what I was seeing. Then a sickening sensation rolled over me and settled in my gut. *David.* My heart pounded. I tried hard to quell the rising alarm I felt. No luck.

"What's wrong? Is it David? Has something happened to David?"

The older and heftier of the two cops pushed his way into the entry, looking around as he did so. Ignoring the rising panic in my voice, as well as my question, he said, "We just need to talk to you for a few minutes, ma'am. Can we come in?"

Despite my fear, I bristled at his boldness. "Looks like you're already in."

A lazy grin crossed the officer's face. I struggled not to slap him. Yeah, I know, not the proper response for a pastor's wife, but this guy didn't deserve proper. Instead, I repeated my question between tightly clenched teeth.

"Is David all right?"

"David?"

"My husband. He left for a fishing trip this morning." I could hear the strain in my voice.

"As far as we know, your husband is fine."

Relief washed over me for a few seconds before confusion set in. Police don't come to my door that often. Never, actually. If David was all right, I couldn't think of a single reason for their visit.

The burly, redheaded cop swaggered—seriously, it was a swagger—into the living room. "This is about Timothy Manter. You *do* know Mr. Manter, don't you, ma'am?"

His tone was so thick with insinuation I half expected him to hitch up his britches and sniffle condescendingly—Rosco P. Coltrane like. It sounded like a statement and not a question. I didn't bother to respond. His sidekick—young and with much better manners—removed his hat and stood on the porch looking apologetic and more than a little embarrassed.

Now that I knew David was okay, I regained a sense of calm. Curious about Tim Manter, but irritated at the unprofessional conduct of the officer, I snapped, "Please step outside until I see your badge. You seem to have forgotten what country we live in."

That wasn't a question either. I tried to match his insinuating tone. Not fazed, the beefy officer stepped back, rolling his eyes as he produced his badge. The younger one also held out his badge for inspection. Satisfied, I nodded.

"Well, Officers McCready and Johnson, please come in and have a seat."

I gestured toward the thirteen-year-old, faded blue couch. Years ago, I had pushed it against the wall to shore up the sagging back. My boys had used it for a wrestling mat, high hurdle, fort, and all-purpose gym. No amount of upholstery would fix it. David and I had planned to replace it with last year's Christmas bonus, but then Jake and Caleb, now in college, called from Anderson needing help with second-semester books and fees. Maybe next Christmas.

The officers sat.

"How can I help you?" The coldness in my voice almost surprised me. Almost. Friendliness was out of the question, even if my pastor's wife conscience was doing jumping jacks on my shoulder and shouting in my ear to be civil. This little guy usually got my attention when I felt like God's reputation was on the line, or the church's, or David's. I had to be extra peeved to ignore it. Evidently, McCready's rudeness, coupled with two minutes of sheer terror, made me extra peeved.

"Timothy Manter is dead."

My mind grappled for a response, but I couldn't believe what he had just said.

McCready's eyes never left my face. "He died two days ago in Anderson, Indiana. Gunshot." He relayed the information in a detached, matter-of-fact way as if the complexion of the world hadn't just drastically changed.

Gunshot? I felt the color drain from my face as I sank into a chair. "Tim? Dead?"

Johnson cleared his throat. "Obviously, you two were pretty close. We thought you might be able to shed some light on this." His voice sounded kind.

It took me a minute to process that. I clenched my jaw. The edge in my voice snapped back like a boomerang. "What are you implying, Officer? Tim and I were close, yes—thirty years ago. I haven't seen him since he left for college."

Officer Johnson smiled. "But you've kept in touch?"

I swallowed, then nodded. "E-mail, Christmas cards, that sort of thing. I was supposed to see him at our class reunion Friday."

"I just bet you were." McCready snorted. "If you haven't seen him since high school, why would he leave you his ten-million-dollar estate?"

"Wha—? What are you talking about?"

I felt like I was swirling down the rabbit hole. How could English suddenly sound so foreign to me? I jumped up and started pacing. I didn't know what to do with my fists. They clenched and unclenched as though they had a life of their own. I wanted to scream but didn't dare. I might never stop.

"The Anderson PD is investigating Manter's death," McCready continued. "Ten million dollars is one heck of a motive, don't you think?"

Tim, oh, Tim. My mind struggled to keep up, but it was failing.

Johnson jumped in, friendlier, not as caustic. "The Anderson Police Department called and asked us to talk to you. Manter left everything to you."

This must be the classic good cop/bad cop scenario.

"As I said, we haven't seen each other since high school. This doesn't make any sense." My mind reeled, trying to latch onto the reality that Tim was dead.

"Do you or your husband own any guns?"

More to myself than the officers, I said, "Who would kill Tim?"

"I couldn't really answer that question, ma'am, I just need to—"

I interrupted again, remembering something. "I have a friend on the force in Anderson. His name's Scott Walters. Call him. He'll tell you I had nothing to do with Tim's death."

"Walters is the officer who called us, ma'am." I felt a huge fist grab my insides and twist. "We need to see any firearms you own, get copies of bank statements dating back a year, phone records for the same period of time, and we need to know where you were on the morning of May 27. We'll check out your alibi and forward the bank statements and phone records to Anderson. If everything checks out, we'll be out of your hair in no time and you will be a very rich woman."

Scott Walters sent them after me? I wanted to laugh and scream all at the same time. This was as close to hysterical as I ever wanted to get. Things like this don't happen to a pastor's wife. You go to church, you come home, you help with the Easter pageant, you bake pies for bake sales, and you teach Sunday school, for Pete's sake! You don't become a suspect in a friend's murder, and you sure don't become a millionaire overnight. You don't even become a thousandaire. You're lucky to score a parsonage as part of the pay package.

Officer Johnson tried again. "About the guns, ma'am?"

I took a deep breath and rubbed my temples. I needed to stay calm. What would David do? I'd never seen a situation that could unnerve him as completely as I was unnerved now. Why did this happen now while he was away?

David had left town this morning for a fishing trip to Alaska. The trip had been planned since I told him about my class reunion. He dutifully offered to attend with me, but I declined. I knew his heart wasn't really in it. Besides, I reasoned, I would be busy with old classmates, and he rarely got away except for the occasional preaching seminar or denominational meeting. A fishing trip might be just the relaxation he needed.

For the last three months, my husband had been under incredible stress. The chairperson of the trustees' board had started picking apart his sermons. The church's youth pastor had died in a horrendous car accident, leaving behind a young wife and two small boys. And his mother had been diagnosed with breast cancer. His usual whistling in the morning had fallen silent. He planned on being gone for a week, and I didn't want to spoil it for him.

All he needed now was a wife accused of murder. I glanced at my Seiko, a fifteenth anniversary present from David. He had spent more than we could afford, but I loved it. Thankfully, it was too late to reach him. By now he'd be thirty-nine thousand feet in the air somewhere over Canada.

"Did we lose you, Mrs. Storm? May 27? Guns?" McCready's mouth curled into a cocky grin.

I suppressed the sarcastic comeback that immediately popped into my head. Instead, I barked out the information like a drill sergeant giving orders. "Of course we own guns. This is Montana. On May 27, I was teaching a women's class at 9 a.m. At 10:30, church started and I was listening to my husband preach a sermon on how the church could experience God corporately. On Monday

I cleaned house, ran errands, bought groceries, and today I'm baking pies. I can give you a list of the people in the Bible study."

"Phone numbers too," McCready said.

"House smells good," Johnson said to no one in particular.

McCready and I both ignored him.

"I haven't been in Anderson since January 15 when I took my two youngest boys back to school after their Christmas break. They go to the university there and live with my mother. In case you don't have a map handy, it's a twenty-six hour drive to Anderson. I couldn't have been there on the twenty-seventh, killed Tim, and gotten back here to teach Sunday school." I made no attempt to disguise the sarcasm that fell heavily on the last sentence.

McCready changed the subject, but not his derisive tone. "You said you e-mailed Manter. Care if we take a peek at your computer?"

Johnson winced.

Enough already. "I think you need a search warrant for that." I didn't really care one way or another if they looked at my e-mails, but McCready's barely veiled accusations really irked me. "Add the bank statements, guns, and phone bills to the warrant too."

Flipping through the pages of the church directory, I hastily scribbled down the names and phone numbers of the Sunday school class participants, and then with a flourish, I handed the list to Johnson, pointedly ignoring McCready's meaty, outstretched hand.

"Now I need to check my pies, and unless I'm under arrest, you know the way to the door."

CHAPTER TWO

Turning my back on McCready and Johnson, I stomped into the kitchen before I went into full-scale meltdown. A moment later the front door slammed. I slumped into the nearest kitchen chair and exhaled a deep breath. Apple pies? Apple pies were the least of my worries. If the church's resident busybodies wanted fodder for gossip, now would be the time to fill up their buckets.

I tried to clear my head. The wall clock ticked off the seconds and then minutes as if it was business as usual. I wanted to scream that nothing was the same. Tim was dead. Not just dead—murdered. I was no longer a pastor's wife. I was a suspect, a suspect in a murder case. Somewhere in the distance I heard a phone ring. Probably Abigail Thornbush with more bake sale wisdom. Just what I *didn't* need.

Snatching the phone off the hook, I hissed, "Abigail, I don't have time for this right now." *Go away!*

"Hello, is this Jamie Louise Waymire Storm?" Not waiting for a response, the masculine voice continued. "This is Stephen Prager of the Prager, Prager, and Adams law firm in New York. My firm represents Timothy Manter."

My knuckles whitened, tightening around the receiver.

"Hello?" The male voice asked again.

"Um, yes, this is Jamie Storm," I said, stammering over the words.

"I don't know if you are aware of it, but Mr. Manter was killed early Sunday morning—shot to death." The voice paused before continuing. "I am deeply sorry for your loss—and ours. Tim was a valued client of the firm's. He left strict instructions that in the event of his death, we were to hand deliver a package to you. My plane arrived in Great Falls late last night. I'm at the Sheraton. Could we meet today at your home?"

Could this day get any weirder? I sighed. "Sure. Come on over." I gave him directions to the parsonage and hung up.

Distracted by thoughts of Tim, I switched to autopilot, wiping the remaining flour and bits of stuck-on piecrust off the counters. The kitchen timer interrupted my turbulent thoughts, reminding me to take the last of the pies out of the oven. Pies. It seemed like a year ago since I'd put them in the oven. I had finished the cleanup and tossed the rolling pin on the top shelf of the dishwasher when the doorbell rang. A pavilion of butterflies fluttered in my stomach.

I opened the door to a tall man who smiled and offered me his business card. Stephen Prager. He stood six feet four, at the least, with salt-and-pepper hair, and smelled of 212 Cologne. His snowy-white mustache was neatly trimmed. Dressed in jeans, a red plaid, long-sleeved shirt, and cowboy boots, he looked more like a ranch hand than an attorney.

"Come on in." I led the way to the butcher-block dining table and pulled out a spindle-back chair for him, then took the seat across from him.

"Mmm. I haven't smelled anything that good since I was a little boy. Pies?"

"Apple. Church bake sale." I picked at the table with my thumbnail. A man in my house from a New York law firm, Tim dead, David gone. I wanted to wake up to my normal, boring life.

"Churches still doing fund-raisers? It's been a long time since I've gone to church." I sat motionless and said nothing, hoping he would get to the point. He didn't. "Is May always this cool in Montana?"

Making small talk was the last thing I wanted to do right now. Under normal circumstances, fine, but chatting about weather and church fund-raisers now seemed absurd.

"It varies. Listen, can I get you a piece of pie or a cup of coffee?" My voice held all the warmth of a frost-covered iceberg. It clearly conveyed toe-tapping, arms folded impatience.

He looked at his watch. Regret laced his voice. "Sounds tempting, but I have a flight to catch."

He opened the briefcase and handed me an envelope with my name scrawled on it in Tim's handwriting. The next thing he pulled out of the case was a bulging, manila, clasp envelope sealed with clear packing tape. It also had my name on it. He set it on the table, then handed me a check for $25,000 drawn on the firm's account.

Okay, yes, the day could get weirder.

I was shocked. *Twenty-five thousand dollars?* I examined the check. My mind refused to make sense of it. I took in a slow, deep gulp of air. I looked at the amount again and took another deep breath. I couldn't speak.

"The money is from Tim. He put it in a special account just two weeks ago."

"But I . . ." The question wouldn't formulate.

Prager checked his watch. "Maybe I'll take that cup of coffee after all."

I walked over to the coffee pot and pulled a mug out of the cupboard. This I understood. I could do this. Getting coffee. Serving a neighbor. Perfect sense in a world that suddenly made no sense at all.

"Are you all right?" Prager asked.

I nodded. Huge lie, but it seemed like the only response to make.

"Maybe he had a premonition or something, because he wanted the check and package in your hands as soon as humanly possible if he died. He was very explicit about that. The rest of his estate, of course, will take time to process."

I handed a mug of black coffee to the attorney. "Of course," I mumbled.

"He was a good man." Prager wrapped his hands around the mug and took a sip of coffee. I hoped he liked it black.

I nodded absently. "I know. Thirty years. I haven't seen Tim for thirty years. Why me?"

Prager shrugged. "Maybe the answer is in the letter." He took another sip of coffee.

I looked at the envelope, but left it untouched on the table.

He glanced at his watch again and scooted back his chair. "Gotta go." Pulling a single sheet of paper out of the briefcase, he handed it to me. "Just a receipt saying you got the items I gave you."

I signed it and pushed it back to him. He stood up and offered his hand. I shook it.

"One more question. Um, I don't exactly know how to say this, but the police were just here. I'm a suspect in Tim's murder." Prager waited for me to explain. "I was wondering . . . could you represent me if I need it? I don't know any attorneys here."

"I'm not a criminal lawyer, but I can put you in touch with one. Don't worry, Mrs. Storm. I knew Tim and he was a good judge of character." He took a card case from his shirt pocket and removed a card. "Here's the name of an attorney in our firm. She's one of the best." He wrote the name on the back of his card, handing it to me on his way out the door.

I nodded my thanks, still too dumbfounded by the money to say much.

He turned back around. "In the meantime, don't talk to the police and make sure they have a search warrant if they come back."

CHAPTER THREE

After Prager left, I slid the deadbolt in place and unplugged the phone. I walked around the table, taking several deep breaths. Picking up the envelope with my name on it, I flipped it over. Slowly, almost reverently, I peeled back the flap. Afraid of what it would say. Afraid of what it wouldn't say. I recognized Tim's boyish handwriting, a cross between cursive and printing.

> *My dearest Jamie,*
>
> *Hey there. I guess if you're reading this I'm no longer alive, but I wanted to explain why I left my estate to you. Estate!!! Back when we were in high school, I don't think any of us thought we would have an estate. You might think you understand why I didn't have a family—that I was too busy making money—but that's not completely true. Or at least it didn't start out that way. I was in love with you, Jamie. I think I loved you from the first day we met after school when I answered your ad in the Tartan to start a Mystery Club. Remember?*

For anyone interested in starting a mystery club, we will begin by discussing the clues surrounding the Son of Sam case. Please meet me after school by the flagpole.

Jamie Waymire—Freshman

29

Being a part of the Cliffhangers was the best part of my life. I didn't realize how quickly four years could fly by. I was so shocked when you married right out of high school that I buried myself in my work. Still, as we have kept in touch and I've gotten to know David and the boys through your eyes and heart, I have such thankfulness that you married him. You seem happier than anyone I know—more settled, more at peace.

You know that I have never embraced the God thing as you have, but I respect how you and David live your lives, how you have raised your boys, and your values. Please use this inheritance in any way you like, even if it is to live in deepest, darkest Africa as a missionary. Pay off your boys' school loans, buy a house, buy a block of houses, whatever, but know that I trust you implicitly and I couldn't think of a better way to spend my resources than to give them to you.

I never quit loving you, Jamie. David's a lucky man. Have fun and as you would say, God bless.

Tim

I broke down and cried then. Cried for my friend Tim, cried that I'd never known his heart, cried that he never knew my God, cried that he was killed, cried that I was a suspect, and cried that David was not here to hold me. Life was full of twists and turns, and on this day, mine had more twists and turns than I could handle. I sobbed until the tears were gone and my breathing came in occasional, short gasps. Fatigue spread through my body. I forced myself to tamp down my emotions. Self-pity would accomplish nothing. I had to do something. An idea slowly took shape.

Looking at the $25,000 check, I said, "God bless you, Tim."

I wiped my nose on my shirtsleeve. Abigail Thornbush would not approve. And at this moment I didn't care.

The phone book held a handwritten list of names and numbers that I seldom used. Now I needed those numbers. The note taped to the inside cover of the Great Falls directory listed six people, all under the heading of Cliffhangers. Plugging the phone back in, I called the first four people on the list and told them the story. I crossed off Tim's name and then placed the last phone call, the one that would be the hardest.

"Yeahhh?"

"Rachel, is that you? This is Jamie. Jamie Waymire from high school."

"Chammie. Chammie Waymire?" She stretched the words out like she was enrolled in a Hooked on Phonics course. Ahh—the joys of excessive alcohol consumption.

The slurred response didn't take me by surprise, but I hoped she would hear what I said. "I've got bad news, Rache. Remember Tim Manter? He's dead."

"Dead?"

"He was killed two days ago."

"Wha—how?"

"I'm going to Anderson to talk to the police. Since our class reunion is this weekend, I want to get the old gang together on Thursday night to talk."

"Tim's dead?" Rachel's voice slurred.

"I need you guys." I lowered my voice. "The police think I may have killed him."

"What?" Although her response was much slower, Rachel's shock mirrored the rest of the Cliffhangers.

"I need your help."

"Why? I can't do anything."

"Listen, Rache, I'll come and get you. I'll fly to Philly, and we can go to Anderson together."

"Uh huh."

"David's on a fishing trip. I can't tell the church people I'm a suspect in a murder case, and you've got the best computer skills of any of us. You could hack into the Vatican's network if you wanted. Tim's murderer is out there. We just need to find him."

I sounded desperate. I *was* desperate. Rachel had computer knowledge, skills, and software that I needed if I was going to find Tim's killer.

There was a brief silence on the other end of the phone. She still resisted. "I don't have the money. I can't do it. I can—maybe I can help from here."

"I've got the money. I'll pay for your ticket, the motel, everything. I really need you. Please, just pack what you have. I'll be there tomorrow to pick you up."

I hung up without another word. Rachel would have to tell me no in person . . . *if* she could face me and still say no.

I hopped into the shower and let the hot water massage my back. Any other day it would feel like heaven, but today it was just a shower. Finally, the knotted muscles in my neck and shoulders relaxed. I made a mental list of what I had to do before I left in the morning. Change my flight to arrive in Philadelphia instead of Anderson and buy an extra ticket for Rachel. Take Tim's check to the bank and get cash for the trip—plenty of cash. Pack for at least a week. And pray. Seriously pray. I wasn't sure anyone but God could get me out of this mess. I wasn't sure what the cops would say when they found out I'd left town. Hopefully, they wouldn't think it made me guilty.

◆◆◆◆◆

At the fund-raiser that night, Abigail just couldn't let herself compliment my pies.

"Well, dearie, not everyone likes apple pies, you know. It would be nice to offer a variety to our customers, but I suppose we'll just make do. Your crust seems a little thin—probably not enough flour. I just hate pies that fall apart the minute you take them out of the tins. Oh well, young people like you will never learn the art of making a flaky piecrust. It takes a little work to be a good cook, you know, and today most people can't wait for the microwave to heat up water, let alone learn to make a good crust. It doesn't work to just slap ingredients together and hope for the best. It's about finesse in baking a good crust—just like in bridge—a little finesse goes a long way."

With that, she'd gone over to inspect Natalie Edwards' brownies. I rolled my eyes and considered the source. Could I just say here that I am forty-eight years old? Not sixteen. Maybe in Abigail's mind, I was "today's youth," but give me a break. If eye rolling had a sound, you would have just heard it.

The evening sale netted the ladies group $1,678 and some odd change.

After the fund-raiser, I dragged myself through the front door, pulled off my shoes, and threw my coat on the end of the couch, relieved the bake sale was over.

Pulling a Dr Pepper out of the fridge and downing a big gulp, I sat down at the table and held the can to my forehead. An overwhelming sense of inadequacy swept over me. Not only about Tim, or about my life, but my role in life—the spouse of a pastor. It's like I was supposed to be this person who is all loving, all understanding, never has a bad day, keeps an impeccable house, and quotes Scripture as a pastime. That was so not like me.

What I really wanted to do with Abigail's critical spirit was pitch it out the window—with her. Instead, I pretended her little jabs didn't hurt, smiled indulgently at her *helpful hints*, and took pies to a church fund-raiser even though my life had shattered into a million pieces just three hours ago. God's sense of humor, I suppose—having someone like me fall in love with a preacher. I didn't know if the joke was on the congregation or me.

Sighing, I emptied the contents of the manila envelope on the table. There were some handwritten notes, a newspaper clipping, and a file folder with the label STEWART, DACIA—05/25/85. Excitement surged through me. I recognized the name. Ms. Stewart had been a student teacher during my last semester of school. She had disappeared the final week before graduation, and the Cliffhangers met a couple of times trying to figure out what happened. We came up empty. Why did Tim have this file? I would save it to read on the long flight to Pennsylvania. I picked up the newspaper clipping from my hometown paper, the *Herald-Bulletin*. The article, a few scant paragraphs, was accompanied by a picture of Mounds Park.

Anderson Police Chief Burke Thompson made the grim announcement today that the skeletal remains of a human body were found Tuesday afternoon in Mounds Park.

Crime scene investigators have identified the bones as those of Dacia Stewart, a former student teacher, who was reported missing on May 25, 1985. Cause of death is not yet known, although preliminary reports indicate blunt force trauma to the head. The skull appears to have been crushed.

Anderson police treated Stewart's disappearance as a missing persons' case at the time, but the case is now considered a homicide. The bones were discovered exactly thirty years to the day that Stewart went missing.

The deceased's parents, long-time Bloomington residents Chuck and Dottie Stewart, took the news stoically. Mr. Stewart said, "Now maybe the police will take us seriously. Our daughter was murdered, and we want some answers. Thirty years and we still love and miss her like it was yesterday."

CHAPTER FOUR

Wednesday

I stared out the window of the Boeing 747, barely seeing the Montana topography below. My thoughts centered on how to convince Rachel to come to Anderson. Her dependence on alcohol had intensified through the years, and I wasn't sure where I stood with her. In high school she would have done anything for me or the other Cliffhangers. But this wasn't high school.

Rachel King was beautiful—at least back in the day. Long, natural blonde hair, generous mouth, ice-blue eyes, and Marilyn Monroe legs. Her complexion was pale, almost milky, and as clear as a newborn's. In school she'd been the envy of every girl and the unobtainable prize for every boy. She didn't use makeup, wore baggy out-of-style clothes, and still managed to look better than the rest of us. She was the smartest of the Cliffhangers and had an ingenious way of looking at things—sort of upside-down and inside-out. She rarely smiled, but when she did, it felt like a gift. And when she smiled, it was always about beating someone at Pac Man or any of the new computer games that were all the rage back in the day. Nothing else seemed to bring her much joy.

When she graduated, her mother surprised her with an IBM personal computer, modem, and printer. It was the talk of the graduating class because her parents had no money. How they could afford the computer no one knew. Rachel was the happiest I had ever seen her when she packed her bags to fly to Philly to the Citrone Institute. The computer-training school had just opened its doors, and Rachel planned on a career with the then intimidating machines. Now everyone and their brother had one, even me, but she could make a computer sing.

I caught myself smiling, thinking back to how surprised everyone was when *Time* magazine picked "The Computer" as the Person of the Year for 1982. As a sophomore in high school, it didn't mean much to me, but it was all Rachel talked about.

The short layover in Salt Lake City allowed enough time to dash into a restroom before boarding the next flight. The lighting above the mirror emphasized why cosmetic companies were in business. Too lazy to apply makeup at five-thirty this morning, I had to take advantage of the stop. I gave my shoulder-length hair a few quick brushstrokes before pulling it back into a ponytail. Strands of gray mingled with the chestnut brown, giving me a dappled appearance. Good in horses, not so good in humans. I leaned in closer to look at the crow's feet around my eyes. Aging—what a wonderful invention. I shrugged off the thought and applied some olive shadow to my eyelids. It brought out the green highlights in my hazel eyes and made me feel younger.

Chasing fifty, I was starting to look like my mother—short and slightly overweight. I say slightly because it sounds good, but my driver's license recorded my heft as thirty pounds north of my bridal weight. But after all, I reasoned, I had birthed four children. People couldn't expect me to stay slender forever, except maybe Sister Thornbush.

Once she said to me, "You know, dearie, I think it would be wise to quit eating so much. You're starting to look like those women who sit around eating bonbons all day. You don't want the congregation to think you're lazy, do you? I remember one pastor's wife. Oh my goodness, she was large. Large, I tell you. I don't really know why we kept them on. Sloth is a sin, and the Good Book makes no bones about it. A person doesn't gain weight bustling about doing the Lord's work. No siree. No time to fill the ol' spare tire when you're doing God's business."

I bought a Dr Pepper, stashed it in my purse, and headed down concourse B to gate 33. Although much larger than Great Falls International, the Salt Lake City airport was easy to navigate, and I had no trouble catching my next plane. I was anxious to check out the police file that Tim had been working on.

After reaching cruising altitude, the seat-belt sign blinked off, the flight attendant brought me a cup of ice for my Dr Pepper, and I opened the file. Although I'd never read a police report before, this one seemed to be devoid of any hard facts.

The police had questioned the entire faculty at Highland High School and many students. The only real facts listed were what the Cliffhangers had already known at the time.

On the day Dacia Stewart failed to show up for school, someone purporting to be her brother called in, said she was sick with the flu, and didn't know when she would be back. When the police spoke with her family, they discovered she didn't have a brother. Her locked car was found later in the parking lot at Mounds Park. It was towed to the police impound and dusted for prints, but only Dacia Stewart's prints were found.

The media reported the police had set up a hotline for anyone who had been at the park on May 25 to call police headquarters.

More than fifteen people responded and were interviewed, but no one had seen anyone fitting Dacia's description.

Tim had highlighted four names of people the police had questioned more than once. Evidently, he was planning on talking to them. I wrote their names in my journal.

The police report concluded that lack of evidence suggested she'd left town of her own free will. Plenty of people just checked out on their lives, and the APD presumed Dacia Stewart ran away with the guy who pretended to be her brother. Although the elder Stewarts from Bloomington strongly disagreed, the case was closed. *And now reopened.*

I glanced at my watch before pulling my overnight case out of the bin above my head. It was 4:42 p.m. The flight was eight minutes late, but that was not much of a problem since I hadn't asked Rachel to meet me.

I disembarked from Delta flight 1930 at the Philadelphia International Airport and followed the arrows to baggage claim to retrieve the rest of my luggage. Luckily, several cabs were parked at curbside. My inability to read a map, complemented by absolutely no sense of direction, excluded me from renting a car in cities I was unfamiliar with. Philadelphia fit that bill. The cabbie tossed my luggage in the trunk, and I gave him Rachel's address and settled back for the ride.

Looking at me in the rearview mirror, the cabbie asked, "You sure? That's a rough neighborhood."

"I'm sure."

"That ain't no part of town for a single woman to be in," he insisted. I didn't recognize his accent, but it was understandable enough.

"Just take me there."

The driver shrugged his shoulders in a don't-come-crying-to-me-when-you-get-mugged attitude, then shoved the gearshift into drive and pulled into traffic.

I sure wished I'd brought my Taser. The stun gun was a gag gift from David on my birthday. The card had read, "To be used on any and all board members, at anytime, anywhere but especially during annual business meetings."

I'd laughed until my sides ached when I pulled it out of the package. Mandatory attendance at annual church business meetings was another part of the pastor's wife's job I hated. I seldom—if ever—came home without a headache. Not only did mean-spirited arguments take place with normally rational human beings, but I had to keep my mouth shut too. That was the tough part.

For instance, I remember Brother Eddy's long-winded diatribe about hymns versus choruses:

"Our young people are losing all doctrinal teaching with these new-fangled choruses. And no, I am not going to call them praise songs. That's just trying to dress up an ugly duckling with swan feathers, and by George, someone has to stand up for the truth. They are choruses, plain and simple—repetitive and boring. With a hymn you get four verses with different words in every verse. The verses tell a story you can sink your teeth into. Not these choruses. You just sing the same words over and over again to a tune that doesn't even flow. And there aren't any notes either. How are you supposed to learn a song without notes? That's what I want to know. I can tell you God is not pleased. He is not pleased at all with this new-fangled music. I will tell you this, there won't be choruses in heaven, I am sure of that."

ZZZAP. I grinned, remembering the amount of mental zapping I did at the annual meeting just two weeks ago. But I went home without a headache and a more cheerful outlook on the whole proceeding. I looked forward to telling David who got zapped with my imaginary Taser and why.

From then on, it had been a private joke between David and me. Now I wished I'd packed the real thing in my checked baggage. I had been to Rachel's apartment once before when David had attended an evangelistic conference in Philly. The driver didn't need to tell me what kind of neighborhood it was in. I knew only too well.

CHAPTER FIVE

August 27, 1964

The smell of hot-buttered popcorn permeated the air. Kids were scattered around tables doing homework or eating snacks. Supervisors bent over them to help with math, English, and science. Now was the perfect time. The adults would never notice the five-minute absence of a little kid. Especially a kid that never caused trouble.

It was the bird's fault. If he hadn't opened his stupid mouth this wouldn't have to happen. Why did birds talk anyway? Stupid bird . . . he brought this on himself.

The rooms in the big, rambling house were built in dormitory style with sparse furnishings. Each room held two bunk beds, one desk, and one overhead light with a bare bulb. A long string attached to the light fixture that even the youngest could reach dangled down in the middle of the room, which was good.

A quick glance both ways revealed the coast was clear. It would be a cinch to get in and out of the room without being spotted. The room itself was like every other room—small. This one didn't have a window, although some did. The walls didn't look like home. They were plain and bare. A cramped walkway littered with dirty socks, *underwear, and shirts was centered between the bunk beds. What a pigsty. The bunks were pushed flush against the east and west walls, each equipped with a pillow, a sheet, and a quilt. Nothing matched the mustard-yellow walls.*

Anger built up like a tornado forming in a black sky. A vicious kick hurled dirty clothes out of the way. This wasn't home. It would never be home. Everything had happened too fast. Life wasn't fair! It took major control to resist the urge to slam a fist through the wall. Why did Mama and Daddy have to die? They didn't have any right to just leave without saying good-bye.

Another stupid thing—books. Stupid happy-ever-after endings. Endings weren't like that at all. The Velveteen Rabbit was a stupid book. Who did it belong to anyway? And if they liked it so much how come they left it lying around? It felt good to rip it apart. First one page and then another and another, until all the pages lay torn and scattered on the disheveled floor in the midst of the dirty clothes. There. Much better. The anger wasn't as strong anymore, but it was still hard to think. It was hard to know what to do, but Petey had to be taken care of. There wasn't much time left.

The small birdcage sat on the cheap desk with the parakeet happily perched by his birdseed. He was pretty. Not boring brown like some birds. Petey had a sky-blue body with a yellow head streaked with black. He looked at the torn book and squawked. He hopped around in the cage like he was mad about something. What right did he have to be mad? He chirped loudly and it was harder to think. His squawks got faster and louder and his wings fluttered with excitement. He needed out of the cage.

"Hey, Petey. Want out of your cage?"

No answer . . . just more screeching.

"You have to promise to sit on my hand. You can't fly away. Okay?"

Petey didn't squawk this time, only looked around with interest.
"Good boy."

It wasn't hard to get the metal double doors to swing open or to turn Mr. Pointer finger into a perch. "Good Petey."

Petey chirped loudly.

"Shhh. They might hear you. We can't have that. You already talk too much."

Louder chirping.

"Stop it, stop it, stop it! Why can't you just be quiet?" The bird had to be silenced. Besides, no one else had a bird in their room. It wasn't fair.

The feathers around Petey's neck were soft to touch. It felt good to squeeze them. His little beak opened in panic, but no sound came out. His vocal chords must have quit working. He really squirmed and fought. He tried to flap his wings, too, but wings are no match against people hands. Especially strong hands, even though the teacher always said how small they were. Teachers always said stupid stuff.

Petey's tiny, black eyes bulged out of their sockets. Still the crushing, pinching, wringing had to continue until the bird didn't move. What a good feeling when Petey finally stopped squirming. The teacher called those feelings warm fuzzies. One last hard squish. A long, blue tail feather drifted gently to the floor, resting on a crumpled torn picture of the Skin Horse. Wonder what the teacher would say now?

Placing the bird back in the cage so he looked like he was snoozing took too much time. It was better to just throw him in. The sooner he was found the better, and maybe—just maybe—a lesson would be learned.

Hopefully, there was some popcorn left.

CHAPTER SIX

anding the driver an extra twenty, I hesitated for a moment, then asked, "Can you give me ten minutes?"

He shrugged indifferently, took the money, and put it in his shirt pocket. "Sure."

With a prayer on my lips and luggage in hand, I walked toward the rundown apartment complex. Groups of tattooed, body-pierced, chains-dangling-from-belt-loops teens clustered on cracked sidewalks. Dusty weeds reached for the sun through crumbled cement steps. Graffiti marked the walls with both artistic and angry strokes. Cigarette smoke permeated the air, and various music boxes warred with each other for airspace.

A lone rapper yo-ed and ohh-like-dat-ed to the beat of a drum I failed to see. His cap lay upside down at his feet, catching any tips coming his way, as he continued to chant his own mix of coded jargon. His jeans rode low on his skinny, little frame. In point of fact, they would hang loose on a sumo wrestler. His boxer shorts displayed tiny little red and pink hearts on a white background. Something about him brought out the mother in me, and I dropped a five in the Sixers' hat.

It was hot. Ninety-one degrees according to the Delta pilot who cheerfully shared the information from the comfort of his air-conditioned cockpit before his passengers departed.

I hurried up the steps and into the building.

The poorly lit hallway in the Fairfield Apartment Complex smelled musty with just a hint of urine. Muffled laughter emanated from the door on my left. I carefully stepped over a fly-covered piece of pizza. It had long since passed its prime. No trouble losing weight here. Just step out your door and take a whiff.

A black spider scuttled across the floor angry at the invasion of his personal smorgasbord. Chills ricocheted up and down my spine. Spiders creep me out. Fear factor-wise, they are far worse than snakes. Throw me in a den of rattlesnakes, and I could fight my way out, but put me in a room with one spider and the terror would paralyze me. Killing them is futile. They simply come back to life and burrow into your brain. It's what spiders do.

Relief flooded me at the sight of door number eleven. After knocking twice and getting no answer, I tried the door. It pushed open easily. This wasn't a good sign. I stuck my head inside and whispered, "Rachel, you here? Rachel? Can I come in?" No answer.

I stepped through the door, stomach churning with trepidation. Dirty clothes, old newspapers, and empty food containers littered the small room. No furniture except for two folding chairs, an oblong table—the kind in church fellowship halls everywhere—and a tattered, black, beanbag chair. The table held state-of-the-art computer equipment, so I felt secure in locking the door behind me. If someone had broken in to rob the place, the computer equipment would be gone. It was the only thing of value that I could see. Kicking clothes and Styrofoam containers out of my path, I walked into the bedroom and in a loud voice called out, "Rachel, it's me. Are you here?"

The mattress on the floor had a lump of bedding on it that hadn't seen a washing machine in weeks. The stench of stale alcohol permeated the pile. I took a deep breath of air through my mouth. Pulling the covers back revealed a mass of oily, tangled, blonde hair.

"Come on, Rache, wake up. I need to talk to you."

Rachel's eyes flickered open and then closed again.

Putting my hands under Rachel's armpits, I dragged her to the bathroom. My passed out, skin-and-bones friend proved harder to move than I envisioned. With much grunting and groaning, I heaved her over the lip of the tub. I turned the water on full blast—cold. Rachel whimpered at the first sting of chilly water, but couldn't find the energy to move.

Wrenching the shower curtain closed, I felt sick to my stomach. How could Rachel sink so low? Why was she living in housing that wreaked of vomit and urine? And where was the church in all this mess? Where were all the Christians? Oh yeah, we were discussing the bigger issues of hymns versus praise songs and whether pre-, post-, or millennialism is closest to the truth. I was angry with the church, angry with Rachel, but mostly angry with myself. Forget about the church, where was I? Back in Montana with my happy little home and comfortable life while Rachel lived in squalor.

Anger and housecleaning go together, at least for me. The parsonage is always cleanest after David and I have a disagreement. Silly, but the madder I get the more productive I become. First, I pried open the windows to air out the place. Checking under the kitchen sink, I found a treasure trove of cleaning products. Windex, Pine-Sol, Endust, and Ultra-flex Hefty garbage bags sat happily unused under a thick layer of dust.

Grabbing a large garbage bag, I tackled the front room with a vengeance, stuffing filthy clothes, molded food, and empty beer cans into it. Within a few minutes, three garbage sacks bulged at the seams, so I attacked the bedroom. Cleaning doesn't take long when you throw almost everything away. I scrubbed the floors until they gleamed.

After several trips to the dumpster, the two rooms looked livable. The only thing left was computer equipment, chairs, table, and a soiled mattress. And if I'd been strong enough, the mattress would have been dragged to the trash too.

My rage finally spent, I walked into the bathroom and opened the shower curtain. Rachel sat under the stream of running water, knees pulled up to her chest, arms wrapped tightly around her legs, and head down. She was shivering and crying, rocking back and forth, but not making any attempt to move. I turned the water to warm and drizzled Pantene Pro-V onto her head. Scrubbing with a gentleness I hadn't shown the kitchen floor, I shampooed her hair.

"It's your turn now, girlfriend. Time to rinse."

Handing her the bar of soap and a clean washcloth from my suitcase, I said, "You need to get undressed and finish showering. Throw your clothes outside the curtain. I'm going to clean in here a bit."

Rachel didn't say a word, but she pulled the curtain shut. Sodden clothes plopped over the edge of the tub to the floor, creating a huge puddle on the filthy, linoleum floor.

I tossed the sopping wet apparel into yet another garbage bag and scoured the dingy, porcelain sink. It looked better, but still couldn't be called white by any means. The toilet required extra elbow grease. The small mirror, hanging on a rusted nail above the sink, had water spots on its water spots. I decided to wipe it down later. Rachel's hair brush, comb, toothbrush, and paste perched on the toilet tank in a plastic bowl, which I scrubbed clean. I added Pine-Sol to the water puddle and mopped the floor. Fetching a towel and clean clothes from my suitcase, I laid them on the toilet lid and spoke to Rachel through the curtain.

"I'll be back in a few minutes, and you need to be ready to go."

"What? Go where? I am *not* going anywhere with you. You can't make—" I shut the bathroom door, cutting off her defiant response.

At least her words weren't slurred. She must have sobered up.

Walking outside and up to the nearest group of young men, I said, "Does anybody want to make fifty bucks?"

Insolent stares.

"I need two strong guys who can carry a lice-infested mattress to the dumpster. I have fifty bucks you can split. Any volunteers?" I waved the money over my head so they could see I meant business.

"Hey, I know what we can do on the mattress, lady. You won't even have to pay me." This out of the mouth of a young man probably not more than thirteen. Still his words and accompanying Michael Jackson gesture brought a chorus of laughter to the group.

I gave him my best, it's-prayer-time, close-your-eyes-NOW glare that I generally reserved for the twelve-year-olds who sat in front of my pew on Sunday. If I intimidated him, he was reluctant to show it.

I repeated the offer. Two guys, who should have been in high school, shrugged and glared at me, but followed me up the walk amidst a refrain of jeers and sexual innuendos. I rolled my eyes at the tough-guy boys, trying so hard to be men. I walked with feigned confidence—like I paid people every day to remove bedding from crummy apartments. It was a bit more bravado than I felt, but I couldn't let them know I was scared. Once inside, the boys gathered up the saggy mattress and hoisted it onto their shoulders. I gave the fifty to the smallest of the duo and out they marched.

I stifled a laugh when I saw Rachel come out of the bathroom. Not that Rachel's five-foot-nine, thin-as-a-rail frame was funny, but with my jeans and large T-shirt as a covering, she looked like the poster child for the reality show *The Biggest Loser*. Rachel held my jeans at the waist to keep them up, but the hem of the pant legs only came to mid-calf.

"Okay, so a fashion statement you're not. A little power shopping at the mall should fix that," I told her.

Rachel's gaze traveled from the clean windows to the empty bedroom. She sighed. "Where's my stuff?"

"You mean the empty food cartons and rotting garbage? Or the filthy blankets and mattress? Gone, just like the cheap wine bottles and empty beer cans. The dumpster behind your building needs to be emptied though."

"How dare you?" Rachel exploded.

"Sober and indignant. That's a change, but it looks good on you."

"Get out!"

"Listen, Rache. I'm sorry if I took some liberties with your trash, but I'll replace the bed, sheets, pillows, and buy a dresser for your clothes."

"I don't want you buying nothing. I want you *out*."

I counted to ten, slowly and not out loud, hoping the quiet would calm Rachel down. As softly as I could speak, I pleaded with her. "I need you."

"Maybe you should of thought of that before you ransacked my place."

"It was a pigsty, Rachel. I was trying to help."

"Sorry Miss-holier-than-thou, but it's my pigsty and I didn't ask for help."

Chagrined and knowing I had no real argument, I changed subjects.

"I really need you to come with me," I said.

"I can't go back to Anderson. I *won't*."

I didn't reply. I just looked at her.

"Why'd you come here?" she asked, still irritated.

"Because I need you."

Rachel avoided my eyes. "I'm sorry you had to see me like this, but this is my life. I didn't invite you into it."

I silently walked over to the glistening window and looked down on the dirt and gravel playground.

Rachel's eyes flashed defiance. "I won't go back to the other life. Not for you, not for a clean place to live, not for anything."

I looked back at her. "I'm not asking you to go back to your old life. I'm asking you to come to Anderson for a couple of days to help me figure out who killed Tim." My voice quavered with desperation.

Rachel shook her head. "I can't do it."

"You can."

"What can I do that you can't?"

"I've already talked to Scott. He'll get you into the police mainframe. We'll meet with the rest of the Cliffhangers to talk. Pick each other's brains, come up with some ideas. I think Tim's death is related to Darcie Stewart's death."

"Stewart?"

"Remember our student teacher in English class?"

"Yeah, but she skipped the country, ran away or something, didn't she?" Rachel asked.

"They found her body a couple of weeks ago. Tim had clippings of the story in the personal effects he left to me. Maybe you can find a correlation between the two."

"It's not that easy," Rachel insisted.

"Maybe not, but if we all work together, we might be able to reason it out. Or at least give you enough data to get started."

Rachel shook her head.

"If you can't find any more info than the police already have, you can come back here to your alcohol-soaked life, and I'll leave you alone." The last statement came out harsher and slightly more self-righteous than I intended.

Rachel studied her feet—embarrassed and silent.

"Come on, Rache, at least let me take you to the mall and get you some clothes that actually fit. Convince me why you can't go to Anderson, and I'll let it drop. Promise." I paused. "Right now my freedom is on the line, and I can't for the life of me figure out why you wouldn't want to help. Can all of this be that important to you?" My arm made a sweeping movement around the bare apartment.

A shadow of pain passed through Rachel's brown eyes, followed by a look of determination. "Give me a belt for these pedal pushers and let's go."

Three pair of jeans, five shirts, underwear, socks, a pair of tennis shoes, and a windbreaker later, we sat in the food court, downing pretzels with cream cheese and Dr Pepper. I'd chattered on about David and the boys during the shopping excursion, but now I was silent. I would wait however long it took Rachel to start talking, or we were kicked out of the mall, whichever came first. At eight forty-five, store clerks started vacuuming the day's grime away, assistant managers checked tills, and the volume of mall patrons decreased dramatically. Rachel played with her food, oblivious to the surrounding commotion. The silence deepened. I dipped the last bite of pretzel into the tiny cheese tub.

When Rachel finally spoke, her words came out barely more than a whisper.

"I was thirteen when it happened the first time—the first time Dad came into my room at night. He sat on the bed and told me my birth had been too hard on Mama and that she wasn't able to respond like she should to a husband. He told me he didn't know what he was going to do, but he needed more out of life. He said if things didn't change, he would leave Mama and me and find someone to make him happy."

Rachel picked up her soda and took a long drink. Her eyes locked onto mine, a dare, waiting for me to blink first. I remained still, not looking away.

"He started to rub my back, and then he put his head down on my shoulder and cried," she said. "Cried like a wounded puppy. I held him until he stopped crying, but suddenly his whole manner changed. He turned different—started pulling at my pajamas and then kissed me on the lips. I was so scared and grossed out, but I didn't know what to do—so I didn't do anything. I just let him do it. He didn't stop with the kiss. It was horrible."

I quelled the gag that came up my throat. I'd never even suspected this.

Rachel's voice carried no emotion. Her words came out evenly spaced, monotone, as if her soul had abandoned her body and only a shell remained—a talking mannequin.

"And then it happened again and again, and I couldn't tell Mama because Dad insinuated it was my fault. That if I weren't such a bad girl, this wouldn't happen, and if I told Mama, she wouldn't love me anymore."

Rage welled up inside of me for the second time today. I wanted to throw something—to scream, to get sick, to kill. What I did, however, was remain silent. I focused on Rachel's lifeless eyes. I'd heard this story in a dozen different forms in David's office. The human casualties were horrific. What was always the same was the incredible amount of damage done to the soul, and how any reaction—good or bad other than listening—would cause retreat and make the victim shut down. I couldn't risk it with Rachel. She needed to talk, so I held my emotions in check.

Rachel took a deep breath. "Then there was the ad from you about the mystery club, and the Cliffhangers became my safe haven. I lived from meeting to meeting. The club kept me from curling up and dying. It was then that I realized I could make it. No one had to know my dirty little secret."

I sipped Dr Pepper, barely able to keep from hurling it as far as I could throw it.

Rachel's voice sounded hollow. "My junior year was worse. One of the teachers started making me stay after class. He said my grades weren't good enough, I didn't try hard enough, and he was going to have to call my parents and tell them about my behavior unless I joined study group at his house. Like an idiot I did. Only when I got there, no one was studying. No one was even there."

"Oh no." The words were out before I could reel them back in.

Rachel picked her napkin to shreds. "It was the same as Dad. He forced me to . . ." Her words trailed off into nothing.

She started again. "He told me it was all my fault. I tempted him, he said. He said if I told anyone he would have me removed from school permanently. I didn't know what to do—so I didn't do anything. I was so ashamed. Something about me was terribly, terribly wrong, and I didn't know what it was."

"What teacher?" I asked, my teeth clenched.

"Does it matter?" Now that Rachel was talking, it seemed like she couldn't stop. The story spewed out of her in the same empty tone.

"I think Mama knew though," Rachel said. "Not about the teacher, but about Dad. Remember when I was the first one in class to get the Pac-Man game? Remember when I got a computer for graduation? They were just on the market for home use and cost a small fortune. I think it was easier for Mama to buy me gifts than to face the truth.

"I don't blame her for not wanting Dad. I vomited afterward—every time. I hope I saved her from feeling like that. Still, something hardened in my heart when I left home. I stopped loving Dad, and I think I stopped loving Mama. I hated them for who they were, for what they'd done to me, and I swore never to go home again."

"I'm so sorry." My words felt grossly inadequate.

Rachel went on as if she hadn't heard me. "Hating them didn't solve anything. I hated myself more. I felt like the whole world could see that I was a bad, bad person. Like it was tattooed on the way I walked and talked. When I graduated from Citrone, I did freelance computer work, and the more computer literate the world got and the more the Internet took over, the less I went out. Now people couldn't see me. Couldn't know I was used goods. Couldn't see my shame. Most of the time I don't even look in the mirror so I can't see it either."

Tears rolled down my cheeks.

"The liquor store delivers my booze, and the grocery store brings my food. It's been over a year since I've been out of my apartment.

The landlord stops by once a month for his check. That's why I can't go back to Anderson. I hate them. I hate my parents. I hate me."

I brushed off my tears, but I couldn't swallow past the lump in my throat. "I am *so* sorry. I didn't know. I don't know how I could not have known—but I didn't. How could we meet every week for four years, and I still not know?" I asked the question more to myself than Rachel. "I don't know what to say."

"I don't need words. I don't need answers—there aren't any. I just need you to know why I can't go back," Rachel said in a flat voice.

I took a deep breath. "I have no excuses for not being the kind of friend to you that I now need you to be for me, but it doesn't lessen my need. I promise you if you come back with me, I will protect you. We can stay at a motel and not even see your parents."

Rachel cleared the table and stood up, saying nothing.

I grabbed her arm. "You can't believe how sorry I am, but for now I need to put your pain on the back burner, unfortunately, like I've always done. I need you to help me, Rache. Please, I'm begging you. I could be arrested for Tim's murder."

Rachel stood still, looked at my hand on her arm, then at the empty tables in the food court. I tried to read her eyes, but couldn't. Seconds ticked by.

"Okay, I'll go. But don't ask me to go to the class reunion."

I let out a huge sigh of relief. "No problem."

"I won't go to your mom's, and I won't go see my parents."

I nodded. "Your call."

"I'd like to see the Cliffhangers though. You can't tell them anything—nothing. I couldn't bear it if they found out about any of this."

I felt sick. I closed my eyes. How could I ever find the right words to make Rachel see the truth about herself? She was the victim, not the villain. "You have nothing to be ashamed of. You didn't do anything wrong. You were a child, but no, I won't tell anyone." *I promise not to tell the group what appalling things you dealt with while I sat by and did nothing.*

CHAPTER SEVEN

Thursday

Our flight left early the next morning. I tucked our small travel bags into the overhead bin, and we settled into our coach-class seats. Rachel's discomfort was still obvious, so I kept the conversation light. Finally, I gave Rachel the letter from Tim.

"I knew it." Rachel beamed after she read it.

Now this sounded like the old Rachel. "Knew what?"

Rachel was grinning for the first time since I walked into her apartment. "That Tim had the hots for you. You just never saw it."

"Oh puh—lease."

"Seriously, he did."

"Well, if he did, and I'm not saying he did, I guess I was too much in love with David to notice."

"Still?"

"Still what?"

"Still in love with David?"

"Of course. It's different now—not the starry-eyed kind—but good. Very good. Not that everything's perfect, but on the whole—good." I knew I answered too quickly, but I also knew that on the whole, what I said was true. Then I changed the subject. "You ever meet anyone, Rache?"

"Nope, and I don't intend to."

Rachel's tone implied that our conversation was over. I reluctantly let the subject drop and tried to enjoy the rest of the flight. Why did I ask that? Of course there wasn't a man in Rachel's life, not after what she'd been through. Why would she ever trust any man? Would I ever think before I opened my mouth?

Finding the luggage carousels in the Indy airport was a simple matter of following arrows. Squeezing between the crush of people proved challenging, but after the crowd thinned, we grabbed our bags and headed outside.

My youngest set of twins was supposed to meet us at the airport. But I only saw Caleb. His dark, thick hair either wasn't combed, or sticky, poky hair was in style. His jeans were custom torn in the knees, and his shirt looked like a Goodwill special, but he looked great. He approached and put his arms around me.

"Hi, Mom."

"Hey, Caleb." I returned his hug and then introduced him to Rachel. "This is my run-never-walk boy."

Rachel smiled and extended her hand. "Hello."

"Hi," Caleb responded.

"Where are Jake and Mom?" I asked.

Caleb put the luggage in the back of his van. "I'll tell you on the way. This is drop-off and pick-up parking only."

Once we pulled out into the stream of traffic, Caleb continued. "Jake didn't have to work this weekend, so he went to Diane's. I don't think you'll see much of him. He doesn't even have time for me. Diane this, Diane that. You'd think she invented the wheel." My son rolled his eyes. "He's staying in Noblesville, but will come down if you *must* see him. He hopes you'll be too busy with the reunion and all."

That's not the half of it.

The driver's seat was pushed back as far as it could go to accommodate Caleb's long legs. "Grandma's baking for the church bake sale. Does every church in the whole world have bake sales? Didn't you just finish with one out in Montana?" Without waiting for an answer, he continued. "Big Guy is playing for the reunion Saturday. We're the entertainment."

"My reunion?"

"Yep."

"And who is Big Guy?" I asked.

"That's what we named our band. You know . . . after the Big Guy. He's the One who gave us the talent."

My heart swirled with warm feelings. Good to see such strong faith in my youngest. "So how's the band working out?"

"Great! We do both Christian and secular music. We're busy most every weekend at some church event or school function. Highland High asked us to perform at the graduation ceremonies. Of course, they want us to play for free, but its exposure. After all—who knows who might be there?"

"Sounds like your plate's full." Maternal pride oozed out of every pore. "I think I'll rent a car when we get to Anderson."

"That would be great, Mom. Not that I don't like being a chauffeur mind you, but I am *really* busy." He flashed that grin that never failed to melt my heart.

"No problem, sweetie. Actually, I think with the reunion, it will be much easier." I kept my thoughts to myself. *Good, then you won't have to see your Mom go to the police station and deliver evidence in a murder investigation . . . or worse.*

Rachel stared out the window in silence. Before I could think of how to include her in the conversation, Caleb spoke up again.

"Did you know the Speaker of the House is going to be there? The Speaker of the House of the United States, Mom. His daughter is graduating. Maybe, just maybe, we'll be sooo good, he'll invite us to Washington for a performance."

I laughed. There was no lack of confidence in my younger boys. Both Jake and Caleb had chosen to come to the university in Anderson. They were ready to see the world outside of Montana. My mother lived there, so I wasn't terribly panicked. For that I was grateful. Worrying, especially about the boys, was second nature to me. Anything that helped alleviate it was gold in my book.

The older twins had been content to go to school in Bozeman. Abe married Kate Tucker right out of college. He stayed on to get his master's in agriculture. Kate supported his endeavors with a nursing degree. Zeb also married after graduation. He married Lisa Minteer of the "Butte Minteers," and they moved to Portland, Oregon where he got a job as an electrical engineer with a small but fast-growing company. Lisa was a free spirit with plenty of money to indulge herself. She volunteered, traveled, and enjoyed remodeling their first home.

I'm not sure my boys realized I was part of the human race. I was a genus known only as Mom. Actually, I liked it that way. It gave me sort of an edge with them, like a superpower or something. I can't imagine how they would react if they found out genus Mom was a suspect in a murder case.

"Well, for your information, I had the Speaker of the House of the United States as my high school government teacher." I punctuated the words with what I considered to be oh-so-cool, body movements.

"You're kidding me!" Caleb said.

"Nope. His name is Phillip House, but we called him—now don't tell him this if you see him—Lousy Housey. He was a real jerk as a teacher, and I don't think *any* of us liked him. Did you like him, Rachel?" I asked, hoping to draw her into the conversation.

"I didn't like much about high school in general," Rachel said softly.

CHAPTER EIGHT

Friday

I looked at the digital clock on the bedside table—5:15 a.m. I was wide-awake, my mind spinning with the events of the last two days. I felt like I had gone from zero to sixty in under a minute with no time to admire the scenery. I know I dozed on and off between one-thirty and five, but it was guilt-sprinkled sleep at best. Regardless of Rachel's broken life, I still convinced her to come to Anderson to try to clear my name. You just couldn't find friends like me on any street corner.

Nor wives for that matter. Guilt tugged at the edge of reason as I thought back to the conversation between David and me. He'd called Wednesday night from Homer after settling in to his motel. I told him about Tim's murder, but left out the part about being a suspect or the possibility that we could inherit several million dollars. I told him I still planned on going to the reunion, but left out the part about going to the police station. I knew he'd fly back immediately and take charge of the situation if he thought I was in trouble.

Not that I didn't like the fact that he took care of so many details in our lives. Normally, it was okay, but lately I had the growing feeling that I was just window dressing. Maybe it was a midlife crisis, or empty-nest syndrome, or whatever the newest psychobabble disorder was, but I definitely wasn't content with my life at this point. Nothing concrete I could lay my finger on, but rather a sense—a gnawing sense—that life was passing me by and I had done nothing of importance. I suspected the words engraved on my tombstone would be: Here lies Jamie Storm: beautiful, fluffy frosting on a world of deep, rich chocolate cake. For once I wanted to be the cake—to be more than just the hugger and kisser of disgruntled parishioners' boo-boos.

David was not only content, but he was also downright excited to be doing what he felt was a sure calling on his life. How marvelous it must be when God calls you to something, anything. I had never shared that feeling. Lately, I'd been impatient, even snappish at times, with David. I couldn't shake the underlying feeling of anger toward him, but the reason eluded me. Nothing outward had changed. Jealousy maybe? He had found his calling, but I hadn't?

Throwing the sensation of unworthiness off with the covers, I headed for the shower. No time to get maudlin this morning. I would let Rachel sleep in, but Mom and I had planned to meet for breakfast at Bob Evans. I'd called her last night to explain why I wouldn't be staying with her. I didn't tell her about Rachel's situation, just that she was exhausted and needed someone to be with her for the week. As usual, Mom understood and didn't ask any prying questions.

I pulled on jeans and a Bears T-shirt and grabbed the rental keys off the dresser. Five minutes later, I pulled into the busy parking lot at Bob Evans. The smells of fresh brewed coffee, honey-cured ham, and sausage gravy filled the air. My stomach growled as I slid into the booth across from Mom after giving her a quick hug in greeting.

My mother, Barbara Waymire, is still a handsome woman at seventy-two. Her eyes are hazel like mine, crinkled a bit at the corners from age, and shadowed with grief. The last ten years as sole caretaker of my dad stricken with Alzheimer's disease had taken its toll. She stubbornly, valiantly refused to take Dad to the Care Center. He was her beloved, and she nursed him to the end. Several weeks after his death, she had secluded herself in her home, only doing what was necessary to tend to the needs of her grandsons. They had been her salvation.

"Grandma, did you see my LeBron jersey?"

"Grandma, can you fry chicken for some of the guys from school? They love your cooking."

"Grandma, wanna come to Brookside Church tonight and hear my concert?"

I knew that if the boys hadn't been there, Mom might have never come out of the dark mist that threatened to overtake her mind and soul when Dad passed away.

"You look great, Mom. I like the new hairstyle. How's it going?"

"I'm good, Jamie. Each day is a little better. I miss your dad fiercely though. I don't think that will ever change."

"No, I bet not." I missed him, too, but the disease had taken him away a long time ago. It wasn't as fresh for me.

"Your kids bring so much life to the house. In fact, the boys are responsible for my new doo. They actually took me to the salon and instructed the stylist to spike and bleach my hair. I have to admit I like it. At first, though, I felt like a Martian in public. I worried about what people would think of me. Two days of five-minute hairstyling ended that anxiety. Now I don't care what they think. It's fun, easy, and I feel ten years younger." She rambled on, obviously trying to convince me she was fine. It wasn't working.

I reached across the table and squeezed her hand.

"How is Rachel?" Mom was a pro at changing the subject. "Did she make it through the night okay?"

I slid my hand back to my side of the booth as the waitress set our plates in front of us. "I guess she's okay. She's still sleeping, and since I had several errands to run this morning, I just let her rest." I dipped a toast point into my over-easy egg.

I avoided mentioning the specifics of my errands. We spent the rest of the meal catching up on Anderson news.

Mom left a chunk of honeydew in her fruit cup—her one-item breakfast. My bacon, egg, hash browns, and toast were gone. I stabbed the melon with my fork and finished it.

"Did you know one of your classmates died here in Anderson in the parking lot of our church?" Mom asked.

"I heard," I said, chewing slowly.

"It was Timothy Manter. He was shot to death. I think he was in your high school mystery club, wasn't he?"

"Yep."

"It was awful, just awful. The pastor didn't even give a sermon that day. We just had a prayer service." The waitress came over to refill Mom's coffee cup, but Mom covered the top with her hand and shook her head.

"So you were at church that morning?" I asked.

"Of course. When am I not in church?"

"Did Tim attend church?"

"I couldn't tell you. Our average attendance is three thousand. I know a lot of people in my age group, but not many others."

"Was anything unusual going on outside?"

"Besides a dead body in the parking lot? Because I think a dead body is unusual." Mom peered at me intently.

I forced a smile. "You know what I mean. Did you see anything odd, anything out of place, besides Tim's body?"

"Cops everywhere and crime scene tape blocking off a huge section of the parking lot. Other than that, nothing different."

"Sarcasm does not become you." I smiled, because in truth it did become her.

The waitress brought our bill to the table and set it between us.

Mom scanned my face. "You're going to try to solve this, aren't you?" I picked up the bill and examined it. "Jamie, this isn't like a high-school game. This is murder." Mom's voice would have been a yellow flag if we'd been at the Indy 500.

"I know." I brushed a piece of imaginary lint off my T-shirt.

Another sin of omission—probably a habit I shouldn't get into. But I didn't want to upset Mom. Not yet, anyway. "I'll be on my cell if you need me for anything. I don't know how much time I'll be at the house. I'll be spending a lot of time with Rachel and at the reunion"

"Be careful, Jamie."

Over Mom's protest, I paid the check, left a generous tip—thanks to Tim—kissed Mom on the cheek, and drove to the police station.

CHAPTER NINE

S cott Walters was the one member of the Cliffhangers whom I'd seen frequently since high school. Whenever we made the trip to Anderson to deliver the boys, or to visit Mom and Dad, David and I made a point to see Scott and his family. We had at least one meal together every visit. Even so, I felt tense approaching his office. He was a sergeant with the criminal investigation division of the Anderson Police Department. Did he believe I was involved with Tim's death? If so, why hadn't he said anything to me when I arranged for the Cliffhanger reunion that was taking place tonight?

I took a deep breath and entered Scott's office. Looking up from his desk, he broke into a warm smile. Scott is my age with short, black hair and chocolate-brown eyes. His skin is the color of cocoa. His pale yellow shirt was open at the collar, a matching tie thrown carelessly across his desk.

"I am so glad you're here, Jamie. I'd get up, but . . ." He rolled his wheelchair back from the desk so we could embrace.

"I think you just use that thing to get sympathy," I teased.

The wheelchair was a pointed reminder of the price Scott had paid for interfering with a bank robbery ten years ago. The bullet had gone through his abdomen and spinal column in one quick, life-changing second. After a six-month pity party, he pulled himself out of PTSD and clinical depression more determined than ever to put the bad guys behind bars. Scott, the only African-American in my high school, had lived a life of challenges. This one hadn't held him back for long.

Not one for small talk, I got right to the point. "I brought bank statements and a flash drive of e-mails to and from Tim. I didn't kill him."

"I know you didn't, but we have to rule out all possible suspects. You stand to inherit a bundle. It's a no-brainer that you're a suspect. You're a friend, so I have to be especially careful not to show favoritism. It can't look like I'm ignoring the evidence." He regarded me with regret.

"I know, but—"

"I'm sure the bank statements alone will clear you. This hit was definitely an expensive proposition. Whoever wanted Tim dead is either a professional or hired one, and they don't come cheap."

"Did Tim come see you last week?"

"He always does."

"Always? He's been here before?"

"Jamie, Tim's been coming down on breaks, vacations, and weekends for the last two years. He'd grown restless, bored with his career. He made enough money. He didn't have to work if he didn't want to. He had no family."

"He never told me. Not that he needed to, but I'm surprised."

Scott shrugged. "He started looking into the death of that student teacher who died the year we graduated. Remember her?"

I studied my nails, pretending the question was rhetorical, choosing to remain quiet about what Tim had sent me via his lawyer. Part of it was shame for being oblivious to the world of my friends. Part of it was fear—fear that Scott might use it against me. If my silence piqued Scott's curiosity, he didn't show it.

"I gave him a copy of the old file and made a few phone calls for him over the past few months," Scott said, "but until two weeks ago, nothing. Then one day out of the blue, he called me to say he wanted me to meet someone. Someone who might have an angle on who killed Dacia Stewart. His voice was edgy, excited. He told me where to look for the body, and sure enough it was there. The fact that he knew about the body made him a suspect—until he died himself."

"Who was this person?"

"No idea."

"He didn't mention a name at all?"

"He planned on bringing whoever it was to the reunion tonight. He didn't hint anything about this in your correspondence?" Scott asked.

"No. I didn't even know he ever left New York."

"Curious."

"Very."

"If you remember anything at all, regardless of how trivial, let me know tonight," Scott said.

"There's a connection between Dacia Stewart's death and Tim's. Must be. He discovered something. He knew where the bones were, and someone shut him up." I tried to keep the edge out of my voice.

"That's what we think. But we don't have any more evidence now than we did when she first disappeared, except for her body. In point of fact, bones. Didn't recover anything else from the crime scene. So far, no other forensic evidence. I'm really hoping that whoever Tim's contact was will show up tonight, but I wouldn't count on it."

"Can you tell me exactly where Tim was shot?"

"The north end of 501 College Drive."

"Mom said it was at the church."

"Yeah, in the parking lot. His body was found at 8:52 a.m. by one of the parishioners on her way to Sunday school. My department was there within five minutes, and we cordoned off the place. You'd have thought we stopped the world from spinning by the reaction of several churchgoing saints."

I could imagine Abigail's response if she hadn't been allowed to enter her church parking lot on Sunday morning. I could hear her now:

"Why you boys had just better remove that yellow tape or else. Do you suppose that God is going to let you get away with these shenanigans? I'm sorry that boy is dead, but it IS Sunday: Remember the Sabbath day to keep it holy. You ever heard of that commandment? There are ten of them, and I don't think God will just willy-nilly let us break one because some poor soul—may he rest in peace—bought the farm on Sunday morning. Now you remove this yellow tape right now, or I'll remove it for you."

I couldn't help grinning when I thought about the police force versus Abigail. No contest. Abigail would win.

I bent down and gave Scott another squeeze. "I've got to run and check on Rachel. See you tonight."

Then as an afterthought, I voiced the most obvious of all obvious statements. "And Scott, we've got to find out who murdered Tim."

CHAPTER TEN

heard the shower running when I opened the door to our room at the Holiday Inn. It was only 10:00 a.m., and I was itching to go to Mounds Park to see the first crime scene. I hoped Rachel would hurry. Time permitting, we could go by the church and see where Tim was killed. Could he have been making a life change? Was God becoming important to him? Why had he been in the parking lot the morning he was murdered, and who would have known to look for him there? The questions came thick and fast, swirling around like autumn leaves in a heavy wind.

Dressed in jeans and a short-sleeved, yellow-knit top, Rachel came out of the bathroom. The dark circles under her eyes weren't as prominent. She wore no makeup, and with her hair pulled back in a ponytail, she looked much younger than me.

"Let's go, girl, back to where all this began," I said.

A trace of anxiety flickered in her eyes. She said nothing, though, and plucked her purse off the back of the chair. She made a slight bow with an I'll-follow-you hand flourish.

It took fifteen minutes to drive to Mounds Park from the motel and another fifteen minutes to walk the trail and find where yellow, crime-scene tape cordoned off an area of about two thousand square feet. It was a good bit off the beaten path, but the path was clearly marked by flattened grass and broken branches. I pictured Gil Grissom and his little band of followers traipsing through the woods with crime-solving kits in hand.

Surveying the area, I said, "I can't imagine what Ms. Stewart would be doing in this part of the park unless she was forced here."

A squirrel raced up a tree. Three birds took flight, protesting loudly at the gall we had to intrude on their morning rituals. Both Rachel and I ignored their protests.

Rachel nodded. "Yeah, I doubt she was sightseeing." A hint of sarcasm laced her voice.

"She could have been killed somewhere else and brought here."

"Sounds plausible, but it wouldn't be easy to not be seen. Scott got a theory?"

"Nothing he told me about." I felt a shiver go through me as I imagined what the student teacher's last images were and how terrified she must have been. "Let's get out of here."

On the way to the church parking lot, I told Rachel what little information Scott had given me. She listened without asking questions. I nosed the yellow SUV rental into a parking space. Rachel, fully rested, and with the effects of alcohol now far behind her, jumped out of the vehicle first and started searching the large, asphalt lot.

"Over here," she called after a quick survey.

The grotesque, white chalk outline was as distinct as those on the crime shows on TV. That surprised me. I'd read that most police departments didn't outline bodies because of the possible contamination of evidence. Maybe they had gotten all the samples they needed, but still needed to mark the spot. I didn't know and didn't care. My stomach was in knots. My eyes filled with tears. This wasn't just chalk. This was my last link to Tim.

I pinched the bridge of my nose and tried to think. It looked like Tim had gotten out of his vehicle and was headed to the church when he was shot in the back of the head. The chalk outline formed a crumpled, fetal position.

I knelt down and caressed the blacktop where his head had come to rest. I didn't bother to brush the tears off my cheeks as I looked at the deep, dark stains that pooled around the area. This was where my friend—who I hadn't seen in thirty years, who had left ten million dollars to me, who I really hadn't known at all—had bled to death.

Lowering my head to the ground, I whispered, "Oh, Tim, I am *so* sorry."

Guilt pressed into me, leaving my chest feeling compressed and tight. I hadn't known Tim at all. I hadn't known Rachel at all. How could I have lived in such a bubble of happiness in high school not knowing what my friends were going through, or who they were on the inside? Had my relationship with Christ blinded me to the pain of others, or had I ignored all His urgings to "Love my neighbor?" And David. Where was David now? I felt my faith crumble into little pieces. I longed for David's confident assurance of the truth. Instead, I felt Rachel's slender hand rubbing my shoulders.

A sudden gust of wind blew a discarded Subway wrapper into the center of Tim's crude outline. I snatched it up, crumpled it, then tore it into pieces, and viciously tossed the shreds into the air.

"Come on, Jamie, this isn't helping. If we want to find the killer or killers, we need to keep it together. You can cry later." The hardness edging Rachel's words spoke of dreams long lost, of trust betrayed, and world weariness.

I nodded slowly and stood.

"We need to find the person Tim was bringing to the meeting tonight. We need to know if he played a part in all this."

Rachel handed me a tissue from her purse. I blew my nose, turning away from her to be polite.

"Do you have a recent picture of Tim?" she asked.

Guilt continued to hammer my chest. "No. I haven't even seen Tim since high school. We didn't exchange pictures, or much of anything else except hi and how are you."

"Let's go back to the police station then. Scott will have pictures of the crime scene, and maybe he has Tim's driver's license photo if nothing else. If we find out where he was staying, we can ask around and see if anyone saw him with someone."

I felt like a traitor for leaving the spot where Tim died. But what Rachel said made sense. I couldn't get bogged down in my feelings. Not now. Not until this was over. Then I'd take a long, hard look at my relationships, my walk with Christ, and myself. Somewhere along the line since high school, I had lost something, and I had a terrifying feeling that it was me.

After we entered the police station, Rachel walked down a hall and entered Scott's office in front of me. "Hey, buddy," she said, greeting him shyly.

"Hey, yourself. Wow, you look good," Scott said.

"Thanks. It's been a long time."

"Too long. Where ya been hiding?"

She slid her hands into the back pockets of her jeans. "I live in Philadelphia now. Just can't seem to make it back. Looks like you've changed a bit." Rachel nodded toward his wheelchair.

"True enough. Life happens. You win some, you lose some. But I've won way more than my fair share." Scott grinned.

"Do you have a picture of Tim?" I asked. "I don't mean to interrupt, but we have a lot of work to do."

Rachel laughed. "That's the Jamie we know and love. Business first, pleasure second."

I wasn't amused by Rachel's comment. Guilt and sadness threatened to overwhelm me. My only escape would be to bury myself in solving Tim's murder case. I repeated the question.

"Picture?"

"Sure." Scott opened the top folder on a large stack of files. He handed me an eight- by ten-inch photo of Tim. "We found this in his apartment in New York. It may be a couple of years old, but it's what he looked like. We have copies in his file, so go ahead and take it."

I looked into the startling, cobalt-blue eyes that crinkled at the corners when he smiled. Gray framed his temples, but the rest of his hair remained dark brown, nearly black. His smile was genuine, even if it was posed for the camera, and I noticed that while his shoulders had broadened since high school, he was not overweight. He must have taken good care of himself.

"Did he tell you where he was staying when he was here?" I asked.

"Sure. He was staying in his old house. When his parents died, they left the business and their home to him. He sold the corner grocery, but he kept the house, probably for sentimental reasons. Anyway, that's where he stayed when he was in town. He'd actually done some remodeling on the old place."

"You serious?" I said.

"Hard to believe you guys ever e-mailed. You don't know squat," Scott observed.

Yeah, and maybe you can twist the knife in a little deeper too.

"Could we get in there?" Rachel asked. "Into his house, I mean?"

I added my two cents. "It would really help."

Scott hesitated for a moment. "My department searched, fingerprinted, bagged, tagged, and cleared the house. It's a bit of a mess, but I don't see how it could hurt. You're technically the owner once the estate is settled, so go check it out with my blessing."

Taking the key from the top middle drawer, he handed it across the desk to Rachel. "Have a field day."

I was excited. "Thanks, I owe you one. We'll go over there now."

"Could we have lunch first?" Rachel asked. "I'm starving."

I wondered whether I'd ever be hungry again until this case was solved, but Rachel hadn't eaten breakfast, so I agreed. Magnanimous of me, don't you think? That's me, always thinking of the other fellow. "Let's go. Where to?"

"Mexican sounds good. Want to come, Scott?"

"I'd love to, but today won't work. Too many irons in the fire, including this homicide investigation. Eat a chicken taco for me." He smiled.

After leaving the station, we ended up at the Taco Palace, and over crunchy tortilla chips, Rachel and I discussed the case.

"I think it's time to divide and conquer," I said. "Maybe Scott will let you go through the case file and do a little background profiling on the four names that Tim had highlighted."

"I'd rather stay together." In spite of her height, Rachel suddenly seemed small and frightened.

"You'll be fine on your own," I assured her. "We can get twice as much done if we split up. I'll go over to Tim's and see if I can find anything."

"Two heads are better than one," Rachel said. Her anxiety was obvious as she nibbled her lower lip.

I shook my head. "Really, Rache, we don't have a lot of time to prove my innocence. What if the police arrest me? While I can-vass Tim's neighborhood with his picture, you can do your magic computer thing at the police station. In fact, why don't we play Nancy Drew here and show Tim's picture at the counter? Maybe they'll remember seeing him with someone."

Rachel offered a weak smile that didn't quite reach her eyes. She grabbed the photo and headed to the front of the restaurant. Both girls behind the counter looked at the photo and shook their heads no.

Rachel scooted back to the table and shrugged. "It was a long shot anyway. I'll drop you off at Tim's and come back for you in an hour."

There was something in Rachel's voice that struck me as odd. "Something wrong?"

"Um, nothing. I'll be okay."

"You're sure?"

"Yeah. I'll go see Scott, get a couple of passwords, and do some background checks from my laptop at the motel."

"Hopefully, he'll cooperate." I handed over the rental car keys and scooted out of the booth. "Okay then, let's hustle."

CHAPTER ELEVEN

t only took a few minutes to drive to Tim's house from the taco place. Rachel dropped me off at the curb, waved good-bye, and I walked to the door. My heart felt like a big, heavy log had plopped down on it. I felt shame and regret for not putting any effort into my relationship with Tim, for not seeing him as anything more than an acquaintance. Now it was too late.

Resolve settled in. I would do my best to find out who killed him. Whatever it took. *And clear yourself in the process,* my pesky conscience whispered. There are times a conscience can get on your nerves.

Once inside I noticed a lot of remodeling had indeed been done since our high school days. The room colors, the furniture, the carpets. Everything looked different. Much brighter and bolder. The wall between the kitchen and living room had been knocked out to make one huge open area. Two bedrooms had been combined to make a master suite with a large bathroom and walk-in closet. Very updated, yet it still maintained the comfortable, homey feeling I remembered when Tim's folks were alive. Only now the house seemed alive with personality. It definitely fit Tim—Mr. Energy himself. And though I felt a little like a peeping Tom, I went through every room, closet, drawer, and box I could find. Nothing grabbed my interest, nor did I detect anything unusual. No surprise there. Scott was nothing if not thorough.

Suddenly, a thought startled me. If Tim's will stood up in court, this house belonged to me now. I felt creepy thinking about it, as though I'd somehow caused his death by inheriting his estate.

I left the house determined to canvass the neighborhood, knocking on all the doors in that block. It didn't take long to find out most of the old neighbors were long gone, and few even knew that anyone ever visited the house at 222 Sycamore. Busy lifestyles and social networking made getting to know your neighbors a thing of the past. Frustrated, I looked at my watch—fifteen minutes before Rachel was due, so I expanded the search to the next block.

A huge, black Labrador bounded out of a small, ranch-style house I approached. A woman, who appeared to be in her seventies, followed him, yelling, "Roger, get back here! We need to put your collar on. Roger, *now*!"

The dog was too busy sniffing me to obey any commands.

I pushed his nose away gently. Dogs had such a crude way of saying hello. This one looked like he'd eaten one too many pork chops, and his tail wagged fiercely. His eyes begged for friendship.

The woman scurried toward me with a bit of a hitch in her get-along. Her rubber-soled, sensible shoes shored up her thick ankles nicely. She wore an aquamarine, polka-dot print dress gathered at the hips. It had short sleeves with white cuffs and a white collar at the neck. Flattering it was not, but she reminded me of my grandmother, and I liked her sense of self if not her sense of style.

"Roger, leave the nice lady alone." Turning to me she said, "I am so sorry. Roger just loves people. We walk every day, and every day he makes a new friend."

"How nice. How long have you lived in the neighborhood?"

"Oh goodness, I've been here for ages, just ages."

She smiled at some distant memory only she could see. If I had to describe her expression, I'd say she looked wistful.

I cleared my throat.

"Do you ever walk down that way?" I pointed down the street.

"Roger and I walk everywhere. They say dogs are man's best friend, but Roger is my best friend. Always will be. You're probably wondering why I named him Roger."

No, no I'm not.

She evidently wasn't telepathic because she kept talking. "Roger was my nephew. Died on 9/11 in New York. Firefighter. So when I got Roger, this Roger, I just had to name him Roger."

"I'm Jamie Storm, and you are . . .?" I tried not to sound impatient.

"Martha—Martha Moss. Pleased to meet you."

I smiled. "Martha, I'm looking for someone who might have visited a friend of mine. He lived just down the street on the next block. His house is blue with white trim and shutters. It also has French doors with rain-glass windows. Do you remember seeing anyone there on your walks? "

"At Tim's house, you mean?"

My interest ratcheted up a notch. "Yes, have you seen anyone visit him?"

"Roger and I see lots of people. Not that I'm nosy, mind you, but Roger makes friends real easy. So did my nephew Roger. That boy had so many friends. You should have seen his funeral. One of the biggest I've ever been to."

"So have you seen anyone visit Tim's house?" I hoped to bring Martha back to the topic at hand.

"Sure, nice guy, too. Roger's a good judge of character. Took to the man in the blue car immediately. Took to his tires, too, if you know what I mean. Now my other Roger—not as good a judge of people. He liked everyone. Never had an enemy. You should have seen his funeral. Biggest I've ever seen. And he lived in New York, too, where people don't make—"

I interrupted again. "The man you saw, can you describe him?"

"Oh, I'm sorry. I forgot myself. Local boy I'd guess. Had one of those bumper stickers with the plaid-skirted man, playing bagpipes. You know, from that school over on the north side. Can't remember the name."

"Do you know what kind of car it was?" I asked.

"Sure do. Blue. And boy, Roger loved those tires. Now my nephew Roger, he wasn't a fan of cars. He was a truck kind of guy. He had a black truck. Black with silver. It was sharp. His momma, that's my sister, she got it when Roger died. My, you should have seen his funeral. It was big. Biggest I've ever seen."

I smiled, thanked the older woman, and walked away quickly before I heard any more stories about the Rogers. Either of them. The bumper sticker had to come from Highland High, my old high school, but who drove a blue car? Looking at my watch again, I wondered where Rachel was. She should have been here by now. It had been an hour and a half. I returned to Tim's house and called the motel. No answer in our room. I called Scott to see if Rachel had decided to stay there and work.

"Last time I saw her, she was with you."

I felt my mouth go dry. "She didn't come back an hour ago?"

"Nope."

A prickling sensation ran along the back of my neck. Something was wrong, dreadfully wrong. "Can you come and get me?"

"Sure, what's up?" Scott asked.

"She's driving the rental, and I'm stranded at Tim's."

"Maybe she's just running late."

"She was coming to see you, Scott. You were the destination." I heard the tinny sound of fear in my voice.

"Maybe she went back to the motel for something."

"I called. No answer."

"I'll be right there," he said. "But don't worry. I'm sure it's nothing."

After I hung up, a sickening revelation hit. Maybe the person who killed Tim knew what Rachel and I had been doing. Maybe the SUV was in a ditch somewhere.

"Oh please, God, don't let Rachel get hurt on my account. Keep her safe." I uttered the prayer in a terrified voice, not the confident one I reserved for Sunday mornings when my Sunday school class was listening. My hands shook as I sank down on the floor to wait for Scott.

CHAPTER TWELVE

May 3, 1980

Crane was a good little berg to watch people. One hundred and ninety-six people, or so the sign said. Too close to Bloomington for anyone to think a stranger was an oddity. Especially a young one—just another student looking for cheap housing away from Indiana University. The sky was bright blue, the wind brisk, and no sign of rain. The breeze felt good against the skin. It skittered the trash from one yard to the next and down Main Street. Torn, crushed Styrofoam cups, cigarette butts, an occasional soda can, food wrappers, and scraps of paper all raced toward some unseen finish line. Springtime in Indiana made a person feel alive, vibrant, and powerful. It was definitely going to be a good day.

The Haskells lived in an unpretentious house across the street from the post office. A smallish, red-brick home with green shutters and a one-car, oversized garage. The funny thing was, it actually had a white-picket fence around the property. A picket fence—how corny. Irritating, really. Such a smug little life. Well, nothing lasted forever, and neither would this. In fact, if things went according to plan, today would be the end of the happy little home era.

It was the perfect day, really. Graduation day—the culmination of hopes and dreams. Time for precious little Craig to start a new life, or so the Haskells thought. Time for the Haskells to receive their reward for being such model citizens.

The streets were quiet in Crane, especially in this small block of houses. An occasional bird squawked or fluttered by, but there was no traffic to speak of and little kids weren't out and about yet. It was only eight-thirty in the morning, and graduation was scheduled for ten-thirty at IU. It was a short thirty-minute drive from here, and on IN-45 there was a wonderful little spot, where if pushed hard enough, a car might just flip several times before coming to rest. Of course, getting into the garage and cutting the seat belts of the '78 Cutlass had been an act of genius. By the time the Haskells discovered the vandalism, they'd be in a hurry to get to the graduation and wouldn't take the time to fix the belts.

It took a lot of patience waiting for the perfect opportunity to accomplish my objectives, but it allowed time to study human nature and meditate on the surroundings. For instance, the Haskells' neighbor to the right appeared to be an alcoholic. He had come out of his house in long shorts, no shirt, and flip-flops. He picked up his daily paper—maybe the Herald-Times *or* The Indianapolis Star. *Then with an attempt at casualness, he looked up and down the street before strolling over to the Ford 250 parked in his driveway. He opened the passenger door with an air of nonchalance, pulled out a small flask from the glove compartment, took a swig, replaced the cap, and put the container back in the truck. Then he slowly strolled back into the house.*

The muffled sound of a dog barking came from several blocks away. A skinny squirrel scrambled down the Haskells' walk hoping, it appeared, to find a source of food. Apparently, winter had been hard for squirrels.

The neighbor came back out of his house, bent down in front of his flower bed, and pulled a few microscopic weeds before indifferently checking out an invisible scratch on his pickup. Evidently, he needed to open the door for a more thorough check and opened the glove box. Once again, he retrieved the flask, and this time he took a longer swig, seemingly unconcerned about who was watching.

The door to the Haskells' garage creaked open. The powder-blue Cutlass backed out onto the street. Mr. Haskell was a solid man with graying hair, a square face, and thick-lensed, black glasses. His brown suit jacket was a nice contrast against the blue interior of the car.

Mrs. Haskell was a small woman in her sixties with mousy, brown-and-gray hair caught up in a bun on the back of her head. Her eyes were close set, and she almost had one eyebrow. Would have, if she hadn't used a mustache trimmer to shave a small streak from the bridge of her nose up her forehead. She held the damaged seat belt in her hand, and her mouth moved a mile a minute. Her purple-flowered, polyester dress clashed with the Cutlass's interior.

It would be an easy task to follow them. They would have no reason to be suspicious of a U-Haul truck behind them. They'd be too concerned about making the graduation with no seat belts to be aware of their surroundings. Like most people caught up in their small, pathetic lives, they had no time to pay attention to what was going on around them. They probably had no idea their neighbor was an alcoholic or that the squirrels had a rough winter. Taking candy from a baby couldn't have been easier.

To be on the safe side, the truck stayed a nice distance behind the Haskells until they left US-23. It was a short ten miles until the spot of contact. The early May tulips and crocuses offered a nice diversion from the pulsating excitement of the planned kill.

Only one problem with the plan. It wasn't foolproof. First, the weather wasn't cooperating. Not a cloud in sight. Rain would've made the roads slick. Still, it would look like an accident at first blush, so getting away should be no problem. But if the Haskells survived, it would be harder to make a second run at them later. Varying the methods of homicide was the key to not getting caught or connected to a murder. Most serial killers felt compelled to leave a signature behind. Now that was stupid. Pretty much asking to get caught. Of course, you can't really call the first two deaths serial killings, but there would be more until a certain person learned a valuable lesson—a lesson of a lifetime.

Renting the U-Haul had been a snap. A quick check of the fake driver's license satisfied the manager. The cash on the counter impressed the dealer more than questioning the idea that a young kid might not actually be who he claimed he was. Of course, the one-hundred-dollar bill to hire the kid to rent the U-Haul and ramps was money well spent. The kid delivered the twenty-four foot truck, took his money, and left the fake ID on the seat of the U-Haul cab. It took some maneuvering to ramp the trailer alone and drive a small sedan into it, but the effort would pay off in the long run.

The Haskells drove Sunday-sightseeing slow. No more than fifty miles per hour according to the U-Haul's speedometer. Time to pick up speed. The sharp turn up ahead would provide the angle needed for a successful hit. The U-Haul's engine shifted with a satisfying roar. No cars coming from either direction. The truck pulled out into the left lane—just another anxious driver trying to get somewhere on time. With a swift jerk of the wheel to the right, the grill of the truck rammed into the side of the Cutlass. The crunching of metal on metal, the screams, the shattering of glass—all music to the ears.

The Cutlass flipped over into the ditch and should have kept on flipping, although now was not the time to look. It took strength and concentration to wrench the U-Haul back onto the left-hand side of the road and continue on until taking a side road. The dirt road looked more like an overgrown path, but with the U-Haul's clearance it was possible to maneuver. Branches scratched the side of the moving van and whacked the windshield. Still not a problem. It wouldn't be returned to the dealer. With a lurch, the U-Haul stopped at a nice wide spot hidden from highway view.

It was time to open the back of the U-Haul, pull down the ramps, get in the car, and drive to the graduation.

CHAPTER THIRTEEN

With sirens blaring and lights flashing, Scott skidded to a halt in front of Tim's house. I locked the door and ran to the customized, wheel-chair-accessible van. I wondered what Martha must be thinking right about now. No matter how nosy you might not be, sirens and lights always aroused curiosity.

"Thanks a lot, buddy." I climbed in the passenger side. "I appreciate the speed, but could you have made a noisier entrance?"

"I don't think so, but I could try," he said with a grin.

"I thought cops could only use sirens in emergencies?"

"True enough. You wanna make a citizen's arrest?" He grinned even wider.

I hit his arm.

"Ow! I wanted to get here as fast as possible. You're the one who acted like it was an emergency."

"Not funny, Scott. I'm scared something's happened to her."

"I'm sure she's fine."

"How can you be sure? Have you seen her?"

"No, but I think you might be forgetting one teensy, weensy detail about Rachel. She's an alcoholic. Why would you let her go off on her own if you wanted her sober for tonight?"

"You think she's drinking?" That hadn't occurred to me until now.

"My guess? She's on a real bender, and the sooner we find her, the sooner we can sober her up. She's probably at the motel with her cell turned off."

"Can't be. She was fine. We just had lunch together."

"Then where is she?" Scott challenged.

"She seemed happy. Interested in solving this case."

"Well then, Ms. Rose-Colored Glasses, you tell me."

"She never mentioned anything about wishing she had a drink." I tried not to sound defensive.

"Yes, I can imagine that she would let you, a pastor's wife, know her deepest desires about drinking."

Although his sarcasm was laced with friendly humor, I felt the reproach slice clean through. "Come on, Scott, I was her friend long before I was a pastor's wife."

Scott shrugged. "Suit yourself. But I'm going to the motel first."

Sure enough, when we pulled into the parking lot, the Ford Escape was parked in a stall near the side entrance.

"Go on ahead, Jamie. I'll be right there."

I didn't have time to acknowledge that leaving a wheelchair-bound friend on his own so I could rescue an alcoholic for purely self-centered motives seared my pastor's wife conscience. I entered the room to see Rachel sitting cross-legged on the bed, back propped against the headboard, face wet with tears, and a Bud Light in her hand. Three empties lay on the bed. Panic rose like bile in my throat. Just what I—*we*—didn't need!

"Rache, what are you *doing*? We have work to do. We have our meeting tonight. You can't be drunk. What are you thinking?" The sentences came out short and choppy in a rush of air.

Rachel brushed the tears off her face with the palm of her hand. Her eyes danced with anger. "This is all so easy for you, isn't it?"

"What's easy?"

"This running around playing detective. Like you don't have a care in the world." Her words weren't slurred, just harsh.

"I thought you were doing okay." *That was lame.*

"You thought wrong!"

"Why didn't you tell me? I was worried about you. I was afraid something happened to you when you didn't answer the phone." I know I sounded defensive.

"Something did happen to me. Hell happened to me."

"I know, Rache, but I thought you were doing good." I softened the tone of my voice.

"Good? You thought because you dragged me down here and let me play amateur detective that I was doing good?" Rachel took a big swig of beer. "Just like that, huh?"

I climbed on the bed and sat next to her. "I don't know what to say." And I meant it. So I just sat.

"I hate this town. I hate every memory I've ever had here. Nothing was good for me here. *Nothing!* I feel like I'm suffocating, and you're playing little Miss Nancy Drew like you don't have a care in the world. Anderson was hell for me, Jamie, and I'm sorry if that offends your sensibilities, but it was hell." The last words came out as a quiet, desperate plea for understanding rather than rage. Tears raced down her face—silent accusations.

I felt hopeless, inadequate, as if nothing I could say or do would help. Week after week in the little town of Great Falls, Montana, people came to me for support. I prayed with them, counseled them, and loved them. Now I felt like it was all smoke and mirrors. There were no pat answers for real problems. None at all.

"Why did you make me come here?" Her question was rhetorical. She didn't expect an answer.

Which was good. I had none. I managed a weak, "I'm sorry."

A knock sounded on the door. I got up to let Scott in. He rolled over to the bed, looked around the room, and said, "Three-and-a-half beers in an hour. Not bad."

"Don't bust my chops. You ain't no saint," Rachel said.

"What I was going to say before I was so rudely interrupted was, do you remember the times in high school when we could do a whole lot better?" He grinned and then reached over and took her hand. "I'm a good listener. If you need to talk, I'm here."

Rachel's pitiful smile didn't reach her eyes. In the quietest of voices, like a five-year-old whispering, she started talking. "I met him there the day Ms. Stewart disappeared."

Scott shot me a questioning glance. I shrugged. It was Rachel's story.

"Met who?" Scott asked.

I reached over and put my hand on Scott's shoulder, silencing him.

"After class he told me that if I didn't meet him at the park and make him happy, he would see to it that I didn't graduate. I didn't know what else to do, so after school that day, I went to the park. He was late. I had almost decided to leave when he got there." Rachel took a deep breath.

Scott clenched his jaws hard.

"When Jamie and I went to the park today, I wanted to throw up. I wanted to run and run and run and never stop, and the whole time, I just kept talking and smiling like everything was okay. But everything wasn't okay. It'll never be okay. I can't do this. I thought I could, but I can't!" She punched the mattress with her fist.

I couldn't believe what I was hearing. Why had I insisted on dragging Rachel into this mess? Dredging up all these old, horrific memories. I had no way of knowing about the park, but I'm not sure ignorance is an excuse. Why hadn't I realized what this would do to her?

Scott's eyes flashed. No self-recriminations for him. Between clenched teeth, he said, "Who was it, Rachel? Who did this to you?"

"What's it matter now? It's over," she sobbed. "I just want to leave this town and never come back. I never should have come here."

"Listen, Rache, did it ever occur to you that Ms. Stewart was in the park and saw what happened to you, and that's why she lost her life?" I said it as gently as possible, but I wanted Rachel to know that she needed to quit protecting the creep who had destroyed her life.

"I never saw her. I swear I didn't, or I would have told someone. I can't believe that it's *my* fault she's dead."

"Let's not jump to conclusions. But *please* tell Scott who it was."

Rachel hesitated for a moment, and then looking down with averted eyes, she whispered, "It was Mr. House. Phillip House." Then as if the mere act of saying his name was like taking a swig of ipecac syrup, Rachel raced to the bathroom and vomited.

Scott's fingers tightened around the arms of his wheelchair.

I followed her into the bathroom and put a hand on her heaving back. Rachel wretched for at least three minutes and then came up gasping for air. With a cool, damp washcloth, I wiped her face. I put some paste on a toothbrush and handed it to her. Not just so she could get the sour taste out of her mouth, but to give her something to do that felt normal. Her eyes were puffy, her nose bright red, and her skin blotchy. I thought she'd never looked more beautiful. And I never wanted to kill another human being as much as I wanted to kill Mr. House. Not exactly a Christian sentiment, but I didn't feel all that Christian right at the moment.

Rachel spoke quietly at first, her voice getting stronger as she talked. "When does it end? When do I stop feeling so dirty? I want to purge the memory of Mr. House out of my system."

She walked back into the room with a glimmer of hope . . . or determination—I wasn't sure which—in her eyes. "Scott, what do I need to do? What do you need from me?"

"Do you think he could have been the one who killed Ms. Stewart?"

"Duh. He *is* a scumbag." My voice was as loud as it was mad. "Ms. Stewart must have seen what happened and confronted him and he killed her. It wasn't long after we graduated that he got involved in politics, and now he's the Speaker of the House."

"I'm asking Rachel," Scott said.

"I don't know. I only know what he did to me." Rachel shook her head.

"Trust me," I said it as if Rachel hadn't spoken at all. "If Tim did find out, House certainly had the means and motive to kill him. I don't think there's any doubt. Listen, Scott, he's speaking at the graduation tomorrow night. You need to go and arrest him now."

"Hold on, Jamie. I appreciate you telling me how to do my job, but you could be wrong."

"Not likely," I snapped.

"I admit this looks pretty bad for House, but right now, all we have is circumstantial evidence."

"Circumstantial evidence? He's a stinking creep, and you know it."

"Yes, judge, I want you to find him guilty. He's a stinking creep.

Jamie said so. I am sure that will fly. I'll advise the DA of your prosecutorial instincts." Scott didn't try to hide his sarcasm.

Rachel laughed a small laugh, but it seemed genuine.

I wasn't amused. I glared at Scott.

"Calm down a minute, will you? I scoured the case file with a fine-tooth comb right after Tim was killed," he said. "The police questioned House twice after Stewart's disappearance. Someone at the park had seen his car there and reported it when the parents of the missing girl posted a reward. They dismissed him as a suspect then. And I checked on his whereabouts last week when Tim was killed. He was in Washington, DC at the time of the murder."

"Big deal, it was a professional hit. He could have hired anyone. Did you knock on his door and ask to see *his* bank statements?" I sounded as indignant as I felt.

"No, I didn't," he said. "He's not inheriting Tim's estate. That's why you're in the DA's crosshairs."

"Thanks a bunch, *friend*." I was adept at sarcasm too. "Take the word of a scumbag, but put me in the suspect pool." I knew I was being unfair. It wasn't Scott's fault, but I couldn't stop the angry words.

"He's a suspect now, though, so stop looking at me like I'm the murderer," he said. "In the meantime, we still need to find out who Tim was bringing to the meeting tonight. He . . . or she . . . might be able to tell us exactly what Tim was onto. We can't arrest House or anyone else without evidence no matter how much we don't like them."

I scowled at him. "What about what he did to Rachel?"

"Statute of limitations is five years on sexual assault of a minor."

"Five years!" I was appalled.

Scott threw up his hands. "I don't make the laws, Jamie."

Rachel interrupted our stare down by changing the subject. "Did you find anyone who knew Tim?"

I shifted my eyes away from Scott's. "Not exactly. But he did get frequent visits from a man with a Highland Scots' bumper sticker on a blue sedan with tires frequently marked by a dog named Roger."

Rachel raised an eyebrow.

"Don't ask." I waved away her unspoken question. "I thought we could swing by the school today and ask around, but we need to hurry before anyone else is murdered—mainly the three of us. I don't want you to come, Rachel, now that I know how hard it is for you, but I'm afraid to leave you alone."

"I'll be fine. I was just caught off guard by the park."

"I need you sober tonight."

"Don't worry. I'll be fine."

"I can see that." I picked up the empty beer bottles and tossed them in the trash.

Rachel ignored me. "Scott, did you bring the passwords I need to get into the mainframe?" He nodded. "Good. Now leave me here with my laptop, and I'll do some research on House and the other suspects. You might be surprised at what I can dig up."

She went to the bathroom, poured the rest of the beer from her open bottle down the sink, and threw the two full bottles in the trash to prove her point.

"I don't want you left alone," I said, unconvinced.

"I'll be fine. Take the room and car keys. You can even take my purse. I won't have any way to go anywhere or buy anything. Please. If Ms. Stewart got killed trying to protect me, I want to do what I can to find her killer."

I looked at Scott, who nodded. He took the two beers out of

the garbage, popped the tops, and poured them out too. "Just a precaution."

Rachel didn't comment. He gave the passwords to her and collected her purse and keys. "My cell number is 555-5309. If you get crazy—want a drink or whatever—give me a call. We'll talk it through. Good luck."

I gave her a hug. "Be safe, girlfriend. I'll be back as soon as I can."

CHAPTER FOURTEEN

D riving through the parking lot at school proved discouraging. Evidently, blue was the color of choice for a lot of drivers, and three out of every four bumpers proudly displayed the Highland mascot blowing on bagpipes.

"This is going to be harder than I thought," I said.

"Not really. Come on. We have a few minutes before classes dismiss for the year. Let's go to the office and let my badge do the talking."

The principal wasn't in his office, but after a conversation with the assistant principal, the secretary made an announcement that blared through the classrooms, offices, library, and gym.

"If you drive a blue sedan and are a friend of Tim Manter, please meet Scott Walters of the Anderson Police Department in the cafeteria. Now."

The cafeteria was long and wide and held three rows of twelve tables each with bench seats. The eight-foot mobile tables had yucky, hunter-green laminate tops and seats. The heavy-duty gray floor tiles were scuffed with black shoe marks from a day's foot traffic. Bits of paper and food littered the area, and I brushed off some crumbs before I sat down. Scott and I waited fifteen minutes after the last bell of the day, but no one showed.

"I knew it couldn't be this easy," Scott said, sighing. "Let's go."

"Just a few more minutes, Scott, please. What have we got to lose besides time?"

For me, coming into the school building brought back lots of memories. The sounds, smells, and sights wrapped me in a warm blanket of reverie. My four years at Highland had been filled with laughter, learning, fun, and comfort. Every recollection—from the school lockers to the principal's office—was good. I couldn't remember a single bad experience. Besides the Cliffhangers club, I had been a part of band, on the yearbook staff, ran cross-country, and was on the drama and debate team. I maintained a 3.5 grade point average and got along with most of the teachers.

How could Rachel's experience have been so radically different? How could I not have noticed? I felt my new best friend—guilt—return with laser focus.

Thankfully, the cafeteria door opened before the feeling leveled me. In walked a tall, lanky man with an air of authority. He wore a well-tailored, charcoal, pin-stripe suit, with a basic white shirt and silk yellow tie with diagonal charcoal stripes. His black shoes were buffed to a sparkling shine. Although his blond hair grayed at the temples, he didn't appear to be much older than his early- to mid-fifties. I noticed an inch-long scar that sliced across his left eyebrow. His face was clean-shaven, but he neither smiled nor scowled.

All business, he stuck out his right hand to Scott. "Craig Haskell, principal. May I help you?"

Scott produced his badge. "Scott Walters—Anderson Police Department. This is Jamie Storm. We're looking into the death of Timothy Manter."

Haskell looked at me. "Your badge?"

"She doesn't have one," Scott said. "Tim's a friend of ours from high school. She's back here for our class reunion and wanted to tag along."

He acknowledged me with a slight nod, his hazel-green eyes veiling any emotions he might be feeling. Almost like he was protecting himself from an invisible enemy.

"What do you need from me?" the principal asked.

"Information. A lead brought us here. Someone from Tim's neighborhood saw a blue sedan with a Highland High bumper sticker. Of course, everybody in town has a Scots bumper sticker, but we had to try. We thought it possible that whoever drove the car might have known Tim and why he was killed."

"I own a blue car, although I'm a little wounded by the blue sedan description. I drive a BMW 320i that tops out at 226 mph." He smiled, but I couldn't tell if it was amusement or arrogance.

"Nice," Scott said, and meant it.

"I'm a friend of Tim's—or was. I'm not sure how I can help, but I'll tell you what I know."

Butterflies fluttered in my stomach. I was anxious for information about Tim. *Please God, let this guy know something.*

"Go on," Scott said.

"Tim phoned me about two years ago out of the blue. He was a stockbroker in New York, single, and interested in my past. Well, not really *my* past," Haskell qualified. "But thirty years ago I was engaged to Dacia Stewart.

Bingo!

Scott and I exchanged glances.

"Tim was looking for answers regarding Dacia's disappearance. When the principal's job at Highland came open, I applied. I moved down here, and he and I have searched for those answers ever since. He told me about the Cliffhangers club and wanted me to come to the class reunion with him."

"Did you find anything?" I asked, more than a little curious.

"We didn't find anything new, but we did become good friends. We spent time fishing, rock climbing, and spelunking together. In bad weather we watched movies, did remodeling projects, and skied. He was like family. Good times. Last week, he called. I think it was Saturday night, and he wanted to know if we could meet after church on Sunday."

I had to interrupt. "Tim went to church?"

Craig nodded. "In the last few weeks he had started going to that big church on College Drive in Parkside. He invited me a couple of times. I declined. I really have no interest in that sort of thing. We used to go on weekend fishing trips, but after he started the church thing, we could only take one-day trips. Had to be back for Sundays. I think church takes up a lot of time, and personally, I don't believe in God and never will. I've seen too many good people hurt for no reason. Dacia is a good example of that. I really can't see how a loving God would let someone like her be killed. And look at Tim. Right after he starts going to church, he gets a bullet to the brain. No thank you. Not interested." Bitterness laced his speech.

I didn't say anything. It was hard. I wanted to pull out the old "God doesn't do bad things. People choose to do bad things" card, but wisely I kept it tucked away.

Craig continued. "I agreed to meet him after church because he sounded so excited. He said he thought he knew who did it and that I would be blown away. Famous last words. Unfortunately, he was the one blown away. That's all I know. I lost a very good friend and wish we'd never even started the investigation."

"What about this idea that Tim was sure he had found the killer. Did he give you any hints at all?" Scott asked.

"No, except to say I would be surprised. He said we'd been looking in all the wrong places."

"Where'd you look?" Scott asked.

"Long story."

"Would you be willing to come to the meeting tonight and tell us?" I asked. "The six remaining Cliffhangers all had Dacia Stewart as a student teacher. Since we've already met, it won't be like coming in cold turkey. I know the others would like to meet you." I tried to sound inviting without being pushy.

"To be perfectly honest, I'm done. I've had enough of this. I loved Dacia, but that was a long time ago. Having a friendship with Tim was great, but I can't help but feel he wouldn't be dead if it weren't for me. I'm just done. Good luck on finding Tim's killer."

Craig turned to leave, but Scott caught his arm, "Could you at least give us the names of the people you checked out?"

"You already have the list. It's in your police report," Haskell said.

"Tim thought none of them did it?" I asked.

"Yeah." With that Craig turned and left.

"That can't be. Phillip House's name is on the list. Tim didn't know what happened to Rachel. How could he be so sure it wasn't someone on the list?" My mind reeled with this last bit of information.

"I told you, all we have on Phillip House is strong circumstantial evidence. We need more. Maybe Tim knew something that led him off the track. If he had known about Rachel, he might have changed his mind. On the other hand, being a child molester doesn't automatically make you a killer."

"No, but I bet being a politician who's also a child molester does. Especially if someone discovers your dirty little secrets. I'm not letting this go, Scott. I'm going to nail the creep if you don't."

Scott grinned. "Ooh, big talk from a preacher's wife. Do they teach you to slay dragons too?"

I laughed, but obstinacy punctuated my next words. "Okay, maybe I can't slay dragons, but I've handled plenty of bad guys at annual business meetings. I have my ways. Seriously, what happened to Rachel was wrong. If he did that to her, how many other girls' lives has he ruined? This isn't some game, this is ugly, and I *will* do what I can. I have to. Rachel deserves better, Tim deserved better, and my guess is Dacia Stewart deserved better. I sat by in high school with blinders on about what was going on around me. I won't do it again."

"I didn't say I was giving up on House. I just said maybe we're wrong. I made a call after we left your motel and someone is already checking on his financial records. C'mon, let's go see if Rachel found out anything."

CHAPTER FIFTEEN

Rachel's hands were flying across the keyboard when Scott and I entered the room. She looked up briefly to acknowledge our entrance. "How'd it go? Find out anything?"

"Oh yeah, we found Tim's mystery guest. You're not going to believe who it is. He's on the list of suspects in the file." I couldn't resist dangling the carrot in front of her.

Rachel made a face. "I found out a lot of interesting info myself. I'll tell if you do."

Scott interrupted. "Listen, girls, I need to run home and see Tanae and the kids before meeting tonight. Why don't you keep the information to yourselves until we're with the gang? That way everyone hears the same thing at the same time, and we won't be playing he said/she said."

"Fine." Rachel looked down and tapped on the keyboard with fast, efficient strokes.

"Give Tanae a hug for me," I said.

"Will do. I'll see you ladies at Todd's."

I was glad the Cliffhangers meeting would be at Todd Davis's house. He lived ten miles out of Anderson on a farm—no bad memories for Rachel. He'd been a farm boy his whole life and was the only one of the group who shared my faith in Christ. He and

I had become friends when we met in Sunday school in the three-and four-year-old class. Our teacher, Miss Lacock, would always ask how our week went, and everyone would say good or great or okay except for Todd. He always, always, always said, "Sorta good and sorta bad." Then he'd say they had too little rain, but that mama cat had kittens. Or his sister picked on him all week long, but his dad let him ride a pig. We loved his stories, but Miss Lacock didn't appreciate them much, I think because we all thought they were so much more interesting than Zaccheus, Moses, or Paul.

As we got older, his stories weren't as fascinating, but by then we were buddies, so I hauled him along to the Cliffhangers' gatherings. He went under protest because he didn't really care about mysteries. He stuck with the group all four years in high school, but his participation was that of an onlooker. He liked things he could understand—a good corn crop, barrows and gilts, moisture—lots of moisture—and combines.

Rachel continued surfing the Internet. "It's amazing what you can find out with a name and social security number. Why does everyone think their children's names and birthdates make good passwords? Personal information is the easiest to find. I even got into some sealed police files. Easy, smeasy for an ingenious hacker like myself."

"And you're modest too. You gotta like that in you ingenious hackers."

Rachel rolled her eyes, though they sparkled for the first time since I'd seen her. If anyone had a calling to be a computer whiz, it was Rachel. Talk about a kid in a candy store. Commandeering private data from various Web sites and sources thrilled her. I could literally see her body relax as the printer spewed out page after page of background data on the four original suspects in the Stewart murder case. She'd also garnered information about Tim's death. In fact, she downloaded his complete file, which was minimal, and printed it out. She was definitely ready for her part of the meeting.

"Let's get a bite to eat before we go to Todd's. It could be a long night." My stomach growled in agreement.

Rachel grinned. "I'd prefer a drink, but if food is all you're offering, I'll take it."

At five-thirty, we left the motel. Neither of us had much to say once in the car. My mind whirled with details of the case. I did manage to ask what Rachel wanted to eat and after a bit of I-don't-care-well-I-don't-care-either, we decided on the Chinese place on Scatterfield. The food was always good, quick, and inexpensive.

Too late, I heard the brakes of the small, red Sunbird ahead of me screech. With a jerk and streak of black rubber on pavement, it came to a jolting stop. I stomped hard on my brake pedal, causing the Escape to swerve. I fought the steering wheel for control. We skidded within a foot of the rear bumper of the front vehicle. The car behind us wasn't so lucky. Rachel's head whipped backward as the car crunched into the rear bumper of our SUV. The impact didn't deploy the airbags, but the seat belts left a few bruises.

Traffic lurched to a full stop. I opened the driver's door and stepped out. The vehicle that hit us was a beige Volvo. The teen-aged driver of the front vehicle was out of the car, sobbing, hands fluttering, her two friends trying to calm her down. I thought I'd better check on them before checking on the Volvo driver. Ever impatient, the unaffected Indiana drivers started their cars and drove slowly around us, giving us curious stares.

Walking to the front of the Sunbird, I saw the problem. I managed to stifle a groan. A kitten, not more than eight weeks old, lay flattened and bloody behind the driver's side tire.

I then walked over to the weeping girl and her friends, using my practiced, pastor's wife's, soothing, it's-going-to-be-okay voice. "Listen, honey, there's no way you could have stopped in time. I'll pick up the kitten. You get back in your car and pull into that driveway on the right so we can get out of the way of traffic. We'll see if we can find the owners. I'll be right behind you."

The three girls were all in tears. I pegged them to be sixteen or seventeen. They were dressed in jeans, too small T-shirts, expensive tennis shoes, and all looked pretty much alike. The driver seemed inconsolable. The slogan on her T-shirt couldn't have been more ironic: "If at first you don't succeed"—written in bold, green letters across her chest and on the back—"Skydiving isn't for you." *Really? Apparently driving isn't for you either.*

Streaks of black mascara and liner slithered down her cheeks. Her friends helped push her into the backseat of the vehicle though it proved difficult. She kept her hands over her face, sobbing in the dramatic fashion that only a teen girl can do. No doubt she was too stricken to drive any further.

I was happy that I'd only birthed boy children. I couldn't remember ever being this fluttery, weepy, or hysterical in all my days as a girl. And neither had my boys.

Rachel had not left her seat in the Escape. Her head was down, probably in an effort to not be seen by anyone who could possibly recognize her. I realized that I wasn't doing a very good job of protecting her from feeling exposed and vulnerable. But I didn't know how I could've prevented this little mishap.

Walking back to the Volvo driver who was busy inspecting the damage to my rental, I asked, "Are you all right?"

The stylish woman was close to six feet tall and looked oddly familiar. She had blonde hair with streaks of gray, wore a pale-yellow pantsuit, yellow sling-back sandals, and yellow earrings. She could've been the cover girl for AARP.

"I'm fine. Just a little shook up. The question is how are *you*?"

"I'm better than the young lady who ran over the kitten. I'm going to pull over into that driveway with her and get out of traffic. If you follow us we can exchange insurance information and numbers."

"No problem. I'll be right behind you."

"You look familiar. Do I know you?" I asked.

Something quick, some emotion, some hint, flashed through her eyes, and then disappeared as quickly as it appeared. I almost didn't see it. Volvo-lady shook her head no. "I'm not from around here. I must have one of those faces." She seemed to choose her words with care.

"Okay, just follow me."

I smiled and walked back to the Escape. I grabbed my sweater out of the back of the SUV and painstakingly picked up the dead kitten. Poor thing. The young driver let out a sound that was half-shriek, half-groan, and started crying again. Quickly covering the lifeless little body, I instructed the new driver, "Okay, let's go."

Rachel took the cat, holding it for me until we could get out of the street.

The teenage girl maneuvered the Sunbird into the residential driveway, with me following. The cat owner had to live around here somewhere. I would help the girls find whomever after I traded insurance information with the Volvo lady.

"She's driving away. She's not stopping," yelled Rachel, twisting around in her seat.

"What?"

"The woman in the Volvo—the one who rear-ended us— she's gone."

I parked behind the Sunbird and got out in time to glimpse the beige Volvo weaving in and out of traffic at a frenzied pace. "Weird. I guess I should have gotten a name. She didn't do much damage to my vehicle. On the other hand she's missing some paint and has a broken headlight."

"Her problem, I guess." Rachel shrugged.

"You happen to see her plate?"

"No, sorry. I wasn't paying attention."

"Very strange. Oh well, I have a cat owner to find," I said.

It took about three houses before the still weepy teen and I found the owner of the kitten—a barrel-chested man in his mid-sixties with shaggy eyebrows and shoulder-length, gray hair held back with a rubber band. He was wearing bib overalls—the kind you associate with train conductors—a white T-shirt, and corduroy bedroom slippers.

I related the story as best I could with Miss Weepy hiccupping through her sobs.

He responded kindly. "Come on in. Set him down on the dining room table."

The feline odor in his house nearly knocked me over. The couch, chairs, and windowsills were alive with the meowing species. There wasn't a piece of furniture that wasn't scratched, frayed, or badly stained. I guessed there had to be over fifty cats. It was obvious it would have taken days for him to notice one small cat was missing.

"I try to rescue these little guys, but occasionally one gets away. This is the first time I've lost a cat."

"Can't you take them to an animal shelter?"

He looked at me like I'd lost my marbles. "Have you ever been to an animal shelter? Shelter? These little guys wouldn't last three days. If they don't get adopted in a preordained time frame, they get juiced."

"Juiced?"

"Killed. Put to sleep. Euthanized. I'd sooner see them get run over." He grunted.

"Oh." I could certainly turn a phrase in a pinch.

"I'll have a service for Puddens tonight," he said, stroking the dead kitten's fur.

"Oh." My second clever comeback in a row.

"We are very sorry," I said. "Thank you for understanding. She really tried to stop in time."

He nodded his head.

I grabbed Weepy's hand. The other girls had opted to wait in the car, and we walked out the door after again apologizing profusely for Puddens' demise. The smell of fresh air was intoxicating, and I took several deep breaths. I waved good-bye to the teary-eyed crew and climbed back in the Escape.

Looking at my watch, I sighed. "That little incident cost us a good bit of time. We'll order takeout and eat at Todd's."

"I am *so* good with that," Rachel said. "The less I have to be in public, the more I like it."

Pulling up to the takeout window, I ordered beef with peapods, sesame chicken, and two egg rolls. "Put chopsticks in the bag too. Please."

"Chopsticks? It'll take us all night to eat." Rachel groaned.

"Come on, Rache. Live a little. Don't you ever watch TV? They eat with chopsticks on *Law and Order* shows all the time. Maybe it gives them special reasoning powers. I eat with chopsticks, therefore I solve crimes." I winked at Rachel.

She shook her head and smiled. "You need serious help, Jamie."

CHAPTER SIXTEEN

Todd Davis lived on the farm he'd grown up tilling, cultivating, and planting. It was a sprawling 2,200 acres of rolling hills. His grandparents had started out with a modest 300 acres, but with good management, hard work, and long days, they were able to buy neighboring land.

Todd's dad inherited the same work ethic and bought two more farms, the owners looking more for the quick buck than the uncertain future of government regulations, nature's whim, or Wall Street futures. When his parents died, they willed the farm to Todd—huge by Indiana standards, but he loved every inch of it. He was determined to give his kids the lifestyle that city living could never afford.

He took pride in Indiana being the fifth largest producer of corn in the country. He was a part of that statistic, and it made him feel good. He also raised soybeans and wheat, but corn was his favorite. He loved the look of the straight rows and would always say, "Knee high by the Fourth of July! Gonna be a bumper crop, Jamie." I must've heard that every summer since we were six. One summer a violent hailstorm destroyed every stalk within a hundred miles. He called it the Great Combine in the Sky.

He'd been offered millions for the acreage by a huge corporation based in St. Louis, looking to expand its brewery operations. He turned them down flat. He'd e-mailed me after the offer: "I can't put a price on my kids' safety or their happiness."

We arrived at Todd's at 6:55 p.m. Four vehicles were parked at the front of his house, including Scott's customized police van. Nosed in next to it was a station wagon with the WNTV logo emblazoned on both sides and the top.

"Well, what do you know. Billy Fisher made it. I don't recognize the brown truck, but guess who owns the blue Beemer?"

I didn't give Rachel time to answer before I grabbed the bag of Chinese food and headed for the house. Rachel trudged behind me like she was headed for the gallows. She held her laptop to her chest like a shield. A mental image of Linus and his blanket flashed through my mind.

"Who? Who owns the BMW?" Rachel asked, a trace of fear lacing her question.

"Come on in, and I'll introduce you to him."

The door opened to the sounds of, "It's been so long. How are you?" and "You haven't changed a bit." Once inside, there was hugging and high-fiving all around. Shawn Norman walked in, and the hugging resumed. When the greetings finally wound down, it was as if we'd just seen each other yesterday. No uncomfortable clearing of throats, no tension, no lack for conversation, at least not for me. I wasn't sure about Rachel. Timid in high school . . . timid here.

Craig Haskell stood back, taking it all in, not joining the conversation. He had changed from a suit to well-worn Levi's and a soft, lime-green Polo shirt. His Nikes were black and appeared to be right out of the box. But however casual his clothes, he looked ill at ease, like he had never seen a group of buddies hug. His face revealed a look that was somewhere between awe, amazement, and distaste.

Before I had a chance to introduce Craig, Billy confronted him. "Hey, who are you?" Billy growled, noticing the stranger for the first time.

"Craig Haskell."

"What are you doing here?"

"I was invited. You?" Craig asked, not intimidated.

"I thought this was Cliffhangers only," Billy grumbled.

I shot him what I hoped was a nasty glare and cleared my throat. "Okay guys, time to get this show on the road. I see everyone could make it but Tim. All of you know why. What most of you *don't* know is that Tim left his considerable fortune to me, which makes me a prime suspect in his murder. I called you guys to this meeting because I thought you could help clear my name. I believe his death is somehow related to Dacia Stewart's murder. For those of you who don't know, the guy here on my right is Craig Haskell—Dacia's fiancé at the time of her death. Tim had invited him to come to our reunion. I'll let him tell the story from there."

Craig nodded at the group.

Todd put his hands up in a time-out gesture. "I know I'm kind of slow, but I wonder if we could take five minutes to catch up on our lives and maybe tell Craig a bit about ourselves. I know it sounds all churchy-touchy-feely, but I need an icebreaker. I haven't seen Rachel in thirty years, and it's been almost that long since I've seen Shawn."

Everyone agreed but me. Of course, none of their lives were on the line. Personally, I was ready to dispense with the niceties and get on with the murders, but that's democracy for you. I was outvoted.

We all sat down at the kitchen table. "I'll start," I said. "Then we'll go around the table from my left, and Craig can end it."

I looked over at Craig. "First, I'll give you some background on all of us. We all went to Highland High here in Anderson. We all graduated in 1985, we all had Dacia as a student teacher in our fourth year of English, and we all belonged to a mystery club called the Cliffhangers. For the last thirty years I've been a preacher's wife and have moved around a bit. I live in Great Falls, Montana and have four boys—two sets of twins. My mother lives here, and my two youngest go to AU.

"I was baking pies without a care in the world when I got the news that Tim had been killed. In an instant my life was turned upside down. I suddenly became a suspect in a friend's murder, complete with ten million reasons for killing him. I called this meeting because I need your help. We were going to meet sometime this weekend anyway during our class reunion. I just bumped up the time frame a bit. For me, finding Tim's killer is very personal."

"Tim told me about the club," Craig said. "Some of the stories were, well, I will just say interesting."

I pulled a box of rice out of our takeout bag. "Rache and I didn't get a chance to eat before we came, so excuse me while I dig into the food." I looked at her.

"I'm Rachel King. I live in Philadelphia. I do freelance research for large companies, anything from employee background checks to in-depth financial analysis of companies being bought out by conglomerates. I've never been married and never intend to be. I wouldn't be here now if Jamie hadn't dragged me here. I'm not very social."

"Shawn Norman here." Shawn stood and shook hands with Craig. "I was a confirmed bachelor until about ten years ago when I met a remarkable woman. Actually, I had met her once before years ago, but that's another story. Anyway, we have a beautiful, nine-year-old daughter. My wife couldn't get away from work, so they didn't come with me. We live in Israel where I work at the US embassy. It worked out for me to be here for the reunion, but frankly I'm anxious to get back to my family and continue my work. I'm all yours, Jamie, as far as the investigation goes until Monday morning. Then it's back to God's country. Literally."

Scott reached across Shawn and pulled a piece of sesame chicken out of Rachel's takeout box. "This is good stuff."

He had also changed out of the clothes he was wearing earlier. He had opted for jeans, a T-shirt with an Anderson Police Department logo on it, and running shoes. I wondered how adept he was at changing and whether Tanae helped, or if he did it on his own. I had no plans to ask him, but I was still curious.

Between chews he continued the introductions. "Scott Walters, Anderson Police Department, paraplegic, father of two, husband of one, hometown boy who still loves his hometown. I took the liberty of making copies of Dacia Stewart's police file as well as Tim's. If you each want to take a copy, it might help you with the discussion tonight. This is, of course, highly against police procedure, so keep your mouths shut and minds open. Hopefully the six . . ." he looked skeptically at Craig, "or seven of us can come up with more than my department did. Sometimes the untrained eye can see what the professionals miss. Also, on top of the Stewart file, you'll notice green Post-it Notes. I took the liberty of making a list of the four suspects, or at least the four people of interest who were interviewed twice about her murder."

"Icebreaking, icebreaking," Todd interjected. "You and Jamie are all business. Give us a break for a minute. The rest of us want to catch up. Go ahead, Billy."

Billy Fisher grinned. "I'm sure most of you know me from Channel 8 News. I do in-depth investigation pieces. I think my high school experience as a Cliffhanger poured 'exposing secrets' into my veins. I haven't been so lucky personally. I've been divorced twice and am currently dating Shelly Andrews from Channel 6. My child support payments total about $1,500 a month. I need to keep finding the next big story. I don't have much time to give this weekend. I'm working on a piece that'll blow the lid off the homeless industry here in Indy. And yeah, I mean what I say when I say industry. You guys would not believe what's happening. The next time we meet, I should be anchoring a national evening news program. Move over Couric, here comes Fisher."

"Modest as always," Todd said. "Hi, Craig, I'm Todd Davis from Anderson. I grew up in a farming family, still farm, and love every minute of it. The sunrises, rainfall, stars, fresh morning air, and my wife and kids are what prove to me that God exists. That He loves me, that getting up every day is worth it, and that I can look forward to an eternity with Him."

"Hey, no preaching," Billy said.

"I let you say what you wanted to say. Now you let me say what I want to say. I'm not much good at mysteries, but I know one thing. Jamie didn't kill anyone, and Scott, I can't believe you haven't cleared her yet. This whole mess makes me sick except for one thing. The night before Tim died he drove out for supper. Sheila fixed her killer lasagna—no pun intended. Excellent meal, if I do say so myself. Anyway, Tim told us that he totally surrendered his life to God—that he'd been exploring the Bible and chosen to give Christ a try. Said he felt as if a weight lifted off his shoulders, like he had more freedom now than ever before. I just wanted you to know you don't have to be sad for Tim. He's in a much better place."

I blinked to stop the tears that threatened to roll down my face. Billy rolled his eyes. Rachel stared intently at Todd, as if she was trying to decide if he was telling the truth. Scott and Shawn both looked down. Embarrassed, perhaps? And then Craig Haskell started talking.

"Well, I guess it's my turn. The only reason I'm here is Tim. I'm the principal at Highland now. I moved here at Tim's suggestion. He called me two years ago and said he wanted to look into Dacia's disappearance. I wasn't doing anything with my life at that time. Highland had a job opening, so here I am. Tim and I had become quite close in the last two years. I didn't do the church thing with him, but we did lots of other stuff. I wasn't even going to come here tonight, but I wanted to honor his memory one last time. He felt he was onto something—something he had to talk to me about. He was murdered before we got a chance. Maybe listening to you all tonight will remind me of something he said. Maybe I'll remember something that doesn't seem important to me but will be to some of you. I don't know. I *do* know that I am sick of death. Maybe if I work with you guys, I can make sense of it all."

"Thanks, everyone," I said, clapping my hands in a let's-get-going gesture. "We'll run through the four suspects in the original murder first and see if anything pops up. After that, we'll run our get-together like a regular Cliffhangers meeting. Agreed?"

Everyone nodded.

"Shawn, you're on the list of suspects in the Stewart murder. How did that happen?" Billy asked.

"I know I didn't do it," the US ambassador to Israel replied, "but I *do* know why they questioned me. On the Friday before Ms. Stewart disappeared, she had recorded all our grades in her grade book. All that was left was the final the following week, and it would be figured in. I had a 56 percent. An F. I went to her Friday night and asked if there was anything I could do to make up the grade. I needed the English requirements, or I wouldn't be able to graduate. She told me it was too late to do anything about it. Said I should have come to her earlier. I begged, but she was firm, and I stomped out of class yelling that she would regret it as long as she lived."

"Appropriate." Billy laughed.

"I was just a young punk then—about as irresponsible as you can get. Anyway, Mr. House heard me yelling at her and later gave my name to the investigators working her case. I don't think it would have been such a big deal, except for the fact that when grades came out after the final, which I did well on, I got an A. Not a C minus or a D plus, but an A. It looked like I had done away with Stewart and doctored the numbers. Fortunately for me it was all circumstantial evidence, and they gave up. To this day, I have no idea how the grade got changed. I've often wondered if someone tried to frame me for her death, but I *didn't* murder Ms. Stewart *or* Tim."

"You never told us any of this back in the day when we were trying to figure it out," I said.

"I couldn't afford to. The grade was great, and my parents were so proud. I kept it to myself. We were trying to find her killer, and I knew it wasn't me, so I didn't think it was relevant. Besides, how many of you would have believed me then?"

Rachel raised her hand. "Trust me, guys, he didn't do it. I changed his grade. I was working in the office, helping get Ms.

Stewart's grades registered in the new school computer. Actually, I helped a lot of teachers register their student data. Computers were so new that I thought even if someone caught the mistake, they would just assume it was a keyboarding error. It was easy, and I thought, who's it going to hurt? All the rest of us were graduating, and I didn't want Shawn left behind."

"Thanks, Rache, you're all heart. Being questioned in a missing person's case—and later a murder investigation—is so much better than flunking a class," Shawn groused.

The group laughed.

"Don't complain. You're the ambassador to Israel," Rachel reminded him.

"There is that," he said.

"Craig, you're on the list." I turned the focus back to the matter at hand.

"Yeah, I know. But I loved Dacia, and I *didn't* kill her. Tim and I were friends, and I *didn't* kill him. You're welcome to look into my background, my finances, anything."

Rachel spoke up. "I've already done that, and you're as clean as Shawn. I did have some trouble locating your family though. Adoptions were still very closed in those days. I'm sorry about your family. I can't imagine losing two sets of parents." Her work was thorough.

"I don't remember much about my birth parents. I was four when they died. My adoptive parents died the day of my college graduation. They were driving up to IU from Crane. Their car was found in a ditch, badly damaged from an outside source. Probably a hit-and-run drunk driver, but no arrest was ever made. After I walked for my diploma, two police were waiting for me. They gave me the news. It was a horrible day."

I smiled at him. "I think we can safely say you're not our suspect. If Tim trusted you, so can we."

"Next up is James Blevins," Scott said. "The police questioned him twice. He was in our class, but I don't really remember him. The original investigation found he'd been sending love letters to Ms. Stewart. The kid was totally infatuated with her. The police even caught him sneaking around outside her window late one night a month before she disappeared. A peeping tom, apparently. She didn't press charges, but the administration removed him from her English class. The day she disappeared, he didn't show up for school. His parents said he had the flu and stayed home. The problem was that both parents worked, and department records show the investigating team couldn't confirm that he stayed home. The interesting thing about James is that he's a multimillionaire televangelist. If he did kill Ms. Stewart, he would have the means and the motive for silencing Tim."

I shook my head. "Not all of us Christians are kooks, you know. He could have made a real life change. When I've seen him on TV, which isn't often, he seems sincere. I think it's too easy and too pat to blame him. I do know that TV preachers don't have a great track record on the moral side of life, but I also know a lot of preachers who are genuine, honest, hardworking people who have truly made a difference in peoples' lives."

Billy looked me in the eye. "So you're saying that if he made a life change he shouldn't be held accountable for murder? Must be a nice world you live in, Jamie."

I was angry now. "I'm not saying that at all. Obviously, if he murdered someone, I want him to pay. But a teenage kid could peek through a window, write sappy love letters, and later become a true Christian. Evil isn't lurking behind every bush. Maybe you've been an investigative reporter too long. Your cynical nature isn't all that attractive."

"Don't be so sensitive, Jamie," Scott said. "We're getting to the person you want to hang. Let's at least try to be open-minded about this."

"Ooh, the good Christian lady wants someone to hang? I gotta hear this." Billy looked amused.

Actually, the good Christian lady would like to knock the grin off your face.

Instead, with stern help from my pastor's wife conscience, I said, "I don't think there's a single doubt that it was Phillip House. He was in the park on the day Dacia Stewart disappeared. I also know that he's a child molester, and my guess is Ms. Stewart found out. Maybe she confronted him and he couldn't risk losing his job as a teacher if the truth came out. He had political ambitions even then. Tim found out, and now the stakes are even higher. His job as Speaker of the House, his family, his financial empire, and his reputation would come crashing down around his ears. He'd killed before. Why not kill again? Only this time he probably had it done. Scott? Didn't the police rule it a professional hit?"

Scott nodded.

I opened my fortune cookie not to read a fortune, but a bit of homespun advice which wasn't necessarily true. *Smile and the world smiles with you.* The back listed my winning lottery numbers. I wadded up the slip of paper and made a perfect swish into the garbage can in the corner. "Ta-da! Three points."

The group ignored my LeBron skills and chewed on the House theory until Scott's cell phone rang. He talked quietly into the phone and then returned to the table discussion.

"I may have to agree with Jamie," he said. "There was a $56,000 withdrawal from House's savings account on May 11, two weeks before Tim was killed. It sounds like blood money to me. I just sent two men over to his house to interview him. If he has nothing to hide, he should be able to tell us where the money went."

"How far back did your guys look?" Rachel asked.

"Just this year. Why?"

"I've done some research myself this afternoon," Rachel said. "That $56,000 is not the first big withdrawal he's made from his savings account. He made several other large withdrawals starting sixteen years ago. It started out at $40,000 and went up by a thousand every year."

Scott looked puzzled. "That sounds more like blackmail than murder-for-hire."

"Another thing," Rachel added. "Every withdrawal was made on the Friday before Mother's Day."

CHAPTER SEVENTEEN

his last bit of information startled the group—me included.
I don't know what made a bigger impression on me, that
Rachel's skills provided such in-depth info, or that anyone
would have that much in a savings account to disperse on an
annual basis. It was beyond my scope of experience. Comments
and ideas flew around the table.

I got up to throw the empty Chinese food cartons in the garbage, and said, "We'll talk about this in a minute, but I need to
know if you all feel good about Craig being here. Tim trusted
him, and so do I. I think he should stay."

Almost everyone nodded agreement. Rachel didn't.

"I'm sorry, but I can't go along with it," she said. "Maybe you
are a good guy, Craig, and just have rotten luck. I don't know. But
I do know that death seems to occur at a regular frequency around
you. Two sets of parents—both dead. Your fiancé is dead. Tim, your
friend of two years, is dead. And there's one other bit of background
information I picked up that you didn't bother to share with us. Five
years after Ms. Stewart was killed, you got married. You and your
wife Angela were expecting your first child when she developed a
bad cough."

Craig's face drained of all color. He looked as if he had just been sucker punched. I kept my eyes on his face as Rachel continued.

"She went into the hospital and died the next day. The baby also died. An autopsy showed she had contracted an unknown virus. The information, medical records, and lab reports were sent to Atlanta to the CDC. Four years later in the spring of 1993, there was an outbreak of the Hantavirus. Although these were the first known cases in the United States, there were thirty-two identified victims. The CDC determined Angela and the baby were two of them."

There was total silence in the room as we processed the bombshell.

Rachel went on. "Too many deaths, guys. All outward signs point to the fact that you couldn't have been involved with any of them."

She hooked his eyes with hers and finished. "But to be on the safe side, I am not sure you should be allowed to know everything we do."

I swallowed. I was honestly too surprised to say anything.

Craig stood up. "She's right, you know. Everyone I've loved has died. I can't deny that. But remember this one thing . . . Tim called the night before he died and said we were looking in all the wrong places. He even had a suspicion that he might know who it was. So you talked about four suspects, but there are really five."

I didn't know what to do. Kick him out, or let him stay. Before I could say anything, he took the decision away from me.

He did a one-eighty and hightailed it out of the front door.

I turned to Rachel. "Why didn't you say something earlier? I thought you said his background came out clean." I could hear the accusation in my voice.

"It did. He hasn't even gotten so much as a parking ticket in the last thirty years. He wasn't implicated in any of the deaths. It's just that something about it makes me nervous. How can one person lose that many people?"

"I don't know, Rache, but he left, so I guess that's that," I said.

Before the meeting, Todd had set up a lightweight, hardwood easel with a large, thick, white pad on it. He had positioned colored markers on the tray. He got up, and taking the black marker, he wrote the word "Assumptions" and underlined it.

"Okay kids," he said. "Let's go. You give me what you *assume* about Tim's death, and I'll write it down. You all know that I have never come up with any ideas on my own, so fire away and I'll be the secretary."

"Tim was killed by the same person who killed Dacia Stewart," Shawn offered.

Todd threw out his own guess. "Neither Jamie or Shawn killed Tim."

"Tim was killed because of what he found out about the Stewart murder." Billy liked clear motives.

"The killer is smart," Scott said. "The police can't even find any clues."

"Tim had some information that nobody else had," Billy said.

The dining room was spacious and comfortable, and Todd had prepared for an all-out Cliffhanger session. In one corner were stacks of pictures in frames that must have previously hung on the walls. The top picture was of an older woman with her head bowed, eyes closed, and a loaf of bread in front of her. The walnut frame matched the dining room table, hutch, and buffet. The walls were sponge painted with light yellows and creams. About twelve inches from the ceiling a wallpaper border revealing antique trucks—not restored—graced the parking lot of a rural general store. You could see windmills and silos in the background—very nostalgic.

Thrust into another corner of the room was a huge vase filled with golden wheat stalks. I imagine Sheila cringed as Todd removed all the wall hangings and shoved furniture aside to make room for our meeting. From the looks of what I'd seen so far, I would say she was endowed with the decorator gene.

Todd scribbled down the assumptions as fast as we yelled them out. He flipped a page and in large letters wrote "Suspects." He numbered them from one to six and wrote out the names that had just been discussed, adding my name and a blank spot. Then he crossed through Shawn Norman, Jamie Storm, and Craig Haskell. He stared at Craig's name, meaning that not everyone in the group had cleared him. Then he put a question mark at the end of it.

Billy grinned. "Remember the case of the missing page 187?"

"Ms. Alexander's class. Junior year. The first day of school and every Algebra II book was missing page 187," Shawn said.

"That's right," I said, laughing. "And we did the same thing. Wrote our list of suspects down and started nosing around into everyone's business. Our list of suspects was long. Remember how we listed everyone in the senior class?"

"And we found out who did it purely by accident," Todd said. "Not much in the way of detective skills there."

"Speak for yourself," Rachel said. "Tim's brilliant mind led him straight to the culprit."

"Oops, my bad. It does take a lot of skill to spend the night with a fellow football player and notice his ceiling and walls are completely covered with the infamous page 187." Todd laughed and shook his head.

"I still remember why the kid did it," Shawn said. "Kind of a quiet guy Tad was. Tough linebacker on the field though."

"Don't keep us in suspense. Why?" Scott asked.

"He found out the answer key in the back of the book was wrong on one of the math problems on page 187. He went to Ms. Alexander, pointed it out, but she wouldn't listen. She told him to take his seat. Then 4.0 Jim called her attention to it later when he couldn't figure it out, and she took the time to run the problem. Sure enough, it was a typo and all the books were wrong. She told Jim how she appreciated his keen mind for catching the mistake. Tad didn't say a word. But with the help of a razor blade and a lot of patience, he systematically removed page 187 from every book—a few at a time—whenever Ms. Alexander left the room."

"Smart guy. Revenge without suspicion. Still, seems excessive for the slight," Billy said.

"Not when you're in high school. Seems brilliant," I said.

"Did we ever tell Ms. Alexander?" Billy asked.

"You kidding? You can't break the we-are-always-against-the-teachers code. Wouldn't be student-like." Scott laughed.

"It'd be nice if we could solve Tim's murder as easily," I said. "Maybe he slighted someone too."

"Big slight," Shawn said.

Todd stuck the "Assumptions" and "Suspects" pages on the dining room wall. Ripping five more blank pages off, he and Billy taped them to the wall. Handing a marker to everyone, he said, "Okay, you know the drill. You'll fire off questions. I'll write one question per sheet of paper, and then as we think of plausible answers, I'll record them under the appropriate question. We'll time this exercise for twenty minutes because we don't want anyone to second-guess his or her answers. Then for the following twenty minutes we'll discuss anything that jumps out at us from the list. And the questions are?"

"Could Tim have been killed for an unrelated reason? If so what?" Scott's detective mind searched out all possibilities.

I added, "What does the Friday before Mother's Day symbolize in Phillip House's life?"

"Did Dacia Stewart and Tim Manter have anything in common?" Shawn said.

When the questions were written down on the large, hanging Post-its, Todd set up a sheet labeled "Facts." While most of us in the group were writing down thoughts that might answer the questions, he wrote down all known information on Tim's death.

Date of Death—last Sunday

Time—between 7 and 8:30 a.m.

Place—church parking lot, 510 College Place

Cause—single .22 bullet to the back of the head

Details—Instantaneous, close range, execution style

Suspects—police have no viable leads

Murder weapon—not recovered

Jamie Storm—sole beneficiary

The six of us settled back in our chairs when the timer went off. The discussion centered on Phillip House and the withdrawals of money.

Billy started. "Is his mother still living? Nursing homes cost a huge amount of money per year. Or what about his daughter? She graduates this year. Does she have an illness that requires medical attention? Is he divorced from his daughter's mother? Maybe it's yearly child support." More questions.

Scott added his ideas. "I think its blackmail, but for what? Did someone see him kill Stewart? If so, why did the blackmail just start sixteen years ago? Why the increase of a thousand dollars a year. Blackmailers need a cost of living raise? When, by the way, did he become Speaker of the House?"

"I think," I said, "that the Friday before Mother's Day must be significant. We need to check out if his mother is still living. Possibly he has a child out there somewhere that no one knows about, and he's trying to keep the mother of that child quiet. Maybe he has more than one child graduating, one with his name, and one without."

Todd jumped in. "Maybe he tithes to his church annually or gives to a charity once a year."

Billy rolled his eyes. "Just keep writing, Todd. We'll ask the questions. You just don't have the knack for this. As I remember in the case of the missing page, you had this whole Genesis, chapter eight, verse seven thing going for you. You were looking for someone who owned ravens in the class. But no Edgar Allan Poes could be found."

Todd didn't even look embarrassed. He just shrugged.

Rachel tapped on her laptop while I nibbled on my lower lip.

"I think we have enough questions to get us started," Billy said. "Why don't we leave Phillip House for now, and I'll look into some of this later tonight and tomorrow morning. We could meet for brunch at nine in the morning before I have to work on my other story. I do need to keep my day job, but I have a lot of sources that could help me find some answers. Tabloid stuff—a reporter's dream."

"So what did Dacia Stewart and Tim have in common?" I asked the question I'd been itching to figure out. "Other than Tim was looking into Dacia's disappearance."

Shawn replied, "The only two things I know for sure are that they were both at Highland High in the spring of 1982, and they both knew Craig Haskell."

"Well, it doesn't really count that they knew Craig because they didn't know him at the same time. They were both killed at the end of May, and they were both killed in Anderson."

"Is there any way to find out if they were part of the same group, maybe a role-playing game, or maybe they invested in the same stock, or subscribed to the same magazine—some connection like that?" Shawn's mind was going a mile a minute.

"Too obvious, Shawn, plus computer role-playing games hadn't been invented yet." I got up and pulled another Dr Pepper from the fridge. It seemed Shawn and I were the only ones participating in this discussion. "Since there's a thirty-year gap between their deaths, it would be hard to find a viable connection for that reason alone. But maybe they both saw something back in 1982, something that Tim didn't even realize he had seen until a couple of weeks ago. Maybe he talked to the wrong person and got killed for it."

"So many questions, so few answers." Rachel looked around the table, finally engaged in the conversation. "I really think that Tim's death is totally unrelated to Ms. Stewart's death. They were killed differently, years apart, and they moved in totally different circles. I think Tim was killed because of money, mistaken identity, or some business-related thing."

"Let's take mistaken identity out of the mix," Billy said. "Whoever killed him followed him to church. You might accidentally kill the wrong person in a crowded bar, but surely not in an empty parking lot. It was either someone who was stalking him, or it was someone he confided in. Why would anyone even know that he went to church? Jamie didn't, and he left her ten million dollars."

"Good point," Todd agreed. "Plus church didn't even start until nine thirty, and he was killed between seven and eight thirty, which means he had to have been followed. Or it was someone he confided in who was lying in wait."

"That's it, that's the connection," I said. "Ms. Stewart was also being stalked, or was confiding in someone. There was no way that someone would have known she was going to the park after school that day. She hardly ever did that. Remember, she always stayed in her room late in case anyone needed help. Someone had to be following her."

"That's all well and good," Rachel said, "but that's a pretty weak connection. If I wanted to kill someone, I would follow them too. I would follow them until they were in an isolated place and then do the deed."

"I agree it's a weak connection. But it's the first sign to me that the deaths could be related. It's the first sign that the MO had similarities, even though the weapons were different."

"MO. Listen to the fancy lingo. You need to come work for me," Scott said, laughing.

"I think our killer is the same person." I spoke emphatically, ignoring Scott's good-natured ribbing. I checked the time. "I also think we should go. It's ten o'clock, and we each have things to do tonight and tomorrow morning before brunch. Who all can make it?"

"The lady speaks, so we're done?" Billy asked in amazement.

"Yeah, we're done," Shawn said.

"About tomorrow?" I reiterated.

"Count me out," Todd said. "I've got the pigs and other morning chores to do. I won't be available until three in the afternoon at the very earliest."

"I can make it for about an hour, then I'll be working the rest of the day," Billy said.

"I go where Jamie goes," Rachel said. "Her wheels."

Scott and Shawn decided they could both make it by nine.

With hugs and handshakes, we said good-bye. Rachel and I were out the door first. I was anxious to put in some thinking time in peace and quiet. Judging by the weary look in Rachel's eyes, I figured the day must have felt like an extra-long marathon. I pulled onto the highway, heading back to Anderson proper. A parade of headlights twinkled behind us. Looking in the review mirror, I made a mental note to tell the driver of the first vehicle behind us that they had a headlight out. It was too dark to see the outline of a car, but I knew no one had arrived on a motorcycle.

Rachel turned to look at me in the dim light inside the SUV. "How do you do it? How do you get everyone so excited about a project and keep everyone on task? You're really good at this."

"Thanks, but I'm not so good. I just love mysteries. It's been a long time since I've done something that isn't church related. I'm not so crazy about this mystery though," I confessed. "The last time I saw Tim was after graduation. He left me millions of dollars, and in the last thirty years, I haven't even made time for him. Or you, for that matter. How did I get this way? So self-absorbed, so into my own little world that nobody else mattered?"

Rachel was good with questions that didn't have answers. She sat in silence, not making light of or excusing my behavior or feelings.

I was grateful.

I turned the SUV into the parking lot at the Holiday Inn, and the one-eyed car zoomed on down Scatterfield without so much as a honk or a wave.

Back in the motel room, Rachel headed straight for the computer while I removed my makeup, slipped into Bears pajamas, climbed onto the bed, and picked up my Bible. I hadn't taken much God-time since this ordeal began, except for the frantic one-line prayers I'd sent heavenward. Tears slipped out of my eyes, and I brushed them away, hoping Rachel was still concentrating on her laptop.

Oh Lord, what have I become? Help me find an answer to all this mess. Help me find an answer for who I am. I'm so sorry for the blanket of comfortable ambivalence I've wrapped around myself.

Long after Rachel turned off the computer and her light, I stared at the ceiling tiles. Not because I found them particularly interesting; my mind just wouldn't be still. My hand trailed across the pillow and down the bedspread. The emptiness I felt without David was incredible. How I needed him. He was such a rock. So solid, so reassuring, so confident. I could use a little of that confidence right now. Rolling over to my side, I brought the extra pillow down and put my arms around it, hugging it tight. Not the perfect spoons David and I made, but better than empty arms. It was funny how I hadn't realized how important he was to me until he wasn't there beside me.

I felt so inadequate. I knew I was in over my head and that the chances of uncovering the killer's identity were practically nil. Not that I didn't have good people around me, but if the police couldn't find Tim's murderer, what made me think the Cliffhangers could? Missing page 187 was not the same as finding a killer. I tried to relax, but thoughts of insignificance, loneliness, and grief trudged through my mind like little soldiers going off to war—relentless and determined.

CHAPTER EIGHTEEN

August 10, 1987

I t was muggy and hot. Oh well, that was Bloomington, Indiana in the summertime. It had been nice to have the weekend to relax. Keeping tabs on the Stewarts was exhausting. Not because they were active. Just the opposite. Watching little or no movement required more concentration because it was easy to get distracted and lose focus. But today was different. The plan was in place. The careful watching and arranging would finally pay off. And then back home for a while where the weather was dry instead of this humid stuff. Even so, it wouldn't last long. There would be others. Some people just never learned. Vigilance was the key. Always watching, always preparing, always on the ready. A good motto to live by.

Driving around the city felt pointless. The Lady in Red was playing on the radio for the umpteenth time, and the lyrics didn't get any better with multiple broadcasts. But it was a time killer and time needed to be killed—along with a couple of nuisances living on Griffin Street.

Minutes stretched into meaningless blocks of time. Nighttime couldn't come too soon. The task ahead required the cover of darkness. Once the police started investigating, they would canvass the neighborhood for eyewitnesses to any unusual activity around the

Stewarts. You could always count on people not noticing unusual activity once they went to bed.

Cruising through the limestone belt of Indiana was good for reflection, but there wasn't that much to see in Bloomington. It was a university town and alive with activity and excitement this close to school starting. Luckily, there wasn't much action around the Stewarts' place.

The trunk was filled with several three-gallon cans of gasoline. It had been no trouble to obtain them. Each of the plastic jugs had been purchased at different stores with cash. The containers weren't traceable, mostly because it had been over a year since they were bought—each procured by a kid who wanted to make a quick ten bucks. The key to not getting caught was planning and forethought. Most people sitting in jails didn't have the patience to be good criminals. Time could be an enemy, but it could also be a friend.

Hopefully, the deaths would be painless. Smoke inhalation should get them before the fire. It would be good if they slept through it all. Burning would be a horrible way to die. After all, it wasn't their fault that they chose to get involved with matters that didn't concern them. It was a pity the woman was deaf. It didn't seem fair somehow. But neither were hurricanes, flash floods, or tornadoes. Life just wasn't fair.

Initially, it seemed like the two dogs would be a problem, but once again careful planning had eliminated the risks. The Stewarts always let the dogs have free rein in the big back yard, which was surrounded by a six-foot privacy fence. At nine o'clock, Mr. Stewart would come out and call them in. By ten the lights were out and the house was silent. With a little ground work laid, the dogs knew to come straight to the fence for their nightly treat of raw meat. The burger was cheap, and the dogs wolfed it down with gusto. Feeding it to them at eight thirty every night for the last week had been child's play. It had been easy to loosen two boards so the dogs could be fed in tandem. A pound for each of them kept them coming back for more. Dogs were simple, so much easier than humans. It didn't take much to make them happy.

The day had not gone exactly like planned, which was worrisome, but probably just a fluke. The Stewarts hadn't followed their daily routine. Usually they left the house around nine and didn't get back until noon. They would bring back a to-go bag filled with fast food— burgers, tacos, or chicken. Today, they hadn't left the house. Maybe one of them was sick. The postman delivered their mail by one thirty and no one came out to get it. Normally, Stewart opened the mailbox on the dot of two to retrieve it. Still it was nothing to panic over. It was too late to change plans now. The disturbing thing was that a young woman let the dogs out to play. She must be a granddaughter. Visiting perhaps, or maybe a caretaker.

An hour had gone by since the last look at the digital car clock. It was time to set the first part of the plan into motion. Careful to tuck the Dramamine tabs all the way into the burger would ensure the dogs swallowed them whole. The tube contained twelve tablets, so each pound of hamburger got six pills. The dogs should sleep through anything—a stranger crawling through the boards of the fence, the sounds of splashing liquid, the strike of a match, the crackling of fast-moving flames. They were pretty big dogs, but six pills was a lot.

Maybe the granddaughter was still there. An unfortunate casualty. The lights didn't go out until eleven thirty, which again was unusual for the Stewarts. Not that a fire could be started until after midnight anyway. The dogs would be fast asleep and it would keep the neighbors from calling 911 until it was too late. Hopefully, the Stewarts were sound sleepers. It wouldn't matter. There would be no way out once the blaze started. The neighborhood lights were all off when the truck pulled up. Sloshing the gasoline around the house was not difficult. Soaking the walls and wraparound porch took about ten minutes total. It took special care and silence.

The best part was the cute little candles that had been retrieved after last's year's Christmas Eve service. A nice little paper protector surrounded the wax to keep hot drips off the hand. Lighting the wick and getting a good flame going didn't shed enough light to wake up the neighbors, made no noise like a bottle rocket would have, and still provided the needed distance for protection from the puddles of fuel.

Candles, however discreet, could not cover up the acrid odor of burning wood, paint, and gasoline. It would feel so good to go back to the motel for a cool shower, to wash away the day's sweat and grime.

CHAPTER NINETEEN

Shadowy, slow, relentless monsters invaded my dreams. My feet seemed stuck in cement. Tentacles of fear clawed at me until I bolted straight out of sleep. Breathing hard, I glanced at the clock—5:00 a.m. I rubbed my hand across my face and pushed my legs over the edge of the bed. If I wanted to make the day count, I needed to clear my head. A brisk walk should help. I shimmied into my rumpled clothes that I'd left crumpled on the chair. I left a note for Rache and slipped quietly out the door. It wasn't quite dawn, but light enough for me to feel safe and see where I was going.

The dream hangover faded when the cool, fresh air hit my face. The sky looked like rain might be in the forecast. The sound of a dog barking in the distance mixed with the repeated *whoit, whoit, whoit* of a cardinal made me smile. The familiar daybreak noises of my hometown wrapped around me like a soft quilt. I felt my steps become lighter.

The breeze, the mourning doves, the quiet hush of a sleepy world spoke to me in ways that no human could. Picking up the pace, I walked with more confidence than I'd felt since this ordeal began. I would find Tim's killer somehow. That was the least I could do—for him and for me. I wasn't in my familiar pastor's wife role now. I was a friend, and I would use every skill I possessed to see this thing through to the end.

Striding past comfortable landmarks, a sense of well-being surrounded me so strongly that I almost wished David's church was located here instead of Montana. Almost. But Montana felt like home, too, and wherever David was, my home was there. I did miss shopping with Mom and having family over for holiday dinners. People in the church always invited us out for Easter or Christmas or Thanksgiving meals, but we were the odd ones out, never quite getting the inside jokes, or understanding the right protocols for special occasions.

With all this determination and good feelings, I felt like I could walk forever. A glance at my watch assured me it had only been twenty-five minutes. Still, it was time to turn around. Dark clouds were rolling in, and I wanted to get back to the motel before the rain started. That's when I saw a tall woman wearing khaki pants and an olive green tunic, her blonde hair cut short. It was the woman who had bumped me from behind yesterday.

"Hey," I yelled.

Volvo Lady wheeled around and started to run.

"Hey, wait a minute. I just want to talk to you." I broke out into a fast sprint, following the green color.

Volvo Lady didn't slow down. She ran all-out. Her legs, long and muscular, took the fluid strides of a distance runner. My legs burned as I tried to keep her in sight. If my feet weren't so busy trying to stay with my legs, I would have kicked myself for the shape I was in. Funny what comes to mind when every muscle in your body cries for relief. I made a mental note to enroll in exercise classes of some sort when I got back to Great Falls.

I ran after the woman for five minutes, although it seemed

longer. I sucked in huge gulps of air. My chest burned. My legs faltered. I felt like rubber, and I gave up the chase.

I gasped out one more time as loud as my overworked lungs could manage. "Hey, wait up, could we just talk?"

It didn't help. Volvo Lady kept running like it was her life's work. I grabbed my left side and bent over in exhaustion. My thigh and calf muscles quivered in protest from the intense labor they'd been forced into. Frustrated, I coerced my body into forward movement. It didn't want to cooperate. I swallowed deep breaths of air, hoping to make it back to the motel before collapsing. After another five minutes of deliberate walking, my breathing returned to normal. My legs stopped burning, and I decided that I might survive after all.

The discussion from last night came back to me. The one thing the murders had in common was that the victims had been stalked. It was too much of a coincidence that Volvo Lady just happened to take a morning stroll at five thirty in the same area where I was walking. Anderson wasn't a huge city, but with 180,000 people, it wasn't small either.

Although I was no genius, it seemed as though this woman had more than a passing interest in my activities. I needed to call Scott and tell him what had happened. Maybe he could find a plausible reason that would pacify the uneasy feeling in the pit of my stomach.

Nearing the motel, I froze. Pulling out of the parking lot and turning left on Scatterfield was the beige Volvo. The woman was alone in the car and clearly in a big hurry. How long had she been following me? I started to run again, hoping to get the license number before the car roared out of sight. No such luck. I did, however, manage to get a glimpse of a bumper sticker with a scientific symbol and white Arabic lettering on a blue background. I also got the first three plate numbers before the car made another left and spun out of sight. I repeated the letters from the license plate over and over until I got to the motel room.

Single minded of purpose, I charged into the room to call Scott. It took a minute for my mind to register Rachel sitting on the bed, rocking back and forth and hugging her knees, tears streaming down her face.

"What's wrong, Rache? What happened?" I raced over to the bed and put my arms around her.

"He called." The words came out in a low moan.

"Who called?"

"He found out I'm here and he called." More rocking.

"Who?" I asked again.

"Phillip House. He called and said if I said one word to anyone about us, I would end up just like Ms. Stewart or Tim. He said 'about us' like it was mutual. Like I liked it and it was my idea as well as his." Her low moan turned into high-pitched hysteria, and with the speed she talked I only heard about half of what she said.

"Slow down and tell me again." I patted her back in what I hoped was a soothing rhythm. I reverted to full mother mode.

"The minute I heard his voice, I panicked. So long ago and I still recognize the voice. Like I'm sitting in government class and nothing's changed." Sobbing now, Rachel couldn't quit talking between hiccups.

I kept patting, staying calm.

"The room got so small, so menacing. I couldn't even look out the window because I was afraid he would be there. How did he get this number? I can't go to breakfast. I can't go anywhere! What if he's out there? What if he's watching the door?"

"I just came in the door. No one's outside."

"Jamie, I know he meant it. He'll kill me in a second if he thinks I've told anyone."

I didn't know what to say to reassure her, so I didn't say anything. I just held her and let her talk. I pushed the chase with Volvo lady to the back of my mind.

"I feel all slimy. I'm so scared—scared that I'll have to keep living like this."

"Rache, it's okay. It's going to be okay." I still didn't have anything to say, but I couldn't stop opening my mouth.

Rachel kept talking like she hadn't heard me. "I'm afraid that everyone is like him and Dad and afraid that it's not really them, it's me. Afraid that when anyone looks at me, all they'll see is a pile of garbage—just filth to step over."

I felt helpless. No easy platitudes would fix Rachel's pain.

"I need a drink. I . . . I really do. I can't do this sober." Her eyes pleaded.

"I'm so sorry, Rache. I'm so sorry. I'm sorry I wasn't here for you, and I'm sorry the creep called, but trust me, you don't need a drink. You need to stand up and fight. You're stronger than he is. You have more guts than he'll ever have, and you don't need to keep living like this."

Rachel eyed me with a look that was a cross between disbelief and anguish.

"Call Scott. He'll know what to do," I urged.

"No, no, no. I can't call Scott. I can't make this public. My parents . . . it will look like I'm, like I'm, well you know. Please . . ."

"Okay, Rache, okay," I conceded. "But you're forty-eight. How long are you going to let Phillip House control your life? Now's the time to take a stand. The Cliffhangers are all here. We won't let him hurt you again. He's a two-bit thug, and we can nail him. But we need your help to do it." We can nail him? I obviously watched too much TV.

Rachel bit her thumbnail.

"Why don't you go take a shower?" I suggested. "I'll be right here. If the phone rings, I'll get it."

I gave her a hug and pushed her toward the bathroom. I had such a hard time understanding Rachel. Protecting the very people who destroyed her life. How hard could it be to stand up against this scum? How hard could it be to turn her father in for molesting her, or her mother for letting it happen?

You've never been there.

Volvo Lady and Phillip House. Were they connected? Where did this all lead? What did they have in common? Were they working together? The thoughts swirled in my head, causing fear to squeeze my guts into knots. Tim was dead. Someone was following me. Rachel's life had been threatened. What did I think I was doing? This wasn't some kid's game—this was for real. I grabbed the phone and started to dial Scott's number. Suddenly, my dad's face came into view. Vincent Waymire—a man who never backed away from anything in his life.

One Sunday morning we were driving home from church when we saw smoke billowing out of a house. Dad stopped the car and ran into the house looking for people. In about two minutes he'd rounded up a mother and two children and brought them out to safety. The woman kept screaming that her baby was still in the house. Dad ran back in and found the baby. Bringing her out, his back caught on fire. He handed the screaming, but unhurt baby girl to her mother before he dropped and rolled on the ground putting the fire out. He was hospitalized for a week with smoke inhalation and second-degree burns on his back.

Two weeks after being released from the hospital, the Anderson Fire Department held a dinner in his honor and gave him a citation for bravery. When we returned home from the dinner, I asked what made him so brave. He smiled. "I'm not brave, Jamie. It's just that when something scares me, I face it and charge."

I looked at the phone in my hand and decided it was time to charge. Sounds of water running assured me that Rachel was taking a shower. Hands shaking, I reached inside the dresser and pulled out the Anderson phone book. There were several Houses listed, but only one Phillip. I dialed the number quickly before I could change my mind.

"I'd like to speak to Phillip House please."

There was a long pause before the voice on the other end replied, "It's early and I doubt he's even here."

"Yes, I know it's early, but he just called. I know he's home. He's the speaker for the graduation this weekend and for my class reunion, so don't give me the runaround. I know he's there. Please put him on the phone." My anger made the words come out clipped and bitter.

"I can't promise you anything, but I'll go check." The person behind the voice sounded irritated at my insistence.

"Thank you, I'll wait." My palms were sweaty. Anger twisted my insides in knots.

"Hello, this is Phillip House."

"Hi. This is Jamie Storm." I continued in a rush of loud, heated words. "I have a message for you. If you so much as touch one hair on Rachel's head, I will take you down. I will go to every media outlet that will listen with all your slimy, little misdeeds. I will find every girl you ever molested, and we will take out huge ads in every Washington, DC paper and every newspaper in Indiana. With any luck you will be in prison for life. If I were you, I'd get out of town, because the minute I figure out how you killed Tim, I'm going to the police."

My voice shook as I spoke, and I could feel my face getting hotter.

"Who is this? What are you talking about?" Surprise and apprehension danced in House's tone.

"I'm Jamie Storm. And you are a murdering child molester, and if you so much as come near Rachel—or try calling her again— you *will* regret it! In fact, if I were you, I would find some urgent reason to leave Anderson now. I'd forget about your speeches to the reunion class and your daughter's graduation. Because if you don't, I might have to make my own speech, highlighting your proclivities for underage girls." *Proclivities?* Evidently, my vocabulary raised a notch when I was spitting angry.

"Now, listen here. You can't threaten me. I am the Speaker of the House of the United States. I have bodyguards. I will not listen to the ranting of some hysterical woman and neither will the media," he warned.

"You don't intimidate me. Your position in the government doesn't intimidate me. Your bodyguards don't intimidate me. I can and will threaten you. And my threats aren't empty. So if you think you're so tough, you just hang around and make your speech. I guarantee . . . you *will* regret it. I'm quite sure your wife and daughter will be intrigued to hear about the sleazy activities you've engaged in."

With that, I slammed down the receiver. My whole body was shaking. I'm not sure I scared him at all, but I felt better. I marched over to the window, then back to the desk, back to the window, back to the desk. Adrenaline rushed through me like a gust of wind. I grabbed a pillow off the bed and threw it against the wall. It wasn't enough. Energy coursed through me, making me feel tough. If my pastor's wife conscience was trying to get my attention now, it would have to wait its turn.

The ringing telephone stopped my arm in midair just as I was going to throw the pillow again. I picked up the receiver. "What?"

"Hey, hold it there, pal. You sound like you're ready to kill somebody. What's going on?" It was Scott.

"Oh, it's you." I tried to calm down. "Sorry, I thought it was someone else. I'm just a little tense. I need to talk to you. Can you come over to the motel before our breakfast meeting?"

"Sure. Can you give me a little clue on the uptight phone voice?"

"No, I'll just talk to you when you get here."

"Sure thing. Rachel all right?"

"No, she's not. I can't talk about that now. She won't let me. I'm not all right either, but I can talk about that, so just get over here." I lowered my voice and added, "Please."

Without waiting for a response, I hung up the phone. The bedside clock read 6:57. I had hung up on two people already, and the day had barely started. *Dorothy, you're not in Kansas anymore.* This was the first time since marrying a pastor that I'd ever hung up on anyone. And boy, did it feel good.

Rachel walked out of the bathroom towel drying her hair. She was dressed in blue jeans, a lime-green knit top, and sandals. Still no makeup, but the effect was dazzling. Rachel really was beautiful.

"I feel better. You're right, Jamie. I'm ready for this to be over. I can't keep taking showers and never feeling clean. I'm done living like this. Will you call Scott for me?"

Her voice and eyes were resolute. She walked over to the window and looked out at the city she had learned to hate. "Maybe

I can reclaim my life. Maybe I can find some way not to despise myself. Do you think that's possible?"

"I know it is." I was going to say more when someone knocked on the door.

CHAPTER TWENTY

I stepped over to the door and looked through the peephole. Craig Haskell, gripping a book, looking like he'd rather be anywhere but at the Holiday Inn face-to-face with room 123. After unhooking the chain and unlocking the deadbolt, I opened the door and ushered him in.

Craig glanced around the room, giving Rachel a curt nod. "I won't be here long. I needed to bring Jamie something Tim left at my house. I thought she might want it."

His eyes were looking for something from Rachel. Approval maybe?

"Don't hurry on my account," Rachel said. "What I said last night wasn't personal. I don't think you killed Tim. I just don't understand all the deaths in your life."

He shrugged. "You and me both."

He looked at me. "Anyway, I'm staying in town long enough to present the diplomas to the graduating class. Then I'm off to take an extended vacation. I don't know when I'll get back, but I assume you'll be gone by then. When Tim and I first started talking about Dacia's death, that's all we did. As we worked together our friendship changed. We got closer. Eventually, we shared a lot with each other about our lives. Several weeks ago he told me about his love for you."

I inspected the carpet, careful to avoid his eyes.

"Last month he brought his senior yearbook over to show me what you'd written. He also showed me the graduation present you gave him. It's here too. He left the stuff at my house because we were going fishing that Saturday, and then he forgot to pick it up. It wasn't a big deal. We saw each other several times a week. He could get it anytime, or so we thought. How wrong we were." He frowned and sucked in a deep breath.

Silence permeated the room.

I cleared my throat. "I don't know what to say."

"There's nothing *to* say. Tim is gone. I just wanted to bring you this stuff. I don't know if I'll ever see you again. I hope you find the answers you're looking for."

"Thanks."

He shoved the yearbook into my hand and turned toward the door. He stopped at the threshold, eyeing Rachel. "I'm sorry we didn't meet under different circumstances."

"Me too," Rachel said, her words carrying a whisper of longing.

"Oh, and Jamie, I hope you find Tim's killer. Good-bye." He walked out, closing the door behind him.

"Did I just see what I thought I saw?" I asked.

"What?"

"He was making a pass at you."

Rachel grinned. "You're crazy."

Rachel sat on the bed, and I plopped down beside her. I rubbed my hand over the front cover of the yearbook, almost afraid to open it. I had no memory of what I'd written to Tim—or anyone for that matter—but did remember the counted cross-stitch bookmark I'd given him and all the Cliffhangers for graduation.

At the top of the bookmark I had stitched the Einstein quote: "Life is a mystery—not a problem to be solved." And then in all my teen, Christian fervor, I added, "But if you want to solve it, follow Matthew 6:33." It had taken three months to finish all six of them, but I was proud of the effort. It was a gift of time from my heart, not just a memento that could be picked off the rack at Walmart. Now it was just plain corny.

"Come on, let's see what you wrote," Rachel said.

"Good segue off you and Craig."

"There is no 'me and Craig.' Now come on, I want to see if you wrote anything gushy."

"No, of course I didn't. I was already in love with David, and I didn't have any idea how Tim felt about me. He never told me." Would it have changed anything if he had? I tossed the mental question aside to revisit another time.

I gingerly opened the front cover and saw the bookmark. It had seen better days. It looked like Tim had used it for more than a bookmark. The edges were worn and raveled. The ivory background was a grayish, dirty color, and some of the embroidery thread had come apart.

A wave of shame washed over me as I realized he must have carried the bookmark with him everywhere. I, on the other hand, scarcely thought of him in the midst of raising the boys, putting on women's retreats, and building a life with David. It wasn't that I didn't care about him, I was just busy, and the occasional e-mails to and from him were sufficient contact for me. Now more than anything, I wished they hadn't been sufficient.

Rachel's arm draped casually across my shoulders in an I-can't-wait-to-see-your-secrets hug. I flipped to the back of the yearbook and was startled to see a big, red heart outlining the sentiments of one seventeen-year-old to another.

"I did not put that heart there."

"Me thinks the lady doth protest too much!"

Holding back the chuckles, Rachel read the long-ago words out loud.

"Tim, can you believe we made it? We did it! I think the only thing that kept me sane was you and the Cliffhangers. I will never forget the last four years as long as I live! Thanks for always being there for me. You're the best! I am going to miss you so much! I know you're going to do great in life! Just think: no more Lousy Housey, no more cafeteria fish sticks, and no more mysteries to solve. At least no more mysteries as soon as we find out why Ms. Stewart disappeared! Then we can begin a whole new adventure in this pony ride they call life. Luv ya, Class of '85, Jamie."

"Tim must have put the heart on it. I sure didn't."

Rachel grinned. "You're right. This isn't mushy at all. The only thing that could sort of be interpreted as love is all those exclamation points you used. You might have been a little emphatic for simple friendship."

"I put exclamation points on everything back then. Let's see what you wrote."

I turned a couple of pages back and found Rachel's inscription. "Tim, it's been great. Have fun in all you do. Forever, Rachel."

"You always were such a talkative thing," I said. "I don't think I can keep up with you."

"I didn't have much to say. Hey, let's go back to the faculty pages. I want to see what Ms. Stewart looked like. I barely remember."

Turning the pages back toward the front, we perused the faculty. It was weird looking at Ms. Stewart now. She looked like one of the kids. Her photo showed an infectious smile, short dark hair, and sparkling eyes. It was strange to think she never grew old. Never changed her hairstyle, never got out of that 80's mode. Death had made her forever young.

"Why would anyone kill her? She looks so innocent," Rachel said.

It was a rhetorical question, but I answered anyway. "Who knows? Killers aren't the most rational people around."

I turned back another page. "I want to get a look at Phillip House too." I looked at Rachel for permission or understanding, I wasn't sure which.

Rachel didn't move. "It's okay. I'm fine. I would rather not ever see him again as long as I live, but I don't think a picture is gonna hurt me."

Phillip House looked into the camera with an arrogant tilt to his head. Black hair parted on the right and long sideburns. He had a stern mustache that made me think a caterpillar had crawled under his nose and decided to take a snooze. His eyes held no light at all. They were dark and foreboding like his character.

Rachel stiffened, but she didn't move away, or quit looking at the page.

My eyes caught sight of the teacher next to him. I couldn't believe my eyes. I turned the book sideways. I pulled it closer to my face. I swallowed hard. "Volvo Lady. That's Volvo Lady! I knew I'd seen her before." My finger pointed down to the young woman in the photo to the left of House.

Rachel squinted at the picture. "How can you tell? That was thirty years ago."

"I know it's her. Look at the eyes. I remember her now. She was a guest science teacher or something. She helped me with some questions on my microbe project our senior year. Think back."

"I didn't do science projects. I was too involved in the new computer stuff to worry about science. After ninth-grade science and biology I was done."

"Cynthia Gilmore. I know that's Volvo Lady. Can you find her address on the Net? I think I need to pay her a little visit. I would say the plot thickens, but that sounds corny. Don't you think it's odd that she's right next to our prime suspect?"

"Yeah, Jamie, I appreciate your deductive powers, but you might notice that H always comes after G in the alphabet. I don't think that makes the coincidence so startling." The sarcasm was definitely not veiled in Rachel's response.

"Oh, come on, I know the alphabet. I'm talking about the fact they were both teaching in 1985, and that's when Ms. Stewart disappeared, and the accident yesterday, and then her following me this morning, and—"

"Slow down. You're gonna have a stroke."

"I'm just saying it's all pretty weird after my morning."

"Whoa, you didn't tell me anything about this morning. What happened this morning?"

I recounted the details of my early morning walk.

Rachel grabbed her laptop and connected to the Internet. Minutes later, she had a report. "There are 207 hits on the name Cynthia Gilmore in the country's white pages. None in Indiana. With a credit card I could search deeper, but that would cost $45.95."

I pulled a Visa card out of my purse.

Two minutes later, Rachel subscribed to People Finder. The search was fast but produced no Cynthia Gilmores in Indiana.

"What about school records?" Rachel asked. "Do you know anyone in the administration who would give you a look at the old teacher files? She could still be on staff for that matter. I could look in the SSA sites if I had a number."

"SSA sites?"

"Social Security Administration, Jamie. Where have you been?"

"Craig might be willing to help. He's still in town and probably over at the school by now. If he won't look up Cynthia Gilmore's social, I'm sure Scott can help. That would take more time, but technically, this Cynthia Gilmore is a perpetrator of a hit-and-run. If I were to press charges, I think the police could get a search warrant for the files."

Rachel handed my cell to me. "Try the school."

"It's Saturday."

"Observant. But with graduation and the reunion, maybe someone's at the office."

I grabbed the cell. "Okay, look up the number." Why not? What did I have to lose? As she read the number to me, I tapped it into my phone, expecting nothing but the constant buzzing of an unanswered ring.

"Highland High School, home of the Tartans. How may I help you?"

After the initial surprise that someone was actually in the office on a Saturday, I recovered. "Yes ma'am. This is Jamie Waymire Storm, and I'm here for my class reunion. I need some information."

"And that would be?" I could hear the snapping of gum.

"I had a teacher, a guest teacher I think, who helped me with my senior science project. Her name was Cynthia Gilmore. Does she still teach there? Do you know how I could get in touch with her?"

"Nope."

"Nope what?" I worked at keeping the frustration out of my voice.

"Nope, we don't have a teacher here by that name." More gum popping.

"Are you sure? Is there anyone else I can talk to?"

"I've worked at the school for seventeen years, and I don't remember any teacher named Cynthia Gilmore." Irritation sparkled in the secretary's voice.

"Could you search the database for teachers who worked in 1985?" I pleaded.

"If she taught here in '85 I have access to the files, but that would take time, and I don't have time today. With the reunion and graduation, my hands are full. Sorry." She didn't sound the least bit sorry, just miffed that someone would dare intrude on such a busy person. Snap, crackle, pop.

"Could you connect me to the principal's office?" I was unwilling to give up.

"He won't have any more time than I do. Besides, this is only Mr. Haskell's second year at the school. He may not even be in his office. This *is* Saturday morning, you know."

I could almost see the eye-rolling at the other end of the line.

"Yeah, I know, and I also know this is a busy day at the school so he might be there just as you are. I'm sorry for the inconvenience, but I'm a friend of Mr. Haskell's and I was hoping to touch base with him while I'm in town for the reunion." I winced as the lie rolled off my tongue. But it was for a good cause, I reminded myself.

With a few more snippy words and loud popping sounds, the secretary, who clearly felt her territory was being invaded and authority questioned, put me through to Haskell's office.

Just as I thought, he was in his office and picked up on the second ring.

"Craig, this is Jamie. Thanks for the yearbook," I said quickly. "Listen, I think I stumbled onto something. I need to find a woman who taught back in '85. Cynthia Gilmore."

"Never heard of her," he said. "What are you looking for?"

"She may have had something to do with Tim's death. Can you check in the old files? I need a forwarding address or social security number, something, anything that might help locate her."

He hesitated momentarily. "Okay, I don't see any harm in that. The old personnel files are on disks by years. It'll take a few minutes. Can I call you back?" Craig cleared his throat.

"No problem."

"One more thing. I'm doing this for Tim, not you, not anybody else. Tim alone. After this I'm done. Don't call me again."

I was surprised by his sudden abruptness, but I couldn't blame him. The Cliffhangers hadn't exactly rolled out the red carpet of friendship to him. I hit the red END button on my cell.

"I need to shower," I said. "My morning walk didn't exactly bring out the best in me. I won't be long, but ignore the phone if it rings. Don't open the door for anyone either. I don't trust House for a second."

I longed for an extended hot soak in a tub to relax my already tight muscles I'd sent into shock from overuse, but I knew there wasn't time. Drying off from the quickie shower, I dressed in casual black capris, matching sandals, and a long black-and-white checked top. I chose the capris for comfort. Applying a light touch of mascara and lipstick, I hoped I was ready for the day and whatever else it might bring.

Rachel, looking nervous but determined, shut down my phone when I walked out of the bathroom. "I just called Mom. I had to call. I need to see her. At least I think I do. She's coming to the restaurant this morning at nine." She regarded me with a look that said, *I hope I'm making sense here.*

"It going to be hard, but we'll be right there if you need us."

"She sounded old and tired. She was shocked when she heard my voice, but she knew instantly it was me. She cried when I told her I wanted to see her."

"Oh, Rache, I'm so glad."

"She's bringing Dad."

A thick silence permeated the room.

The ring shattered the stillness. I don't know who was more relieved, Rache or me. I grabbed my phone. "Hello."

Craig rattled off Cynthia Gilmore's social security number. "I'm breaking the law doing this, you know. She didn't have a forwarding address listed on the exit interview, and she only worked that one year at Highland. Best I can do."

I thanked him, hung up, and handed my note with her social to Rachel. "See what you can do with this."

She looked grateful for the change of subject.

Within minutes, Rachel printed out a social security statement. The heading read: PREPARED ESPECIALLY FOR CYNTHIA GILMORE. Flipping to page three she read the YOUR EARNINGS AT A GLANCE columns. "Look at this. This is really weird. It looks like she only earned money during five of all the years listed."

I looked at the listing. "1982, 1984, 1985, 1992, 2004, and then nothing. It lists the years up through last year, but nothing was recorded on those years. We know what she did in 1984 and l985. She taught school at Highland, but how did she live all those years she didn't work?"

"I suppose she could have inherited a bundle and doesn't really need to work. Or she could be married to a Mr. Gilmore and is a stay-at-home Mom like you. Maybe in the years that the statement lists earned income, she was bored and tried her hand at different jobs. It's obvious she didn't teach in 1982, 1992, or 2004," Rachel said.

"Why is that obvious?"

"Because those years don't have a consecutive year listed either before or after them. A teaching contract goes from August to May, doesn't it? It's always a two-calendar-year period of time."

"Ooh, you're good, girl. Did you glean anything else from the report that I might have missed?"

"Look at this heading: WE BASED YOUR BENEFIT ESTIMATES ON THESE FACTS. It shows her date of birth as February 4, 1958. That might be useful. Other than that, unless she works a little more in the future, her social security benefits aren't going to amount to much."

"Can you do anything on your computer, using her birth date, social, and name that might help us find out anything else?"

"I can try. I don't know how much more I can find. There are a couple of family tree and ancestry sites I can check. When do we leave for our breakfast meeting?" Rachel asked.

"In about fifteen minutes. Find out if there's anything else, and we'll head out. It's probably just my imagination, but knowing that Cynthia is also Volvo Lady is more than a little unnerving."

CHAPTER TWENTY-ONE

Billy had insisted on meeting the group at the café.com. It had opened before the age of 4G phones, but its client base hadn't diminished. It was a coffee shop and breakfast bar, catering to white-collar business people. The booths, circular in shape for privacy, had wi-fi and curved screen TV's with accessibility to all network and cable news channels with business, financial, crime, and sports channels. It opened its doors at 4:30 a.m. and closed at 11:00 a.m. Café.com did more business in those few morning hours than most of the regular restaurants in Anderson. Just one more way for business warriors to get ahead of the competition: work and eat at the same time.

I put my arm around Rachel as we walked into the coffee shop. "You can do this." A lame—although good-intentioned—attempt to make her feel as though she wasn't alone.

Rachel looked like she was going to be sick.

"After you're done talking to your mom, come over to our table."

The host greeted us with a smile. "Good morning, ladies. Seating for two?"

"Actually, we're meeting the Kings and the Cliffhangers," I replied.

"The Kings are seated in booth 17, and the Cliffhangers are in booth 28. Enjoy your breakfast." After handing us each a complimentary copy of the *Wall Street Journal*, he looked at the couple behind us.

"Here goes," Rachel said, taking a deep breath as she glanced toward booth 17. She set her copy of the newspaper back on the host's podium. I put mine back on the stack with hers, then I gave her hand a squeeze, and we parted ways.

I wound my way through the maze of circular cubicles until I found number 28. I know the restaurant had good intentions, but the booths made me think of the giant teacup ride at Disneyland. They didn't make me think business, on-the-go, up-and-coming professionals. On the other hand, I lived in Great Falls, Montana where up-and-coming professionals left and went to up-and-coming states with more than 900,000 people.

Scott, Shawn, and Billy had already been served cappuccinos and were in deep conversation.

"It's about time you got here. Where's Rachel?" Billy said, peering around me like he might find a pot of gold hidden behind my back.

"Good to see you too. She's busy. It's just me——Chopped Liver." I sounded more piqued than I felt.

"Oh, come on. I just assumed you'd be together."

"She's taking care of family business. She'll be here."

"Todd called," Scott said. "He's coming after all. He'll only be able to stay a few minutes, but he says he has a timeline of events for us. Did any of you find out any info last night or this morning?"

Before I could open my mouth, Billy was already talking. "I have a report on James Blevins. He's the chaplain for the reunion banquet tonight. We went out for a late-night interview.

"The guy is squeaky clean. Or at least I couldn't find any dirt on him. He was in New Orleans doing a three-day crusade when Tim was killed. He has about 32,000 witnesses to prove he wasn't in Anderson on that day. He called his financial guru for the ministry and gave the guy the go-ahead to let me see the books. After the class reunion, Blevins is holding a crusade in the Indy Coliseum."

"Good work," Shawn said.

A slender waitress came over to the booth with an order pad in hand. The petite woman with wide blue eyes flashed a quick smile. "It looks like your other party has arrived. Are you ready to order yet?"

I hadn't looked at the menu yet, but ordered Dr Pepper, hash browns, and bacon.

The guys ordered enough breakfast to keep a table of eight happy. The waitress grinned and went to the kitchen to place the order.

Billy continued with his rundown of Blevins. "Unless they have a different set of books, I gotta say this guy is on the up and up. No big payouts on or around Tim's death. Blevins and his wife take a salary of $70,000 a year, and the rest is all tied into the ministry, missions, and several—22 to be exact—small-town churches around the country. I called ten of those churches and received the same answer. Blevins supports small churches that can't afford a pastor on their own. He dumps about $100,000 yearly into each of the churches I called. I actually think the guy is what he says he is."

"Don't act so shocked," I said. "Not every televangelist is a bad guy."

Billy shrugged while Scott and Shawn laughed at his discomfort.

Todd's entrance interrupted the chuckles and took the focus off Billy. "Sorry I'm late. I can't stay long. I wanted to give you this." He put a stack of papers on the table. "I have a ton of work to get done today if I want to go to the reunion tonight with a clear conscience."

"Before you leave, I need to ask you something," I said. "Do you know anyone who drives a beige Volvo?"

"Not that I can think of, why?"

I looked around the table. "Do any of you have a headlight out?"

"That's a bit personal, don't you think?" Billy laughed, but no one else found my question funny.

Shawn shook his head.

Scott looked me in the eye. "What happened?"

"I think I'm being followed. I noticed a one-eyed car behind us immediately after we left Todd's last night. It tailed me until I turned into the motel parking lot."

"It wasn't any of us," Scott said. "We stayed for another hour reliving our high school sports triumphs, such as they were. Why did you think the car was following you? And how could you tell it was a beige Volvo at that time of night?"

I recounted the story of the dead kitten, the fender bender, the early-morning chase, the yearbook discovery that Cynthia Gilmore was a teacher in 1985, and of her current earnings. I told the story in great detail, including the numbers I'd seen on the license plate and the bumper sticker.

The waitress brought out our breakfasts and set the multitude of dishes on our table. "Enjoy." There was barely an inch of free table space left.

"Describe the bumper sticker again," Shawn said.

"It was a molecule or atom, with these circles around the atom and Arabic-looking writing. Blue background, white atom, white writing."

"The bio-tech department at the University of Israel has

bumper stickers something like that. But I couldn't tell you for sure unless I saw it or you could copy the writing."

"Sorry. Memory's not that good," I said.

Scott grabbed a pen and wrote down the partial plate number that I'd remembered and called them into the station. "I'll hold the line while you pull up an address," he said into his cell. "Okay, thanks." He scribbled down the address the dispatcher had given him. Taking a big bite of ham omelet, he muffled, "Anybody want to ride with me while I go have a chat with Ms. Gilmore?"

"I know you're super cop and all," Billy said, "but it's not like she's going anywhere in the next few minutes. Chill for a minute, and let's finish this. I have to get back to the studios to finish my homeless piece. Some of us have regular jobs, you know." He sounded almost envious.

"Sorry, I can't go with you either," Todd said. "The farm is calling. I don't think I'd have much to add except clever conversation anyway. I'll see you guys tonight at the reunion banquet." He grabbed a piece of toast off one of the many plates and left.

"We can't leave without Rachel either," I said. "I think we need to look at all the other info we have and add it to the timeline Todd worked up for us."

Each of us picked up a copy of the timeline from the center of the table stuck under Billy's side order of buttermilk pancakes. Maple syrup had slowly dripped on the top page. Todd had worked on the chronology of the case before he went to bed. He'd used a spreadsheet and had left adequate spaces between each entry to add other dates. I added in everything I could think of that Todd had missed.

Our table was quiet for several minutes as the four of us ate breakfast and tried to find any clues that popped out at us from the spreadsheet.

"This looks like one of those brain teasers in the crossword puzzle books," Billy said. "You know, the deductive thinking puzzles."

I took a small sip of Dr Pepper and said, "I still like Phillip House for it. His name appears the most times, and we have yet to find out what the payments are for around Mother's Day. Also, he's a general sleaze. I think there has to be a connection between him and Cynthia Gilmore. She could be a private investigator working for him, she could be a hired killer, or she could be . . . who knows?"

Shawn shifted in his seat. He swallowed a good-sized bite of his ham-and-cheese omelet and then stated his observations. "I don't know if it means anything, but most of the dates are in May. Again, death seems to follow Craig Haskell, and I noted that three of the deaths took place in years that Cynthia Gilmore had income. But I don't think she was paid to kill anyone, because the amounts she made aren't nearly enough to justify contract killing."

Scott nearly choked on his water. "Do you really think contract killers report their income to the government? You've been in Israel wa-a-a-y too long."

"Good point. I wasn't thinking."

Movement outside the cubicle caught my eye.

"Could you use a slightly emotional Cliffhanger at this booth?" Rachel appeared at our table, trying to grin. Her nose was red and her eyes puffy. She scooted into the circular booth next to me.

Shawn answered her. "Of course we could. Just don't offer any thoughts that aren't logical, or you might get skewered for your efforts." He shot an exaggerated dark look at Scott.

"How are the folks?" Billy asked.

"Actually, I'd rather not talk about them," she said quietly. "I haven't seen my parents since I left high school, and my dad had a stroke ten years ago. He can't speak, or walk, and I hardly recognized him. Mom has had a lot on her shoulders, and I haven't been much of a daughter." An uncomfortable silence followed. "So if you don't mind, just update me on the case."

I pushed the spreadsheet of dates and names over to her. "Right now, we're just discussing our observations about what we see on the timeline Todd made for us. He's back on the farm, but will join us tonight for the banquet."

"Did you tell the group that Craig is leaving after graduation and plans to take an extended leave of absence?"

Scott looked up from his plate where he had been scooping forkfuls of splattered hash browns into his mouth. "Whoa, whoa, whoa. Craig's leaving town? What if he's our killer? Rachel, is there anything else you found out in his background check?"

"Not that I didn't already mention. I think if we want to know any more in-depth about him, we need to interview friends or family. A computer search can't tell us everything."

"But the problem is, from what I can see, he doesn't have any family or friends. They keep dying off." Billy grinned when he said it.

I felt excitement course through my body. This was going to work. We were going to find out who killed Tim. We were going to clear my name.

"You said Craig was adopted. Do you know his birth name?" Scott asked Rachel.

"Not yet. I'm still trying to find that out. His birth records are sealed."

"Did he have any brothers or sisters? This is top priority if he plans to leave after graduation." Not waiting for Rachel to answer, Scott wiped his mouth with his napkin, took a big gulp of coffee, and pushed his wheelchair away from the table. "I'm going to interview him right now. Jamie, can you and Rachel take a quick trip up to Bloomington and talk to Stewart's parents—see if they know anything about Craig's background?"

"Sure," I answered.

"Maybe go to the school there and see if he left under suspicious circumstances. Billy, I know you're busy, but if you have time, could you take this address and run over to check on Cynthia Gilmore? See if she was following Jamie." Scott was in his element now, shelling out orders.

"I'll do it on my way to the studio," Billy said.

"Shawn, I need you with me."

I looked at my watch. "Okay, its 9:45. Rachel and I will be gone at least four—maybe five—hours. Can we meet again at three o'clock to compare notes?"

"I don't think I'll be able to make it," Scott said. "I think we'd better just stay in phone contact. We're all going to see each other tonight at the banquet. We can talk then." Scott seemed in a hurry to get started.

Plugging her laptop into the printer provided at the table, Rachel said, "Everyone, give me your cell numbers." As we called them out, she typed them in bold and hit PRINT. She handed out the sheets to each person.

The Cliffhangers left the table with the same excitement we felt when we were back in high school about to solve some mystery. Rachel and I jumped in the SUV and headed south to Bloomington.

I looked over at my passenger and laid a hand on Rachel's arm. "How was it really?"

"I don't really know. It was scary until I actually saw Dad. He looked so pathetic in his wheelchair, his head lolling to one side. Mom had to keep wiping drool off his chin. He's not strong or frightening any more, just pitiful. It was horrible. I feel bad for Mom. She has no life outside of taking care of Dad. She's more trapped than I ever was, because she won't ever get to move out. Now I don't know what to think or feel."

I kept my thoughts to myself. The early morning rain had vanished as quickly as it had come. White, puffy clouds drifted aimlessly in the blue sky, and vibrant greens streaked past the window at sixty miles an hour. No matter the turns, no matter the highway, I would never be able to make it right for Rachel. Listening and loving was all I could do, and even though I hadn't done a good job of it in the past, I was determined to do it better in the future.

It wasn't long before I brought our conversation back to Tim's murder and the timeline that Todd had worked on. "Rachel, did anything jump out at you at all?"

Before Rachel could form a reply, her cell phone rang. After listening for a minute, she said, "I'm not surprised. Thanks for calling. Keep us posted."

She turned and looked at me. "The address the DMV has on record for Cynthia Gilmore is a non-address. Just a vacant piece of property with no house on it at all. We are back to square one with her. This doesn't necessarily put her at the top of my list, but I *am* beginning to think she's involved somehow. I just need to figure out how. My computer knowledge hasn't been all that helpful in tracing her."

CHAPTER TWENTY-TWO

November 13, 1989

I t was the perfect setup. No one would ever suspect foul play. No one had even heard of HPS or Hantavirus Pulmonary Syndrome in the United States. Of course, there had been outbreaks of it for decades in Europe. Russia, Scandinavia, and Finland were hit with it, but no cases had appeared in the US. This was so perfect. Luckily, there had been a recent case in Edmonton, Alberta, which was a reminder of the disease and the spark that created the lightbulb idea. It wasn't always easy to come up with new ways to eliminate a problem.

The first symptoms of HPS are general and flu-like—fever ranging anywhere from 101 to 104 degrees, headache, stomach pain, pain in the joints and lower back, coughing, and sometimes nausea and vomiting. Nothing much to worry about. Probably wouldn't even warrant a trip to the doctor. The main symptom is difficulty breathing as the lungs fill with fluid. Getting to the doctor now will probably be too late. It can quickly lead to an inability to breathe and, in severe cases, death from suffocation. That is the goal. The average time between contact with the virus and the onset of illness is two to three weeks. So much the better. Who would ever connect an electrician to an illness that happened weeks later? No one.

The plan had gone off without a hitch. "Ma'am, this is Pat Island from Indiana Power and Light. We will be in your area around ten this morning. There seems to be a short in some of the wiring in your neighborhood. Both the house on your left and right have experienced problems. We need to chase down the problem."

"Why would that affect me?"

"Well, I don't know that it will. But if it was wired by the same electrician, and it seems likely since you're side-by-side in the same subdivision, it could be a problem. Your neighbors smelled something burning and called us. They were lucky. It could have caught their houses on fire."

"I'll only be home for another hour. I'm meeting my husband for lunch."

"I kn . . . It will only take a few minutes." Almost a mistake, a slip of the tongue, but a quick recovery. And that was all that was needed.

"Okay. I definitely don't want the house burning down."

"I'll be there in five minutes."

After a quick survey of the house, the nursery seemed the appropriate place to spread the contents of the little black box. It appeared to be a nursery, although there was no furniture in it. The walls had gotten a fresh coat of light celery-green paint. Baby booties, rattles, and giant diaper pins were stenciled on the walls in muted Easter colors. Evidently, they didn't know whether it would be a boy or a girl. No solid pinks or blues. Not that it mattered. The baby would never see the light of day.

The best part of the room was the sewing machine and ironing board. Angela must be busy being Mommy of the Year and making baby clothes herself. What a waste. But on the upside, she probably used the room often. That would almost guarantee a good dose of Hantavirus would infect her lungs.

It only took a quick glimpse into the living room to ensure privacy. Angela was chatting on the phone. Very good. Half a minute to don the gloves and mask. Another minute to spread the lovely, little, lab-infected mouse droppings in the closet and in the corners of the room, and the task was finished. A quick holding of breath, removing the mask and gloves, shoving them in a pocket, and a polite good-bye. No one the wiser.

There would be lag time before the kill was finished, but that didn't matter. One could keep up with the news via the daily paper. A quick smile, a thumbs-up gesture at Angela, and out the door. The entire operation took less than five minutes. The consequences would last a lifetime. The very thought was balm to the soul.

CHAPTER TWENTY-THREE

The address in Bloomington led us through a tidy neighborhood where flowers spilled out of pots, lawns sprouted no dandelions, and hedges lined property boundaries at manicured heights. Two robins flew into the next yard over in hopes of catching worms without being disturbed by the human race. A blue jay followed the robins but not before giving us a piece of his mind. They really do scold.

Rachel and I were uneasy as we approached the small, yellow house with white shutters on Oak Street. It seemed wrong somehow to barge into someone's grief, however old, and reopen a painful wound. I was getting good at opening old wounds. With a sigh, I rang the doorbell. Then a curious thing happened. Lights flickered on and off, both inside and out, like a warning of some kind.

"What's that all about?" I asked.

Rachel shrugged.

A short, robust woman opened the door, wearing a bib apron with splotches of flour scattered on it. Her hair was the kind of white that people envied. No yellowing around the edges that spoke of too much color, just beautiful snow-white hair, cut short, and permed into loose curls. Wrinkles laced her face, and her eyes crinkled around the corners. Not saying a word, her eyes went from Rachel to me and then back to Rachel.

I cleared my throat. "Mrs. Stewart, my name is Jamie Storm and this is Rachel King. Could we come in and speak to you for a minute?"

Mrs. Stewart looked quizzically at Rachel, said nothing, and then looked at me.

I plowed on hoping to elicit a positive response. "A friend of mine was killed in Anderson last week, and we feel his death could possibly be connected to your daughter's." I knew the statement lacked diplomacy, but there was no easy way to do this.

Mrs. Stewart's hands flew into action. She signed her response after evidently reading my lips. Her voiced words were incomprehensible—just a series of nasal-sounding grunts.

Ahh, now the blinking lights made sense. Mrs. Stewart was deaf. I didn't know sign language, and I looked at Rachel. She shook her head.

"I don't know sign." I spoke slowly, loud, and with exaggerated lip movements. My shoulders shrugged in a helpless gesture. Too late I realized she'd read my lips before. Exaggerated speech was probably an insult.

Mrs. Stewart smiled at us and stuck up her right index finger in the universal one-minute-please gesture I did understand.

Still standing on the porch, we waited until Mrs. Stewart came back leading a seventyish, balding man. Yawning and rubbing the sleep out of his eyes, he smiled at us. "You have news of our Dacia?"

"Not exactly, and I do hate to get your hopes up. A good friend of mine was killed, and I believe their deaths may be connected. Could we talk to you—see if you might have some information that could help? Your daughter taught my English class the last semester of high school." Then I added, "I'm here from Montana for our class reunion. I only have a few days."

Mr. Stewart's hands moved as he interpreted for his wife. "This is my wife Dottie. Call me Chuck."

"Rachel King."

"Jamie Storm," I said and stuck out my hand.

We shook hands with the elderly couple.

"Dottie can read lips just fine, but I like to interpret just the same. Come on in." He opened the door wide, gesturing for us to enter. We followed them into the living room, where the conversation continued.

"Have the police contacted you yet?" I asked.

"Just to say they've recovered her body. They haven't released her to us yet, but it shouldn't be long before they find her killer." Chuck's voice was full of hope.

Dottie started signing again, but she didn't look as hopeful as Chuck. He voiced for her. "I don't think the police will look any harder now than they did when she first went missing. We told them over and over something terrible had happened to our Dacia, and they didn't so much as lift a finger thirty years ago. All those ridiculous excuses—she probably just got tired of teaching and took flight. She's young. Young people don't have any sense of responsibility. She'll call when she's ready to come home. They didn't try then, and I don't expect they'll put much effort into it now."

Chuck put his arm around his wife's shoulders in a protective gesture. "If you have a friend who was murdered, and they have a body, you might be more fortunate than us."

The loss of hope swam in Dottie's eyes.

I studied the floor, wishing I hadn't come. Dredging up the past seemed pretty tough for the Stewarts and they'd been through enough. But I was here and it seemed silly to leave without getting as much information as possible.

Rachel must have felt the same way. She continued the questioning. "Did you know Craig Haskell very well?"

"Oh my, yes," Dottie signed as her husband interpreted. "He was everything we had hoped for in a future son-in-law. He loved Dacia."

"Did you trust him?" I asked.

"Of course. He couldn't be over here for a minute without finding something to do. He was always helping Chuck fix up the house. They built the entire porch by themselves. It went completely across the front of the house, and then they built a huge back porch for Sassy and Molasses."

I didn't remember seeing a porch when we came in. "Sassy and Molasses?"

"Our golden retrievers. They were the best dogs. We lost them when we lost the house."

I decided it was none of my business how they lost the house, so I redirected the conversation. "We know that Craig was adopted. Does he have any siblings that you know of? Or do you know what his name was before he was adopted?"

The constant signing that Chuck and Dottie conversed with began to feel normal for me. I quit watching their hands and concentrated on their expressions.

"Why all these questions about Craig? You don't suspect him, do you? I can tell you, he wouldn't hurt anyone. He's got more character in his little finger than most of his generation has in their whole body," Chuck said.

I was not offended at the aspersions leveled at my generation. I often felt the same way. I tried to soothe his concerns. "We don't have any idea who killed your daughter or who killed our friend Tim. We figure if we ask enough questions, look hard enough in the right places, we might be able to find out what happened to our friend and Dacia."

Chuck looked hard into my eyes. He must have decided I was telling the truth so he opened up. "Craig didn't talk much about his life. To be perfectly honest, I don't think he remembered much about his birth parents."

"Names?" Rachel asked.

"I don't know. He didn't mention names, and we didn't ask."

"Brothers or sisters?"

"I think he had at least one sister. I'm not sure though. He loved his adopted parents. It nearly broke him when they died."

"You knew him back then?" Rachel asked.

"He and Dacia started dating two months before he graduated, so Dacia never met them. Neither did we, but he talked about them all the time. Very respectful."

"How well did you know him?"

"After Dacia disappeared, Craig spent a lot of time with us. He helped us breathe. When you lose your only child, and you can't make sense of it, the world just stops. You can hardly move. Craig helped us keep going." Tears streamed down Chuck and Dottie's weathered cheeks. Neither tried to brush them away.

"Do you still see him?" I asked.

"Not since the fire. He just disappeared after that. We tried to call him, but an answering machine picked up. He never called back, not even once. We went to the school where he worked, but he wouldn't see us. Maybe his pain was too much."

I felt a click of intrigue but was careful not to show it. "There was a fire?"

"About three years after Dacia disappeared, Craig fell in love with a young woman. He told us about her." Dottie's hands were moving as fast as Chuck could interpret. "We didn't see him as much as before, but he still came by on a regular basis, checked in on us. He never failed to send cards on Mother's Day, Father's Day, and Easter. He still brought Christmas gifts, and even brought Angela down for Thanksgiving the year before they got married. She was a lovely girl. They invited us to the wedding. Then the fire happened, and that was the last we ever talked to him."

"What happened?" Rachel asked.

Chuck reached over and squeezed his wife's hand, then let go so he could speak and sign at the same time. "It was about a month before their wedding when my mother passed away. She was one hundred and one. She got a birthday card from President Reagan, God rest his soul, when she turned one hundred. It had the presidential seal, Mr. Reagan's signature, the real deal. She kept the card in her Bible, and they read it at her funeral."

"The fire?" I interrupted.

"Anyway, we were at the funeral down in Champaign, Illinois, and Kelly, a young gal from our church, came over to stay with Sassy and Molasses. Nicest girl you'd ever want to meet. We asked her to feed them, keep them company, and walk them. We planned to be gone for three days. How I wish we'd taken the dogs with us." Mr. Stewart cleared his throat. Hesitated. Continued, slower, more tears.

"The night after the funeral our house burned to the ground. The police called us at about two in the morning. The place went so fast, the only thing the fire department could do was protect the nearby houses. Ours was too far gone by the time they reached it. Kelly died in the fire . . . so did our dogs."

"That's horrible."

Mr. Stewart nodded. "It was worse than horrible. It was arson. Fire marshal investigated. The porches had been soaked with gasoline. Our home burned in a matter of minutes. Nothing anybody could do. They still don't know who did it."

"Not good," Rachel said.

"That's the last we saw of Craig. Never came around again."

"Did he know you were going to a funeral?" I asked.

"No, we couldn't reach him the day Mom died. We left as soon as we got our clothes together."

Dottie chimed in, hands in action. "That's when he walked away from us. I think he blamed himself, but there was nothing he could've done. Nothing."

"What makes you think he blamed himself?" Rachel asked.

Dottie and Chuck made such a good team it was hard to tell when one finished talking and the other began.

"Shortly after that we got a curt note from him, asking us not to come to the wedding. He wrote that he needed to distance himself from the past and look to the future."

"That must have hurt," I said. My mind raced with possibilities. The unraveling pattern put Craig right smack-dab in my most-favorite-suspect category.

"We honored his wishes, but we still checked on him through friends. When his wife and child died, we went to the funeral. He acted as if he didn't see us. The last we heard, he was seeing a psychologist and had taken a leave of absence from the school. Poor Craig. Too much death."

I stood up. "Well, we've bothered you long enough. Appreciate all you've told us. We'll get back to you if we find anything that ties Dacia's murder to Tim's." I couldn't wait to get outside to talk to Rachel alone. I wanted to test my theory on her.

"One more thing," Rachel said, always thinking of the next move. "Do you remember what psychologist Craig went to see?"

"No, sorry, I don't. Some fella down in Indy. Worked in an office with lots of other head doctors. I wonder how much good it did him. Sometimes you just have to buck up and accept life as it comes. No psychologist in the world would have made us hurt less when our Dacia disappeared . . . unless he could have brought her back to us. And that sure didn't happen."

"Thanks for talking to us," I said.

Mr. Stewart nodded, took my hand for a moment, and walked us to the door.

I tried to organize the jumbled thoughts that spun in my head. Another death had occurred surrounding Craig that we hadn't known about. He was seeing a psychologist—mental problems or just grief? He might have a sister somewhere. Was she alive or dead?

Back in the vehicle, I said, "This is creeping me out. Anyone who gets near Craig dies."

"The Stewarts' aren't dead," Rachel said.

"You know what I mean. They'd be dead if they hadn't gone to a funeral."

"I know. But they don't suspect him in the least. They still love him."

"Doesn't make him innocent—makes them trusting. I gotta tell you, he's fast rising to the top of my suspect list."

"So now House is Mr. Nice Guy?" Rachel sounded defensive, angry, and small—all at the same time.

"I didn't say that. I don't think it. He's the scum of the earth for what he did to you. I'm just not sure he killed Tim. We need to look at Craig with an open mind."

"I know. I was just hoping . . . well, it doesn't matter. You're right. We need to look at Craig." Rachel sounded like she was trying to convince herself. Her eyes that just moments before had sparkled with interest were flat and lifeless. She looked hopeless. I needed to change the subject.

"Let's stop in Indy on our way back to Anderson and see if we can locate Craig's shrink. Maybe he can give us some answers." I knew confidentiality laws might prohibit getting much, but anything might help at this point.

"That would have been back in 2000, 2001, or so. Do you think he's still seeing someone?" Rachel asked.

"I don't know. I don't even know how to approach a psychologist to find out if Craig was a client." I thought hard but couldn't come up with a workable idea.

Rachel looked over at me and smiled. "Well, Mrs. Pastor's Wife, I have an idea, but you might have to close your ears while I do it. Get me to a wi-fi hotspot. I need an Indianapolis directory."

We pulled up outside a Starbucks and logged on to her laptop. After searching under the listing for psychologists, Rachel punched in the numbers on her cell. I listened in disbelief to the one-sided conversation. Rachel was very good.

"Hello, ma'am. This is Rachel King of King, Storm, and King out of Champaign, Illinois. We represent a Mr. Craig Haskell who passed away several months ago. We need to find out which doctor treated him back in 2001.

"Yes, ma'am, I am sure that is confidential information, but Mr. Haskell left a considerable share of his estate to, and I quote, 'the shrink who helped me find the light.' If we can't locate the doctor he is referring to in his will, his share will go to one of the other beneficiaries. We've tried all the normal procedures to find out this information, and we sure could use your help. I suspect if your doctor is the right one, he'll not be too happy if you let this drop. Please look up your client list from 2001 and check to see if there is a Craig Haskell on it. We'll do the rest."

Rachel was silent for a minute and then said, "Okay, thank you. I appreciate your help." Hanging up she told me, "No luck on my first try."

I didn't know what to say. I was impressed with Rachel's gutsy methods, if not her truthfulness. My pastor's wife conscience had given up doing jumping jacks on my shoulder, and I sat shaking my head. I hoped God wouldn't give up on me. I had a brief moment of being glad David couldn't see me. As Rachel continued down the list of psychologists, I let my thoughts drift back to Great Falls and the simpler, gentler life. I caught myself smiling at the thought of Sister Thornbush's reaction if she could see me now.

"Well, well, well, it' a fine how-do-you-do when the pastor's wife condones lying. My gracious, it's a good thing the good Lord raised up from the dead, or He'd be turning over in His grave at such sinfulness. I knew it was too good to be true. Just because a person can bake a couple of apple pies don't mean she'll get to heaven. Serving the Lord is more than bake sales and mission trips. Quite the example to set to the youngsters in this congregation. The next thing you know, she'll be clapping during the singing."

Rachel's question broke into my drifting thoughts. "Do you think there's a way to narrow the search? How can one city have so many psychologists, psychiatrists, and therapists?"

"Try looking under death, or grief counselors, or loss victims—something like that. Medical doctors have specialties. So do head doctors."

"Okay, let's see. Huh. There are psychiatrists and psychologists for everything. Aging, addictions, bi-polar disorder, physical- and sexual-abuse victims, grief, PTSD, and every other dysfunction known to man."

My voice softened. "Maybe you should see someone about the abuse you experienced. It might help you see the truth about what happened."

"Good segue—not off the topic at all. I . . . I don't know. I don't know if I could betray my parents like that after all they did for me."

"Woo-hoo. They gave you a home and food. Real big of them. Parents are supposed to do more than that—like protect you from the bad guys and not be the bad guys." Sarcasm poured out of my mouth. "Your dad did things that are unspeakable, and you still think it's your fault. Maybe a shrink could help you see the truth. I know the truth, Rachel, but I don't think you do. Not in your heart of hearts. And I want that for you more than anything."

Rachel turned away and punched in the number for the third grief counselor. Nine doctors were listed as being a part of the Healing Hearts Clinic. I realized our conversation was over. Listening to Rachel chat about the phantom estate, I wondered if I would have coped as well if the circumstances had been reversed. It made me shudder to think of my dad, the gentle and loving Vincent Waymire, degrading me in that way as a child. I had no business thinking I knew what was best for Rachel. No business at all.

"Yes, ma'am, we'll be right over. Could you repeat the address for me?" Furiously motioning to me to hand over a pen, Rachel wrote and repeated, "478 North Meridian. Dr. Julianne Trueax. Got it. Thank you."

"It looks like our carrot dangling did the trick," Rachel said. "We have one eager rabbit ready to nibble. The receptionist at this clinic serves all nine doctors, and in about thirty seconds, she con-firmed Craig had been a client of the clinic back in 2000 and 2001."

"So this Dr. Trueax was his shrink?"

"She didn't specifically say. She just said Trueax was who we needed to talk to. She also warned us that all client information is privileged and that the doctor would not be able to give us any information regarding Haskell. And one other thing, we'll have to pay the going rate for the doctor's time. And we can't mention how we got her name, but other than that, we're good to go."

"So what you're saying is that this Dr. Trueax doesn't even know we're coming, or what we want to talk to her about. We simply have an appointment with her like any other Joe Blow off the street?"

"That's correct, and her fee is $340 an hour, and I promised the receptionist $100 for the information."

I swallowed. "I guess it's a good thing Tim left me plenty of money to come out here this week. That's a weeks' pay for David and me. How can people afford to get mental help?"

The drive to North Meridian was spent chatting about the cost of health insurance, frivolous lawsuits, and a country obsessed with self-esteem and personal awareness.

Pulling into the clinic parking lot, we could see where much of the money went. The clinic sat on more than an acre of land. The grounds looked like Adrian Monk was the gardener. A large fountain splashed water onto the backs of geese swimming in the huge, man-made pond. Shrubs and flowers lined the walks, and tall maples provided shade for waiting clients. The clinic itself looked like an inviting mansion where one could imagine bread baking in the oven rather than minds being dissected, redi-rected, and put back together again. Here, in the busiest part of

Indianapolis, was a respite from the hurried and frenzied pace of a world gone crazy. A little ironic.

The reception area was as inviting as the grounds had been, with beautiful marble and oak flooring with comfortable leather furniture sprinkled throughout. Plants of every size and shape were tastefully displayed in brass and marble pots. Classical music floated out of the hidden wall speakers, inviting muscles to relax and clenched jaws to unclench. It had an almost sanctuary feel. Peaceful, serene, and soul mending. Rachel and I walked to the middle of the room where a round oak desk with several flat-screen monitors hummed and three receptionists sat.

"We have an appointment with Dr. Trueax," Rachel said to no one in particular.

A plump redhead with just a touch too much lipstick motioned us over to her station. "Are you the woman who just called?"

Rachel nodded.

"You need to pay up front," the receptionist stated. "For the visit and my computer research services."

I pulled out five one-hundred-dollar bills from my pants pocket and laid them on the desk. Redhead beamed and handed me back three twenties.

"Walk down that hall to the right and enter the door labeled Green Room. Dr. Trueax is waiting for you." The nametag on her muted orange shirt was labeled Teena.

"Could I have a receipt please?" My voice was firm—no nonsense.

Teena pulled out a book and made out a receipt for $340.

"And I need a receipt for computer research," I added. If I was going to be robbed in this plush office, the least she could do was give me a receipt.

The other two receptionists looked up from their tasks and eyed Teena. The redhead scribbled on a piece of plain, white paper: "For services rendered, $100." She dated and signed it, but her signature was unreadable.

I gave her what I hoped was an amused smile, and we walked to the Green Room. And green it was. The walls were painted with sea-foam green, lighter green, and a smattering of vanilla. The couch and recliner in the office consisted of plush, forest-green fabric with oak and brass trim. Plants contributed a serene feel to the room. Dr. Trueax was a small lady with an extremely short haircut. It was shorter than the average flattop had been in the '50s. Her eyes sparkled, which lessened the severity of the haircut, and she asked, "What is on your minds today?"

Evidently, Teena had not explained anything about our interest. Rachel started and finished with the lie. "So if we can just ask you a few questions to make sure you are the psychologist who helped Craig Haskell find some peace, we can issue a check from his estate and be on our way."

I couldn't believe my ears. Surely Rachel understood that we had no check and that this was merely a figment of her overactive imagination. It would be practically impossible to back away from this situation with any credibility at all.

Dr. Trueax smiled at both of us. "Well, I'm sorry to disappoint, but I purchased this practice from Dr. Rice's wife. If Craig was treated in 2001, Dr. Rice would have been his doctor."

"Do you know where we can find Dr. Rice?" I asked.

"You can find him at Crown Hill, but I don't think he'll be of much help to you."

"Crown Hill?"

"Crown Hill Cemetery. Dr. Rice died in January of 2002. One of the anthrax victims in the wake of 9/11. Sorry."

I couldn't believe my ears. Another death surrounding Craig? This was unbelievable. This could no longer be a coincidence. Rachel was at a loss for words also.

Dr. Trueax stepped from around her desk. "Listen, ladies, it looks like you are both pretty shocked. Is there more to this inquiry than meets the eye?"

"No, no, we're just shocked that we can't follow Craig's wishes." Rachel lied with ease.

"Anthrax death? Was the killer ever found and convicted?" I asked.

"Well, that's the tricky part. The anthrax that killed Dr. Rice was not the same strain that killed the other victims. You would think that anthrax is anthrax, but there are several strains, and several methods of delivery, and Dr. Rice's differed completely from the others. At first the police were afraid of a copycat killer, but it seems Dr. Rice was the odd one out. Gastrointestinal anthrax. Ate contaminated meat. The other deaths—all inhalation form—were related to the man whom the FBI finally caught. He was charged in every death but Dr. Rice's."

"So was Dr. Rice's killer ever found?" Rachel asked.

"Not as far as I know. But the FBI got warrants for all his client files, and they didn't find anything compelling enough to make them warn me about anyone."

CHAPTER TWENTY-FOUR

achel and I hurried out to the Escape. "We have to warn Scott. He should be interviewing Craig right now." Rachel grabbed my cell and dialed Scott's number. No answer.

"I have a bad feeling about this," I said. "You keep trying to reach him. Call the others and see if they have heard from him. Hang on!"

With adrenaline surging through my veins, I weaved through traffic until I reached Interstate 69 North. With little regard for the posted speed limit, I reached Anderson in twenty-eight minutes. Taking Scatterfield to Highway 32 took longer than the entire drive from Indy. With stoplights, ongoing construction, and congestion, I couldn't catch a break. Drumming my fingers on the steering wheel, I prayed, "God, let Scott stay safe."

Rachel tried to calm me down. "Scott is going to be fine. He's got a gun, he knows how to use it, and he's a cop. I'm sure when he questions a suspect he's always on the lookout for trouble."

"I was just so sure it was Phillip House. Craig seems like such a nice guy. But then that's what they said about the Son of Sam and Ted Bundy."

"Okay, now I think you're getting a little carried away. None of the deaths surrounding Craig are serial-killer deaths. There

was nothing similar about any of them, and some were acciden-
tal. He wasn't even around when most of them occurred. I think
you need to take a deep breath and chill."

I turned left onto Range Line Road and headed toward Highland High. "Too many deaths to be coincidental. Craig is right in
the middle of all this, and I don't know if he paid someone to do it
or what, but he's involved. Scott's in danger. I can feel it."

Rachel knew it was useless to argue with me when I got like this.
She sat back in her seat and watched the road for Craig or Scott's
vehicles. When we arrived at the school, Scott's van sat in the front
parking lot. For a Saturday, the parking lots were busy, but with
the reunion and graduation weekend, it was not a surprise. Driving
through the lots, we didn't see Craig's blue Beemer anywhere.

I double-parked the SUV in front of the school offices and ran
inside. An air of excitement rushed down the hallways as non-stop
chatter filled the building. People walked down the hallways with
boxes of decorations. Two young guys pushed a big rack stacked
with folding chairs into the cafeteria. A well-tanned blonde with
striking blue eyes walked past with a clipboard, stopped, and
looked directly at me.

"Jamie, is that you? Jamie Waymire? Wow, you look good,
girl. Breathing that fresh Montana air must keep you young."

It took me a second to recognize the 1982 class president, Lisa
Ivy. Giving her a quick hug, I said, "Lisa, so good to see you. It looks
like you're busy so I won't keep you. I need to talk to the principal
before tonight, but we'll chat later."

Lisa would not be deterred. "It's Lisa Blevins now. I married
James after college. Can you believe it? I'm a preacher's wife too.
I just can't wait to tell you about it. My life and all the changes I
made since high school. God is just tooo good."

If I hadn't been on a mission, I would have found this discussion more than interesting. Lisa was from one of the wealthy families in Anderson and had all the clothes, cars, and friends money could buy. She was not noted for a moral lifestyle in high school, and her path rarely crossed mine. "I really am sorry, Lisa, but I have to go. I'll talk to you tonight." I gave Lisa a quick hug and stepped into the office.

"Can you tell me where I can find Principal Haskell?" I directed the question toward the forty-something woman wearing a bright-green, button-down shirt. She looked to be in charge.

The secretary looked up from the computer. "Sorry, you missed him. He left some time ago. Maybe I can help you. What do you need?"

"Actually, I just need Craig." I hoped the use of his first name would suggest to the secretary we were more than friends. "We were supposed to meet later, and I'm not going to make it. I really need to let him know what's going on." Lying, I realized, wasn't hard at all once a person got started.

Green-shirt wasn't fooled. "Mr. Haskell asked that he not be disturbed. He didn't mention anything to me about meeting you this afternoon. Now if you don't need anything I can help you with, you need to move along." Authority rang in her voice, tinged with superiority.

I gave it one last effort. "This could be a matter of life-and-death. Please just tell me where he is. I need to talk to him."

"From meeting with you to life and death. Wow. How do you ever keep it all straight? I'd be happy to call security if you've forgotten where the door is." Her icy words bit into the air.

"Please, ma'am, I'm sorry to make you angry, but I'm worried about a friend of mine. Craig might have seen him." Again I lied.

"For the last time, I am not to disturb him. He's fishing with a friend, and he'll be back in time for all the festivities tonight. You can reach him then if it's important. Now I have lots of loose ends to tie up before I go home." Green-shirt turned back to the computer, clearly ending the conversation.

Fear clutched my heart, and I walked outside. I would never forgive myself if I'd put Scott in harm's way, being so insistent that the murderer was House. I trotted over to Rachel waiting in the SUV.

"I'm going to put a note on Scott's van telling him to call us. Then we need to figure out what to do next."

"I already know what to do next," Rachel said. "Hurry up. We have places to go and people to see."

I taped the note on the driver's side window of the van, jumped in the shotgun seat, and asked, "So where to? What about Scott?"

"What about Scott? We don't even know if he's in trouble."

"If something happens to him . . ."

"We need to do what we can do. Finding him now is not one of those things."

"I guess you're right," I said.

"We need to find out if Craig had a sister, where she is, and if she knows Craig. Maybe she can explain what's going on. We also need to find out more about Cynthia Gilmore, or Volvo lady as you call her. She has something to do with all this, or at least she knows something important. I need to get back to the computer and do some more research."

"How much more can you do on the computer?"

"For starters, I'll pull up Craig's driver's license with my access to DMV records and find out his birth date. Then I'll use that info for a search to determine how many Craigs were born in Indiana.

Then I'll use their last names to see how many death certificates were issued four years later. I might find something.

"From there I'll search local newspapers for articles about the accidents. I might be able to pin down which social-service agency took care of him, or even which adoption agency he went to. For Cynthia, I have to do more checking on her social security number. Something is running around in the back of my mind that I need to check out."

"I'll drop you off at the motel then," I said. "I need to check out Tim's house again, and then I'll pop over to Craig's. Maybe Scott is over there. I have to do something, and I don't know the first place to look for them fishing." I hesitated for a minute. "Will you be all right in the motel room by yourself?"

"You mean am I going to get drunk? You can say the words. It won't hurt my feelings. I'll be fine. Seeing my parents, seeing my dad like that, it was a shock, but freeing somehow. I can make it through the day, maybe the week. I don't know. I'm not saying I'm quitting, but right now I'm okay. You do what you need to do. I need a little cyber time anyway." Rachel reached over and laid her hand on my shoulder and gave it a little pat.

After dropping off Rachel at the motel, I drove to Tim's place. I didn't have a key, but I decided to walk around the house, looking in windows, checking to see if anything looked disturbed. The yellow, crime-scene tape was gone, and the place looked deserted.

Rounding the southeast corner of the house, my face exploded in pain. I fell to the ground, stars spinning in front of my watery eyes. I felt a vicious kick in my stomach, and a male voice snarled, "If you know what's good for you, you'll get out of Anderson today. If you're still butting into other people's private lives tomorrow, you won't have any more tomorrows to worry about."

My mind cleared just long enough to grab his nearest pant leg. Twisting my head into position, I sunk my teeth into the pants, sock, leg, and all. I heard a scream and bit harder. A hand reached down and grabbed a handful of hair and slammed my head on the ground. I felt my teeth loosen before the world blacked out.

I woke later to someone vigorously rubbing a wet cloth across my face. It wasn't cool, gentle, or soft. Whoever it was, they were in a big hurry for me to wake up. I heard a faraway voice echo. "Roger, Roger. Stop that. Come over here."

I opened my eyes to see a large, black lab eagerly licking my face. "Roger?"

A wave of dizziness swept over me when I tried to sit up. I fell back, which Roger took as an invitation to give me a big, wet, sloppy kiss. Yuck. I pushed Roger's head away and tried again. This time I made it to an upright position. Fighting nausea, I pulled my shirt up and wiped dog slobber from my face.

"What happened?" I looked up at Martha.

"I don't really know, dear. Roger started barking, and by the time I got myself turned around to see what was happening, I saw a man running away—kind of gimpy like. Roger got loose and ran over to you, and I've been trying to get him off you ever since."

"Do you remember what the man looked like?"

"Like I said, I only saw him briefly, but I didn't notice much."

"Any distinctive features?" *Please, please God, let her remember something.*

"Well, like I said he ran kind of funny like. Almost dragging one leg, but as he picked up speed the leg was doing better. He puts me in mind of that guy who stands behind the President when he makes speeches. Of course, this guy was shorter and not as handsome, but he had the same color hair, same color eyes, and the same square jaw."

Phillip House? Out loud I asked, "Did you see what he was driving?"

"Oh my, no. By that time, I was trying to get Roger off you. He's so like my nephew—always trying to save the world. That's my Roger. I sure named him right. They say you always live up to the name you're given. It just goes to show you they're right. Now my Momma gave me the name Martha. Now how do you live up to a name like Martha? There's no way I can be like the first First Lady, so I wonder what am I supposed to be like? Course, if she would have named me Elizabeth, I would have had to be like the queen, and I think that's rather snobbish, don't you? Yes, I think all in all Martha is better. Solid, honest, dependable, not running around with silly hats on my head even if they do match all my clothes."

My scrambled brain struggled to focus, and Martha's talking was making it more difficult. "Martha?" I put the question out there hoping to deter further name conversation. It was a mistake.

"Martha Sue Baker. Well, that was my given name—Baker. I'm pretty good at baking. Brownies are my specialty . . . well, any kind of cakes really. Of course, when I married Stanley, I became a Moss, but I still bake really well. And how do you become a Moss? It's not like you can grow on trees." Martha laughed at her joke.

I tried to stand, and after the second attempt, I finally made it. I still felt nauseated, but I needed to get away so I could think. How long had I been out? Were Phillip House and Craig Haskell working together? I still needed to find out where Scott was. Maybe I should report the assault to the police and tell them my suspicions. *Oh, David, where are you? I need you so much.*

"Stanley, though, he did grow on a person. When I first met him I didn't really like him, but the more time I spent around him the more I liked him. Of course, that was back in '45 when guys were scarce with the war and all. One couldn't be too choosy if they wanted to get married. And I did. Wanted to get married I mean. Anyway, Stanley Moss lived up to his name, and we got married."

I butted in. "I'm sorry, Martha. I really need to go. I appreciate Roger coming to my rescue, but I need to report this to the police."

"Goodness, you're going to have one heck of a shiner. Want some ice?"

"No, thanks. I gotta go."

"Oh sure, no problem. I want to get Roger some water anyway. It sure is a warm one." Martha looked up at the sky in an accusatory glare. "Well, come on, Roger. Let's go."

If Roger was thirsty he clearly didn't let on. He sniffed around the ground, ignoring Martha's voice. Suddenly, he let out a sharp bark, his nose pushing at something.

I looked down to see him poking a man's handkerchief around. "Hey thanks, Roger. That might help."

Bending down, I patted Roger's head, grabbed the wrinkled linen, and stuffed it in my pocket. I walked away to the sound of Martha telling Roger more about names and characteristics and who did or didn't live up to what *they* said.

CHAPTER TWENTY-FIVE

January 12, 2002

The idea of injecting the anthrax spores directly into the steak was genius, pure genius. It didn't come without risk, of course, but on the whole it was the best plan to ensure innocent bystanders didn't get hurt. That had happened before, and it was no good. No good at all. Not that the bystanders got hurt, but that the real culprits got away scot-free.

The difficulty came in designing a scheme to get the doctor to a cookout. After only two weeks of surveillance, the answer presented itself. As it turned out, Glenn Rice had one flaw—hopefully a fatal one. He liked women, a lot, and not just his wife. The good doctor was not a man to let the Seventh Commandment get in his way. Always sucking in his gut and pretending to be a stud around women half his age. So childish. So pathetic, but oh so convenient.

It only took two appointments filled with stories of overwhelming grief to be considered a legitimate client and an acquaintance. Accidentally bumping into Rice at a grocery store, followed by an apologetic invitation to a barbecue using the old I-must-bring-my-twenty-five-year-old-sister-because-she's-lonely gambit—was perfect bait. The doctor swallowed hook, line, and sinker. Evidently, overactive libidos overrode professional ethics and the psychiatric code of conduct. Finding a good-looking young woman willing to play the part of a forlorn sister was a piece of cake. A quick call to an escort service and paying the two-thousand-dollar fee solved that problem. A bargain at twice the price. It was almost too easy.

Luckily, it had been the warmest January on record, and parks were filled with Frisbee enthusiasts, young children, and frazzled parents thankful for the seventy-five-degree weather. The Fort Harrison State Park was not especially pretty at this time of the year. The massive hardwoods stood naked and stark. But it was just the place for the two lovebirds to get acquainted while the steaks cooked. It didn't take long before Rice was tripping all over himself to appear young, engaging, and sexy. Pseudo-sister turned on the charmed, giggly, and appreciative act. They strolled over to a short hiking path, promising to be back by the time the steaks were done. There was ample time to lace the beef with an abundance of the lethal anthrax.

A quick stop at County Market had supplied potato salad, baked beans, and fruit to complement the meal. The other half of the cooler contained chilled beer. The grilled steaks looked delicious. All was as it should be. It was pure joy watching Dr. Rice eat with such gusto. He complimented the meal several times between drinks and bites. The "kid sister" joined in the praise. How very refined. Not that the doctor would feel refined in a few days. By then he would be showing initial signs of nausea, loss of appetite, vomiting, and fever. Later other symptoms would develop—abdominal pain, vomiting of blood, and severe diarrhea. Given the time delay of symptoms, Dr. Rice would never connect the steak to his illness. It was hard not to smile.

CHAPTER TWENTY-SIX

O nce I got in the SUV, I sat for a moment. The last thing I remembered before Roger's slobbers was zipping around the corner of Tim's house. I couldn't remember any vehicle following me, but I hadn't paid attention. If it *was* Phillip House, what did it mean? What was he doing at Tim's place? Had he followed me? Was there a connection between House, Haskell, and Gilmore? I couldn't wait to get back to the motel and have Rachel cross-reference the three names and see if there were any hits.

I realized I was jumping to conclusions by deciding that Martha's description of the man she saw running was Phillip House just because he "sort of looked like the guy that stood behind the president during speeches." Still, it was better than nothing. I pulled the wrinkled, stained hankie out of my pocket and stretched it out. In the bottom right-hand corner were the initials PHH. Now my conclusion-jumping didn't seem so ludicrous.

I looked in the rearview mirror at my face and noticed my eye was already turning bluish-black. Whatever hit me had split the skin on my left eyebrow. Roger must have licked most of the blood off, but I was still bleeding a little. Before starting the engine, I grabbed a Kleenex from the glove box, spit on it, and wiped off the blood Roger missed. I applied a little pressure with the tissue against my eyebrow.

"You haven't seen your class for thirty years, and now you're gonna look like a puffy, lopsided raccoon. Jamie, Jamie, Jamie."

Shaking my head at the image that looked back from the mirror, I put the car in gear. With a quick readjustment of the mirror, I started the drive back to the motel. Less than a week ago I was baking apple pies, and now my head was bleeding from a vicious attack. I had poked someone hard—possibly the Speaker of the House—and I was trying to solve a murder case.

Unbelievable though it was, emotions surged through me I hadn't felt in a long time. Excitement, energy, fear, and something else I couldn't quite label. What I *didn't* feel was boredom. I don't remember when boredom had slithered into my life, snaking its way into every waking moment, but it had.

My life had become a jumble of David's dreams, the children's needs, and church people's troubles. My dreams, needs, and emotions had long been forgotten in the consuming need to take care of those I loved. The consuming need that I assumed was God's will for my life. Was I mistaken? Could God want me to have those things and something else too? Could it be okay to have a passion for something besides husband, home, children, and church family? The questions flooded my mind so fast it surprised me. I needed to put them aside until later. I had a murder to solve and a friend to save. I couldn't help Tim, but maybe I could help Scott.

Everything led back to Craig. Every death could be related to him in some way. It reminded me of the theory of six degrees of separation. I wondered why I didn't have some sense when I met him that he was not all he seemed to be. Normally, I accurately sized up a person in the first ten minutes of meeting them. David called it the gift of discernment. On rare occasions I did change my mind after a first meeting, but it was not the norm. I knew that more often than not my perceptions of people proved right. Now when it really counted, I was wrong, dead wrong, and I prayed Scott would not pay for my mistake.

I thought again of calling the police. *I think Scott is in grave danger. He went fishing with the principal of Highland High School.* Yeah, that would work. I imagined the skeptical looks as I tried to explain about the deaths surrounding Craig: his adopted parents died in a car crash on the way to his graduation, his fiancée died here in Anderson by blunt force trauma to the head, his wife died of Hantavirus, his best friend was shot in the back of the head, his psychiatrist was poisoned with anthrax, and now Scott is with him.

Even as I reviewed the list, I knew the police would not take me seriously. I would have to find some hard evidence that proved Craig was an active participant in at least one of those deaths and not just a recipient of the worst case of Murphy's Law ever.

Thankfully, I reached the motel and pulled into the parking lot. I was having trouble with the vision in my left eye. Examining myself again in the rearview mirror before getting out of the SUV, I could see why. My eye had swollen shut. *I definitely lost round one.*

The Holiday Inn's lobby bathroom held one large paper towel dispenser. Ignoring the intellectual graffiti carved into the walls, I grabbed four paper towels. The vending machines supplied the ice I needed. At this point, the poor man's ice pack felt heavenly on my eye. I hoped the swelling would go down before the reunion dinner. At least the black eye would match my dress. Woo-hoo. I'd be "styling," as Jake would say.

Knocking on the door to the room I called out, "Rachel, open the door. I've got my hands full." I waited a minute and knocked again. No answer. Setting the ice pack down and sliding the key through the lock, I opened the door.

One glance around the room made my heart stand still. The laptop computer was open and on. Papers were strewn all over the floor. The bathroom door was open, the light on, and no one was in the room. Rachel's purse lay open on the bed with the contents scattered out.

"Oh, Rachel. Oh no, what happened?" I cried out.

I picked up the papers off the floor and noticed it was part of her research. There was no note. For once, I hoped Rachel *was* out drinking. It was better than the alternative. Maybe she was in a hurry and didn't want me catching her.

That's when I noticed a phone number written in Rachel's handwriting on a hotel pad. Digging my cell phone out of my purse, I punched in the number.

"Anderson Taxi service. How may I help you?"

"This is Jamie Storm. I'm at the Holiday Inn on Scatterfield. A friend, Rachel King, just left here in one of your cabs in a big hurry. Could you send a car for me? I need to go to the same place, but I've lost the address. I'm not from around here."

I hoped that sounded convincing. I figured if the cab company got another fare, they'd be willing to cheat a little. I was counting on the power of greed.

"Yes, ma'am, we'll be right there. The hospital isn't far."

CHAPTER TWENTY-SEVEN

H*ospital? What do you mean, hospital?*

I wanted to scream, but opted to hang up instead. Firm fingers of dread clamped onto my stomach and twisted. Fear and bile rose in my throat. My head throbbed above my eye, but I didn't have time to give into it. I glanced in the mirrored dresser. The swelling on my eye had gone down, but it was still shut, black, and puffy. I ran to the bathroom and swallowed two ibuprofen before the taxi arrived. I pulled my hair back in a ponytail, which revealed the extent of the bruise, but right now I didn't want even a strand of hair in my face.

Throwing the purse strap over my shoulder, I marched toward the door determined to do something—anything—to help Rachel. I wasn't sure how fast a taxi could make it, but I would be out front waiting. My mind whirred with thoughts of what could have happened. Every fiber of my being screamed for Rachel to be okay.

The cab pulled up after what seemed like an eternity of pacing, and I hopped in the backseat. The driver didn't say a word, just pulled onto Scatterfield He crept along at about twenty miles per hour. Could he go any slower? Looking at my watch, I realized it had only been a minute since I climbed in the back of the old yellow car. Several minutes later, the driver pulled up in front of St. John's Medical Center.

"Ya want me to wait?" the cabbie asked, not really looking at me. Not really wanting to wait, because it was 98 degrees out with the humidity at about 70 percent.

Pulling a twenty-dollar bill from my wallet, I said, "No, don't wait. I'll call again if I need a ride." Without waiting for change, I ran into the hospital entrance to the front desk. "I'm looking for Rachel King. Do you know where she might be?"

"Honey, you look like you need to see a doctor for that eye. The emergency room is just down that hallway and to your left." Pale blue eyes surrounded by wrinkles and bifocals looked at me sympathetically.

"Please, I'm looking for Rachel King. She's the emergency, not me." Tightness gripped my chest.

"What's she in for?" the seventy-something volunteer asked. Her voice was calm, kind, patient, and gentle.

"I don't know that she was admitted. I just know she took a cab here and was dropped off."

For the first time since leaving Montana, I broke down. Maybe it was the soothing, tender voice of the volunteer, but suddenly everything seemed hopeless. Unwelcome tears slipped out of my eyes, and I bit down on my lower lip. The harder I tried to keep them in, the faster they fell. I turned, looking for a bathroom in which I could take refuge, but found none. Through blurred eyes, I found a seat and sobbed into my hands.

I felt an arm slip around my shoulders and squeeze. "Now, honey, everything is going to be fine."

"I can't do this. Really, I can't." With a hiccupping sob, I looked at the volunteer. I'm sure my splotchy, red face—one eye red-rimmed and the other black and swollen—cried out for sympathy.

"No, I expect you can't. But I know who can, and it's going to be fine."

"Please, is there any way you can find Rachel King for me? Can you page her or something?" Between blowing my nose and sucking in air, the words came out jerky. I was beyond caring about the curious glances from others.

"I'll go page her, honey, and in the meantime, why don't you say a little prayer? You know God is the only one big enough to handle the things that are out of our hands, and I know He cares about your friend and about you."

With a tender squeeze to my shoulders, JOANNE/ST. JOHN VOLUNTEER, according to the nametag pinned above her left breast, walked resolutely back to her desk and picked up the phone, pushed the intercom button, and said, "Rachel King, please come to the front desk. Rachel King, please come to the front desk."

I was so startled that someone was comforting me instead of the other way around that I stopped crying. I could get used to being incognito as a pastor's wife if this was the way things worked. I looked over at Joanne and mouthed, "Thank you."

Looking around with my good eye, I flinched when I saw Rachel—pale, bone-pale—walking toward me. She looked smaller, like a shadow trying to creep behind a bush and not be seen. With shoulders slumped and dry-eyed, she moved steadily toward the information desk either not seeing me or not recognizing my battered, ballooned face.

"Rache, I'm over here. What happened? What's wrong?" I stood and put my arms around her.

Joanne bowed her head slightly and whispered a prayer that was camouflaged from the ever-constant flow of people coming and going.

"Dad's dead," Rachel said in a monotone voice. "Mom called me from the ambulance. She left a message at the motel. I didn't notice the phone light flashing until I started the computer search. I came as soon as I got the message. He either had another stroke or a heart attack. They won't know until the autopsy. Maybe it was the shock of seeing me this morning. I don't know."

"Rache, Rache." I folded my arms around my friend in a helpless gesture. I had no words, no reassurance, nothing.

"I don't know how to feel. I've wanted him dead for so long. I've spent nights lying awake, wishing he would be hit by a car . . . drowned. I even wished he'd be so sorry for what he'd done he would kill himself." Rachel took a big gulp of air. "And now—now he's dead. And I feel nothing. No sorrow, no joy, no relief, nothing."

I held on to her, my hand moving in small, slow, caring circles on her back—the soothing back rub, a standard in the pastor's wife's bag of tricks.

"I need to go to Mom's. I can't let her go home alone. She's in the emergency waiting room. She hasn't moved or spoken since they told her the news. I told her I'd be right back. Can you send my suitcase and computer over to the house?"

"Of course, Rache. Let's go see your mother, and then I'll take care of everything." Slipping my arm into the crook of her arm, we walked back to the busy waiting room.

The pungent odor of hospital-strength disinfectant disavowed the cheerful outlook the brightly-colored hallways tried to convey. No problems here. This is a happy, happy place. Rachel's body stiffened as she prepared to enter the waiting room. It was then that she must have noticed my face.

"What in the world happened to you?"

"Now's not the time. I'll tell you later."

I approached Rachel's mother. "Mrs. King, I'm so sorry." The older woman was stoic, her purse on her lap, her lips sealed in a thin, white line. I knelt down on the floor and took hold of her tightly-clenched fists. "I'm so sorry." It still seemed lame the second time around, but it was all I had.

"We were about to eat lunch, you know," she said. "Not much . . . just a ham sandwich with chips and lemon-meringue pie. Jack always liked something sweet with his meals. I don't care if it was breakfast, lunch, or dinner. He had to have something sweet to eat. I think I'd better throw the sandwiches away, don't you think? I put mayo on Jack's. I just eat mine plain. Maybe mine would be okay? I'm not sure. I can't think. Should I eat my sandwich?"

"Mom, forget about the sandwich. I'll fix you something to eat when we go home," Rachel snapped.

I patted Rachel's leg, and she stopped talking. "Jack won't mind if you throw out his sandwich. It would probably be better than saving it. But you might keep the pie. I imagine you'll have lots of company in the next few days. I'll have my mom bring over some fried chicken and potato salad. You go home with Rachel. She'll help you make some phone calls. It's okay to cry, you know."

"Cry? Oh no, I really couldn't. Jack didn't like it if I cried. Said I wasn't a little girl anymore and crying wouldn't do me any good. Jack always just kind of told me what to do, and I'm not sure . . . ."

Pain radiated from Rachel's eyes. "Let's go home, Mom. We'd better start on those phone calls. I need just a minute to talk to Jamie, and then I'll be right back."

Rachel took my arm and led me across the room. "Before Mom called I managed to find the orphanage where Craig lived. I didn't find out who his sister was, but I got the name of a gal who worked there when Craig was adopted. She's in an assisted-living facility in Indy. Her name and address are on some of the papers I printed out. I was planning to go there with you, but now . . ."

"I'll drop by later," I said. "I'm sure the last thing on your mind is the reunion dinner tonight, but if you want to come, I know my mom would love to sit with your mom."

"We'll see. Give us the rest of the afternoon, okay? I feel guilty about not feeling sad, but I can't pretend something I don't feel."

I gave Rachel a hug. "It's okay. Don't worry about it now. You'll have plenty of time to sort it all out later. I'm going to see if I can find the lady from the orphanage. I'll bring your stuff by later."

I walked over to Rachel's mom and planted a kiss on top of her head, gave her a quick hug, and left the hospital. I'd see somebody later about my face.

CHAPTER TWENTY-EIGHT

After stopping at the motel to find the address, I called Mom to fill her in on the death of Rachel's dad. True to form, she told me she would bake a cake, fry some chicken, and make both a potato salad and a veggie tray. She assured me that she would be happy to spend the entire evening with Rachel's mother and help her with the company that would be stopping by to give condolences. I don't know if good moms are hard to come by, but I wouldn't sell mine for a million bucks.

At three forty-five, I pulled into the parking lot of the assisted-living facility. After explaining my purpose, the front-desk clerk called Celia Leeds and spoke to her for several minutes. I heard her describe what I was wearing, explain that Celia was under no obligation to talk to me, and cautioned her that I looked a mess. Perhaps my ensemble—a black eye mixed with wrinkled, grass-stained clothing—wasn't her style. When she hung up the phone, she muttered, "Apartment 137. Down the hallway, take a left, then another left. Celia's place is at the end of the hall."

The apartments all had names above the numbers on the doors. The hallways were painted a light caramel color and decorated with a sentimental wallpaper border of china dolls, drums, wagons, and toy soldiers. Bulletin boards hung about every twenty-five feet, sporting announcements of every kind. It didn't take long before I knew when the next Bingo night was and what the residents would be eating for their dinner meals for the following month. Lessons for ballroom dancing, crocheting, and Chinese cooking were offered. Bridge games were on Tuesday and Thursday afternoons from 1:00 to 5:00 p.m. in the activity lounge. *Activity lounge. Now there's an oxymoron.*

Rapping on door 137, I prayed Celia Leeds would be receptive to questioning. The door opened to reveal a thin woman with silver-gray hair pulled back in a loose chignon. Her ill-fitting housedress, the color of mountain bluebells, sagged off her shoulders. Perhaps she had once filled it out, but in the way of so many frugal seniors, she refused to part with it although it no longer fit. She wore gray slippers with white anklets. She was about five foot eight and had a pleasant smile.

"Jamie Storm?"

"Yes, ma'am. Thanks for seeing me."

"What can I help you with?" Ms. Leeds asked.

"I was wondering if you could answer a couple of questions for me."

"Depends on the questions. What about?"

"Lost Lamb Orphanage. You worked there in the '60s?"

"Whew, that was a long time ago," she said.

"I need some information on a brother and sister who lived there."

"I'm not sure I can remember much from back then." Then as an afterthought, Ms. Leeds continued. "You look harmless enough except for your black eye. Come on in. Some bruiser take a swing at you?"

"It's a long story."

"Humph. I bet."

Celia lived in a small, two-bedroom apartment with a tiny kitchen, but a spacious dining-living room combination. The furnishings were simple, comfortable. I settled on a glider-rocker that matched the blue couch. A quick glance around the room confirmed that Celia didn't believe in clutter. The end tables, bookshelves, and coffee table were all free from accumulations of paper, magazines, or mail. The infamous Sister Thornbush would have approved.

Without another word, Ms. Leeds filled two glasses with ice and poured tea into them. I accepted and took a long drink. "Now what can I do for you," she said.

Not wanting to appear rude, I started with small talk. "When did you first go to work for the orphanage?"

"That was a long time ago. Let's see, I graduated from high school in the spring of '53. I wasn't ready to go to college, so I thought I would work for a year, save some money, and then go. Lost Lambs was my third interview, and they hired me, first to clean rooms, help the cook, and do whatever odd jobs needed done. Then I fell in love with those poor lost kids, and they fell in love with me. I soon found myself in charge of a group of girls, fifteen in all, as a housemother of sorts. Later on, I was given another group. By the time I had been there ten years, I was housemother to the twelve housemothers and fathers working there. I loved every bit of it.

"Never did get married. I guess I felt like I couldn't leave those kids. So many had been hurt or abandoned by people who should have loved them. Some could hardly trust me, let alone strangers. My heart wouldn't let me leave them, so I never let it get entangled with a man."

"When did you retire?" I asked.

"Two years ago I slipped and broke a hip. Not so good at seventy. This business of getting old is not all it's cracked up to be. No diapers yet, thank goodness." She smiled when she said this.

I smiled back and took another long sip of tea.

"Since the hip, all sorts of health problems have crept up though. I resigned one month after the fall and rented this apartment. Help is available if I need it, but it isn't nursing home status yet."

Miss Leeds creaked over to the west wall. Pictures covered it, both in frames and pinned up with brightly colored tacks. Old black-and-white photos with scalloped edges, Polaroid shots, 35mm full-colored pictures—all of them children.

"These are some of my kids."

I followed her to the photo-splattered wall. It looked completely out of character in the pristine room.

"Nice," I said.

Pointing to one of the Polaroid snaps, Miss Leeds reminisced. "Here's little Amanda James. She came to us when she was just two. Her mama died giving birth to a baby brother. He didn't make it either. We never did find a dad."

Good memory. This might be my lucky day.

"I'm looking for information on a Craig Haskell and his sister. I believe the state put them into the orphanage in 1964 sometime after their parents were killed. I don't know their birth names or even the sister's name. His name, as I said, is Craig, and his adopted name is Haskell. He may have been adopted in 1965 or 1966. I'm trying to find out if his sister was adopted and what her name is."

"That was a long time ago," Celia said. "Many adoption records were sealed, but in the case of children whose parents were killed, the regulations were not as strict. Let me think back. We had a lot of brother-and-sister combinations. One in particular that I remember might be who you're looking for. The young boy's name was Craig if I recall correctly. Craig Blanchard. His sister's name was Rella. Actually Cinderella, but we all called her Rella. Can you believe what some folks will name their children? Rella was the oldest. Wonderful girl. One of the sweetest we ever had."

"Why do you remember that brother-and-sister combo so much?"

"Mostly because Rella was so loyal to little Craig. He was four—just a scrap of a thing—and she was six going on sixteen. He never said a word the entire time he lived in the orphanage. Not to his sister, not to anyone. One day some folks came in and wanted to adopt Rella and Craig, but when they realized the psychological problems Craig had, they only wanted Rella. She wouldn't go without him."

One more notch in the Craig-is-the-major-suspect belt.

"When you speak of psychological problems, do you mean that he wouldn't talk, or was there something else?"

Miss Leeds looked through me, seeing something in the distant past that only her memory could view. "I had a parakeet once named Petey. He could say a few words, but mostly he just chirped away and kept me company. I thought if I brought him to Craig it might help him speak again."

"And?"

Miss Leeds eyes filled with tears. "Not two days after the couple left without adopting Rella, I found Petey dead inside the cage. He had been strangled. I felt sick and sad all at the same time. But Petey was a bird after all, and Craig, a very hurting little boy, so I didn't tell anyone. Just took the cage out of the room and never said a word."

My stomach twisted.

"Two weeks later a couple came in and wanted to adopt Craig. We couldn't get them to adopt Rella, although we tried. They felt like they wanted to see how well they did with one before they tried two. They weren't concerned about his inability to speak, and I didn't tell them about Petey. Craig wouldn't talk to us. He wouldn't say yes or no, so we let them adopt him. The light went out in that little girl after that. She was never adopted. She left the orphanage upon high school graduation. I've never heard from her since."

"What made her unadoptable?"

"She did. Plenty of couples came by that would have taken her, but she consistently turned them down. Like I said, the light just went out of her when her brother left. I don't think I ever heard that girl laugh after that. She was pleasant, got straight As in school, and worked hard. She helped all the other kids, especially the young ones who were new. She would read to them at night and hold them when they cried. She was better than most of the paid help. I guess she treated them just like she would have treated her brother if he had stayed. All of us loved her, but nobody could get close to her. She didn't let anyone in after her Craig was gone. She didn't have any best buddies. She just had Rella, and it appeared that was all she needed."

"Did she know who adopted her brother?"

"She saw them the day they picked little Craig up. I don't think she knew their names. She never asked, and we never told. She hugged him good-bye, turned, and went into her room. She didn't come out of her room until the next morning. I tried to talk to her, but she acted like nothing happened. She never once mentioned his name again or asked about him. Rella was only seven at the time, but she grew up overnight."

"Do you have any idea of where she might have gone to college?"

"Funny you should ask. She didn't apply to any universities in the States. She applied for places out of the country and got accepted at major universities in England, Germany, Israel, Kenya, and Belgium. Maybe others I didn't know about, but I have no way of knowing if she went to any of them. I don't see how she could afford it."

"Scholarships?"

"She was valedictorian of her class, so yes, she qualified for academic scholarships, but I don't know about the rest of the costs. It isn't cheap to get an education, you know. She worked her last two years in high school and could have saved some, but I wouldn't think she had enough to go to college overseas."

Something tickled at the edges of my memory, but I couldn't bring it to the surface. I couldn't see how any of this would relate to the murder of Tim Manter. Still, I didn't want to leave any questions unasked.

"Do you have any idea how I could get my hands on her social security number? I might be able to trace her that way. It's very important that I at least speak to her."

For the first time, Celia looked suspicious. "She was a wonderful girl whose childhood was filled with hard knocks. From the looks of your eye, you've experienced a few yourself, but I can't just hand out information without knowing why. I don't want Rella hurt any more than she already has been. Why, exactly, do you need this information?"

I figured with Celia's experience around children she could spot a lie a mile away, so I gave her the truth in its condensed version. "I think it's possible that Craig killed someone, possibly more than one. Right now he's out with a friend of mine who's confined to a wheelchair. I'm afraid he might kill Scott if I can't find him, but I have no idea where he is. I thought if Rella is still around, he might have contacted her."

"Do you actually think little Craig could have killed someone?"

"I not only think it's possible, I think it's probable."

Celia searched my face for signs of falsehood. Finding none she went to the phone and dialed a number. She wrote on a pad and gave the sheet to me. "The school still had her social security number on file. Here it is. I hope you find her."

"Thank you, Miss Leeds, I hope so too."

CHAPTER TWENTY-NINE

Cars lined the street on Fentmore Avenue where the Kings lived. I pulled up behind the Channel 8 news van. Good old Billy Fisher. He might sound gruff, but he was a real softie. He loved every one of the Cliffhangers, and groundbreaking story or no, he would stand by Rachel in a time of crisis.

I gathered Rachel's suitcase and laptop from the backseat and walked up the cracked sidewalk to the small, three-bedroom house I remembered from high school. Lemon-yellow paint peeled away from the wood siding like shavings on kindling. The roof sagged with the weight of ten years of neglect and not enough funds to hire help. My heart lurched to think what Rachel felt as she walked her last few steps up to the front door.

Mom opened the door with a smile that turned to shock when she saw my eye. "Where have you *been*? What happened to your eye? *What* is going on?" she demanded.

"Mom, now's not the time. I'll explain it all later. I'm sorry about not being here right away, but I had an errand to run before coming over. How's Mrs. King?"

Mom still frowned despite my attempted cavalier attitude. "She'll be okay," she said. "Right now her world is spinning out of control, but she has a good network of people who will help out.

I'll talk to my pastor about getting her into some grief counseling. He's got several good contacts. Rachel has decided to stay here for the rest of the summer, maybe for good. That will give her mom some time to adjust to life alone before she has to make any major decisions. It's not easy to lose a lifetime partner, no matter the circumstances."

I knew Mom was thinking of living with a stroke victim or an Alzheimer's patient, not a child-molesting creep, but now wasn't the time to set her straight. There probably wasn't ever a good time to set her straight. I knew from experience Mom's wisdom was usually right on target, even if she didn't understand all the circumstances.

I gave her a hard, tight hug. "I'm so glad you're here, Mom, but I've got to run over and say hi to Billy. Will you excuse me for a minute?"

Mom nodded but brought her hand up to my purpled eye and softly touched the swelling. "I love you, baby. If you need my help, I'm here."

I wondered why so many daughters had problems getting along with their mothers. I couldn't think of a deeper, more satisfying relationship than the one Mom and I experienced. It was freedom wrapped in love. Trust covered with a coating of pure admiration. Mutual friends wrapped together by the bond of mother/daughter loyalty. I hoped that someday I would impart that same relational freedom to the boys.

But I had a murder to solve, and here I was waxing poetic.

Setting the suitcase and laptop down in an unoccupied corner, I eased between grieving visitors to get to Billy and Rachel. Billy was just leaving. Hugging Rachel tightly, he said, "If there's anything I can do, anything at all, just call me."

"I will," Rachel said.

It was a lie, I was sure. When people are grieving, you need to call them, not expect them to call you. And I would tell Billy that very thing when I got a chance.

"Rache, I'll be right back," I said. "I want to talk to Billy."

We walked out into the sunshine. Billy took one glance at my face and quipped, "You might want to use a mirror the next time you apply mascara. Your one eye looks a little overdone."

Ignoring his wit or lack thereof, I said, "I'm so glad you came. Rachel needs us now more than ever. And I need you too. Can you pop this social security number in your computer and see what surfaces? I have a name too."

Without waiting for an answer, I jumped into the passenger side of the van. The back was equipped with video equipment, computers, and still cameras—everything a self-respecting journalist needed and more, including wi-fi. He typed in the name Rella Blanchard, added the nine-digit number that I had given him, and hit enter.

It took less than thirty seconds to get an address, telephone number, and interestingly enough, a Web site.

Billy looked at me. "I doubt this will help you much. She lives in Jerusalem. It's an overseas number, and the Web site is posted in Hebrew or something."

Again something tingled at the edges of my memory, but nothing concrete came into focus.

"Let me try something else," Billy said. He typed in *Jerusalem* *Rella Blanchard* in Google under advanced search.

"Woo-hoo!" he shouted. "We hit the jackpot: 6,572 hits. Let's just take a peek. Ugh. She must be a brainiac. Looks like she has several articles posted in the high-IQ science magazines. She has a doctorate in chemical engineering, teaches at the university in

Jerusalem, and has more than one patent on pharmaceuticals that are responsible for combating the HIV virus. Craig's sister, huh? I could get interested in brains like that."

"I doubt it's the brains that interest you—more like the cash behind the brains."

"Ouch, that hurts."

"Is there a picture of her?"

"I'm not going to look through all these sites to find a picture. Sorry, Black-eye, I gotta go. Child support won't pay itself. Why don't you talk to Shawn? She looks really well-known over there. I think you can safely take her off your list of suspects, living in Israel and all."

"She isn't on my list. Her brother Craig is, and he has Scott. I hoped she would be able to help me find him."

"What do you mean, he has Scott?"

"Supposedly, they're fishing together, but the more I look into Craig's past, the more skeletons pop up. And I mean skeletons in the *literal* sense. Bones and more bones."

"I think you underestimate our policeman friend. He's not without resources just because his legs don't work. Why don't you call this Rella person in Jerusalem? It might ease your mind." And in the manner of all good reporters, he handed her his satellite phone after punching in the collection of numbers listed as Rella Blanchard's phone number.

The recording said, "This is Dr. Blanchard. I will be out of the office until July 15. Please leave your name and number, the reason for the call, and I will get back to you as soon as I can. If this is an emergency, please call my service at 011-1000-2323-011. Thank you."

I called the service number to find out that Dr. Rella Blanchard was in the States on a teaching sabbatical. She was speaking at several conferences nationwide on the prevention of AIDS and the role of research in the fight against the disease. This particular weekend would find her in Chicago at the Hyatt Regency. Probing further, I got the operator to give me Dr. Blanchard's room number. I handed the phone back to Billy and gave him a big bear hug.

"You're the best. I'll see you tonight at the dinner." I jumped out of the van and sprinted back to the King house. Billy grinned and waved.

Weaving my way through the throng of mourners, I gave Mom a quick hug and told her I had a couple more errands to run before the reunion dinner.

I caught Rachel's eye and noticed that at that very moment a large, robust gentleman with a handlebar mustache was hugging her. "Yes, siree, I knew Jack back when he as just a young pup. He and I played football together in high school. He quarterbacked, and I was the center. We were quite the team. Anyway, a better man there never was. The world is a sadder place today. I remember one game, this was back when he was a senior and I was junior, we were playing for the championship and—"

"Excuse me," I butted in without remorse. "I need to speak to Rachel a minute if you don't mind. Actually, I need to speak to Rachel whether you mind or not." I smiled with those last words, hoping to take the sting out of them. Handlebar Mustache didn't even notice. He just turned and continued reliving his high school glory days with the next unsuspecting victim.

Rachel gave me a grateful hug. "I need to get out of here. I thought I could stay, but if I have to hear one more word about how wonderful he is, I mean *was*, I'm going to puke."

"That's why Mom's here. Don't worry about leaving. No one will notice. I need to check on a couple of things before the reunion dinner, so grab your computer and let's go. We'll come back here to change for dinner and make sure your mother's okay."

Conversation resumed after I called for a cab and we went outside to the curb to wait.

"I thought I could handle this," she said, "but I'm not doing very well. I want to scream at everyone—where were you? Where were you when I was being destroyed bit by little bit? I can't think straight. He's dead. He can't hurt me now, but I'm so angry. Why, why, *why*?"

I knew Rachel wasn't asking for an answer. She just needed to rage. I let silence fill the air. It covered us like the pall that would cover Jack King during his funeral next week. We were both relieved at the sight of the yellow taxi pulling up beside us.

CHAPTER THIRTY

The silence in the cab only lasted a few seconds before the driver started humming and then singing along with his radio. He wasn't good, but what he lacked in tone he made up for in volume. I recognized the song as *I Am Mine* from an old 2002 release of Pearl Jam's. Not that I'm up on rock and roll, but the bass player came from a little town north of Great Falls, and Montana embraced the band like it had birthed it from its own womb.

Over the cover of hideously flat notes, Rachel said, "There's one more detail I want to check out about Cynthia Gilmore. Remember her sparse social security filings? I'm going to check with Ancestry.com and see if I can find a death certificate with a matching social."

"Why? We know she's alive. She's Volvo Lady, remember?"

"But is Cynthia Gilmore *really* Cynthia Gilmore? Maybe she took on a dead person's social. Why did she show up now? Why is she tailing you? There's more to her than meets the eye, and even though you're more convinced than ever that Craig is guilty, I think we need to check out all possibilities."

"You can check on that while I try to reach Rella Blanchard in Chicago. I need to know if she and Craig have even talked to each other over the years. She might have some clue where Craig is right now."

The cab driver stopped singing with Pearl Jam long enough to take my money before he drove away, singing off-key to his heart's delight. Not a soundscape I would miss.

Rachel went to work with the laptop while I used the phone. It only rang once before a soft-spoken woman answered, "Hello?"

I could feel my pulse pick up speed. I needed to be careful. I didn't want her covering for Craig. With a quick introduction about me, I explained that I met Craig after coming to Anderson for a class reunion, that an emergency had come up concerning one of my friends who was out fishing with him, and I tracked her down via Miss Celia Leeds and then her Web site.

"I really need to find Scott. Would you know of any place that Craig fishes on a regular basis?"

The line was silent for a moment. "You went to a lot of trouble to find me, Mrs. Storm. This must be a pretty serious emergency."

"More serious than I can say," I said without a speck of lying.

"He loves to fish at Geist Reservoir near Indianapolis—good bass fishing. Why don't you try looking for him there? If you don't find him, I'm driving down from Chicago this evening and we're meeting at Grindstone Charley's for a drink. Come and join us."

"I might just do that if I don't catch up to him at the reservoir. Thanks."

I couldn't believe I just agreed to go to a bar for a drink with someone I'd never met. It was a good thing David was in Alaska fishing, or he'd be absolutely opposed to the idea. I'm not sure he'd be more opposed to the drink or me meeting up with someone I knew nothing about. The longer he was in the pastoral ministry, the more overprotective he became. He didn't invite me to the jails with him, or down by the riverfront where the homeless were, or even on most of the domestic violence calls he handled. I know bars and pubs would be on his list of "places Jamie doesn't need to go." But it was all for a good cause, I rationalized, and besides David wasn't here to go with me so what else could I do?

Before I could tamp down the memories, I thought back to the first years of our marriage. We were going to change the world. No fears then, only the excitement of following Christ into every nook and cranny. We would feed the hungry, clothe the poor, change the world one person at a time with love and more love. And when we were done we would sit on our front porch, put our feet up, and talk about all the wonderful things God did in our lifetime.

Then reality set in, and we took a church. David put in long hours, I birthed boy babies that got into every imaginable bit of trouble they could, and my hands were full with family and church work, leaving the world to take care of itself.

Still, it was up to me to help Scott. I hadn't been there for Tim or Rachel, but I would do my best for Scott.

Even as I let my mind slide back into reality, I knew David and I would need to have a real talk when he got back from Alaska. Somewhere in the shuffle of church duties, baby bottles, T-ball, puberty, graduations, colleges, and the marriages, we quit talking about real things. Or at least real things that mattered to me.

I couldn't remember a single conversation about my goals, my dreams, and my life for years. And maybe that's the way it is when you raise kids—the way it has to be—but it couldn't be that way for me anymore. I couldn't be the good little pastor's wife anymore. I had to become an active participant in life. The sense of shame I felt for being swallowed up in my own daily events without a thought to the rest of the world threatened to engulf me.

"Bingo!" Rachel yelled. "I was right. That social was registered to a Trista Echo who died May 11, 1980 at the age of 14. Let me check real quick and see if I can find out how she died."

Using her access to the police department database and the obits in the Marion County registry, she went to work. It didn't take long to find an answer.

"She died of an overdose of Valium—apparent suicide," she said. "The Valium was prescribed for her mother. She left no note, but her obit has one piece of information that might interest you."

"What?" I said, impatient at Rachel's attempt to drag out the suspense.

Rachel read one sentence out of the many that made up the obituary of a short-lived life. Just one, but it had the weight of a ticking time bomb.

"She was survived by an uncle, Phillip House, a schoolteacher at Highland High."

Rachel read it flatly, like the name was just another name, any name. Not the name of a molester of young girls, not the name of the monster who added to Rachel's descent into a world of drugs and booze, nor even the name of the Speaker of the House of the United States.

This news almost made me dizzy. So many pieces of a puzzle I couldn't put together. I'd try to process this information on the way to Geist Reservoir. My main priority now was finding Scott.

"Let's go, Rache. We'll deal with that later. We need to find Craig and pray that he hasn't killed Scott."

Rachel looked at me intently for a minute and then said, "I understand your fear, but I keep thinking about all of this and

I can't help but come back to the same thing— motive. What is Craig's motive for killing all those people? He wants to die the world's most lonely man? All of the deceased were close to him in one way or another. Aren't most crimes of passion limited to a spouse or lover? If we assume that you're right, then he killed his fiancé, wife, unborn child, psychologist, best friend, and adopted parents. Why? Did he benefit financially?"

"I don't know . . . I don't know. Could we take this discussion on the road? Maybe I am way off base, but I'm not going to sit idly by while one of my friends is in trouble." I softened my voice. "I've already done too much of that in my life. I won't do it again."

Rachel looked straight into my guilt-ridden eyes, gave me a quick hug, and said, "Okay, you're the boss."

Just as I reached to open the door, a loud, persistent pounding on the other side echoed into the room. I rolled my eyes at Rachel and swung open the door. What now?

"You're going to the banquet dressed like that?" Billy said, his voice playful with mock disgust. Next to him, Shawn, Todd, and Scott grinned in unison. Each wore a suit and tie and looked like they had been freshly scrubbed. Their colognes and after-shaves were having a little aromatic war, not entirely pleasant, but it didn't matter one whit to me.

My legs went weak with relief. "Scott, where did you come from? Are you all right? I'm so glad to see you." I bent and hugged him so tight, I doubt he could breathe.

Pulling my arms from around his neck, he said, "I'm glad to see you, too, but I kind of expected to. It is our class reunion, remember? What in the world happened to your eye?"

Before I could answer, Shawn—usually the quiet one—said, "I hope the other fella looks as bad as you."

I felt tears welling up behind my eyes. Not so much as a result of their voiced concerns about my eye, but because Scott appeared alive and well. The pent-up tension of the last hour whooshed out of me in a babble of words.

"I'll explain it later, guys. Give us a few to get ready. We'll meet you there. And by the way, I'm happy to see you all. I thought Scott was with a killer. I didn't know if he'd make it back alive."

Scott made a choking sound. "You thought *what*? Are you crazy? I went fishing with Haskell. I think you might want to give this case a rest. You're getting a little paranoid."

"I know but—"

Todd came to my rescue. "Come on, guys, let's go and save a table. These girls look like they need a minute or ten to freshen up. Our wives aren't coming until the banquet starts at eight-thirty. They don't want to hear all our high school memories. Can you imagine? Free entertainment and they turned it down."

I mouthed a silent thank-you to him.

CHAPTER THIRTY-ONE

The parking lot at the sprawling, red-bricked Highland High School was filling up rapidly as I nosed the yellow Escape into one of the few remaining slots at the front of the building. Rachel and I looked up at a giant Scotsman with sword drawn above the entrance. Arced above the red-and-white tam perched on the head of the swordsman were the words HOME OF THE SCOTS. Underneath it read: PRESENTED BY THE CLASS OF 1982. COMPLETE RESTORATION BY THE NATIONAL HONOR SOCIETY AND THE CLASS OF 1998.

I felt a surge of pride as I eyed my alma mater. I knew that as much as I loved this place, Rachel hated it and all it represented, so I said nothing. The old gym/cafeteria was decorated in Scottish themes with plaid tablecloths. Kilts, tartan wall hangings, and bagpipes were displayed at one corner of the gym. Color copies of the senior pages of the yearbook were scattered liberally on the tables. Classmates I hadn't seen in years milled around looking at pictures, laughing, drinking, and in general enjoying the cocktail hour. I thought most spouses must have opted for the route of coming later to the banquet because there were very few people I didn't recognize.

As we walked to the table the male Cliffhangers had commandeered, the four guys let out appreciative wolf whistles. So politically incorrect.

They stared at Rachel and rightly so. She wore a simple black dress that complemented her features. It was short, showing off her long, slender legs. The capped sleeves and scoop neckline added to the elegance of the dress. She had borrowed a pearl necklace and matching earrings from me and had even used a touch of mascara, eye shadow, and almond lip glaze. While completely out of character for her, she was a knockout.

I wore my usual Sunday fare. An ankle-length red skirt, cream tank top underneath a red jacket, matching earrings, and two-inch red pumps. With an eye nearly swollen shut, I felt a little like the ugly duckling next to Rachel, but I enjoyed her moment in the sun.

"Where have you been all my life?" Billy quipped, looking straight at Rachel.

"Shut up," Rachel said.

"Seriously, you look good."

I laughed. "If she has two legs and two arms, any woman looks good to you."

"I'm hurt," Billy said.

I sat down and tried to resume my conversation with Scott. "I uncovered more information about Craig. He has some serious mental issues."

He wasn't in the mood to listen. "Listen, Jamie, we can talk about all that later, okay? Right now I want to know what happened to you."

You could hear a pin drop. Suddenly, the attention at the table was focused on me. I recounted what happened at Tim's. "But I'm all right, I think the bigger question is who killed Tim?"

"Dollars to donuts, both events are related. Tell you what, Jamie, you're safe with us tonight. Let's tackle this in the morning. Right now I think we all need a break. Let's spend the evening talking about the good old days. Let's reminisce and enjoy this party."

"Look at my face, Scott. Does it look like I want to make small talk? Rachel's dad died today. I'm under suspicion for murdering a good friend. I thought you were in the hands of a killer all day and I didn't expect to see you alive, so forgive me if I'm not in the mood to reminisce about our high school escapades." I was trembling with anger.

Rachel laid her hand on my arm. "He's suggesting a *break*, not stopping the investigation. An hour or two at the most to talk about normal things with old friends is not much to ask. Surely if I can do it, you can do it too."

Shawn, ever the diplomat, added his two cents worth. "Why don't we spend our time both ways? What law says we can't do some mixing and greeting and then come back to the table and do some detective work?"

Billy joined the discussion. "One night is all we're asking. We haven't seen our classmates in years. Jamie, you need a break from it too. Look in the mirror. A night away from murder and mayhem won't hurt."

"You wouldn't be so cavalier about this, Billy, if you were the one accused of murder."

"A little self-righteous, are we?"

His teasing tone put me on edge. "Point taken."

With a churning stomach, I grabbed my purse and headed for the ladies' room. I felt ready to explode. That wouldn't look good on the ever-present pastor's wife resume. I would have liked to hand Billy his head on a silver platter. As I applied a quick dash of lipstick and rubbed my lips together, I realized I couldn't go back out to the group and make small talk. Maybe I could slip outside and drive around for a couple of minutes and cool down. Hopefully, God would give me some direction, because right now I felt lost, confused, and angry.

Self-righteous? Billy wouldn't know self-righteous if it came up and shook hands with him. You have to know the meaning of the word "righteous" in order to know what it meant to be self-righteous, and I was willing to bet the farm Billy didn't know anything about being righteous. I seethed all the way out of the restroom to the entrance of the school and outside to the Escape. I unlocked the driver's side door and yanked it open, all the while muttering to myself.

My anger blinded me to the dark form that slipped silently behind me and covered my nose and mouth with a chloroform-soaked handkerchief. For a second I was so stunned I didn't do anything. I tried to struggle against the arms that held me, but I was overpowered by the drug. I felt my purse slip out of my fingers. Pure panic filled me right before everything went black.

CHAPTER THIRTY-TWO

May 2

T he gentle wind blew hot, swishing the branches of the nearby almond trees, rustling the leaves. The blossoms had long since dropped in favor of the almonds. Honey buzzards flew in swarms overhead, making their annual migration to the forests of Eastern Europe from their winter home in Africa. The elusive raptors punctuated the crystal-blue sky with giant Vs, swooping and fluttering, searching for wasps and other delicacies. Birdwatchers would have a field day. But bird watchers did not come to Israel in May. Too bad. They didn't know what they were missing. These birds were stunning with their variegated brown-and-white underbellies and wings.

No, most visitors came because of faith. They wanted to breathe hallowed air. To perhaps walk the paths the great men of God walked. Or to catch a glimpse of the Sea of Galilee and visit the manger where Jesus first drew breath. Faith in a higher power fit into these people's rosy view of life. They would be better off watching the birds. To forget faith and believe in personal destiny. This business of God as creator and sustainer of life was definitely not a theory of intellect, but rather a fairy tale to be woven and spun into the minds of little children at bedtime. But fairy tales are fairy tales, and they have no power to right

245

wrongs, or make the world a better place. It took willing hands and heart to do that.

Hiring a hit man was surprisingly cheap. Easy, too. A little research, a few phone calls, and voila. If the target were a famous person with detailed security it might be different. But for the average no-name who could be followed with little or no trouble, a thousand bucks could insure a quiet demise. Of course, the price jumped a bit when Manter started getting suspicious, but it was still doable. Luckily, his distrust only lasted a short time from onset to death. Unfortunately, he'd found Dacia's bones and alerted the police before he'd been eliminated, but not every contingency could be planned for.

The call had come in relatively early, considering the miles between the two countries with a time-zone difference of nine hours—6:00 p.m. and not a moment too soon. Anxiety had started to creep in, but it was for naught. All had gone according to plan. No hitches or miscues. The caller followed Manter early Sunday morning, hoping for an opportunity to present itself. It did at a little after eight in the morning, Indiana time.

Manter seemed absorbed in his own thoughts, and the caller managed to get within two feet of him. It was as easy as pie. A simple shot to the back of the head. Manter didn't even know what hit him. He was probably dead before he heard the plopping sound of the silenced pistol being fired. His brain would not have had time to send any messages to his ears, the caller stated. How very lucky he was not to have to think about death.

The hit occurred in a church parking lot, of all places. Manter must have felt completely at ease. Probably didn't turn at the sound of crunching gravel, or soft footsteps. No reason to suspect that attending church could be fatal to one's health. It's just unfortunate that death had to happen at all. How hard could it be to learn? Why did it take *so many times to teach a relatively simple concept? Oh well, one more lesson would have to do. It would be the coup de grâce of all lessons.*

Time to bid the birds good-bye. It was a pleasant walk, but now there was work to do. Travel plans to be made, funds to be transferred, evidence to be planted, and repercussions to be watched. And in the end, peace. When it was all over, there would be peace.

CHAPTER THIRTY-THREE

izziness and nausea dazed me when I awoke. Everything was black, but I could tell I was moving. I forced myself to lie still and try to remember what happened. Despite the grogginess, within minutes of waking I could tell my hands were tied behind my back, my feet were bound together, and my mouth was gagged. Not a happy way to wake up. *Maybe it wouldn't have been so bad to meet and greet old classmates after all.*

Nausea swelled into my throat, but I knew if I gave into the feeling, I would most likely drown in my own vomit. *Calm down. Think.* The smell of grease and fumes convinced me I was in the trunk of a car. I still had my clothes on, for which I was thankful, although I was missing a shoe. Terror threatened to override the calm. I needed to think clearly, so I started doing what I always do when I'm scared stiff—singing in my head. I hardly ever sing out loud. I sound like a screech owl with a bad cold.

Jesus loves me this I know, for the Bible tells me so. Little ones to him belong, they are weak but He is strong. Yes, Jesus loves me, Yes, Jesus loves me, Yes, Jesus loves me, the Bible tells me so.

Breathing more evenly, I tried to think of what David would tell me to do. He loved cars and taught me little things like how to change the oil, how to change a tire, how to check the air pressure in the tires, and how to use my rearview mirrors effectively. I didn't remember anything about how to get out of the trunk of a car when you're hog-tied. I would have to chide him the next time I saw him for neglecting to let me in on that little tidbit.

Oh God, please let there be a next time.

I couldn't hear anything coming from the front of the car. Maybe it meant there was only one kidnapper. I would have to watch for an opportunity to escape, and I needed all my mental abilities focused to do that. Obviously, if my captor wanted me dead, I wouldn't be in the trunk of a car trussed up like a turkey. Or at least he didn't want me dead in the school parking lot. Where there's life there's hope. I wasn't sure where I heard that, but it would become my new motto if I made it out alive.

The trunk was stuffy and hot. Sweat dripped into my eyes, and my back was soaked. I wondered how long it would be before Rachel noticed I was missing and come looking for me. I doubted the guys would notice . . . ever. I hoped the kidnapper had not picked up my purse or shoe. If not, Rachel would know that something wasn't right. But even if she did, would it be possible to trace where I'd been taken? I didn't think so.

The pitch-black world of the trunk confused my senses. I couldn't tell if the car turned left or right or went straight. My sense of timing disappeared along with the feeling of security, and I couldn't gauge how long I'd been in the car.

My right leg was numb, so I rolled from my side to my stomach, hoping to get some feeling back. I tapped my toes on the floor of the trunk, trying to hurry the process of waking up my leg. Needles shot through my feet, and I felt the urge to laugh. It was so mundane as to be ridiculous, having a sleeping limb while you were being kidnapped. Adrenaline is supposed to shoot through every fiber of your body, and you're supposed to miraculously fight off the bad guys and become a hero, not have your leg fall asleep. Television was really letting me down in this real-life scenario.

When the car slowed to a stop, I tensed. I couldn't escape, but possibly I could catch a glimpse of my assailant, which might give me some insight into my predicament. I rolled back to my right side and kept my eyes trained on what I assumed would be the trunk lid. Although it was night, the minute the trunk cracked open, I could see my captor coming at me with another rag. I squirmed and made as much noise as the gag would allow. Instead of a scream, my throat emitted a low moan that could be mistaken for a dog growl instead of a human in trouble. I fishtailed my way as far back as the trunk would allow, twisting my head constantly, trying to escape the anesthetized rag. Just before blacking out, I caught a glimpse of cold, green eyes.

In an instant, I recognized the kidnapper. Then I succumbed to the blissful darkness.

CHAPTER THIRTY-FOUR

M y first sensation was a pasty-dry cottonmouth and parched throat. My head leaned forward with my chin resting on my chest. I didn't want to move a muscle until I could take stock of my situation. The gag was gone, and I was perched on a tall stool and strapped in with a bungee cord, arms pulled behind the stool back, wrists duct-taped to each other. My feet were tied to the stool legs. I couldn't see much, except light beige, plush carpet. I could tell there was a lamp behind me with a dim bulb. The dizziness that accompanied my drug-induced sleep had passed, but I ached for a drink of water.

Fear raked across my chest and settled in like unwanted company. *God, help me know what to do. What possible skills have You prepared me with to handle this? I can bake a pie, write a tithe check, hug one hundred people in less than ten minutes, and sit through church meetings like they're more enjoyable than a day at the beach, but how do I get away from this panic that's crawling through me, not to mention the bad guy on the couch? I don't even have my Taser with me.*

Looking up, I saw the kidnapper watching me from a black, leather recliner. The room held a matching couch and a wide-screen TV, state-of-the-art entertainment center with surround sound, and a variety of high-end faux plants and trees. The room, the captor, being tied to a bar stool, it was more than I could stand. I felt tears well up in my eyes. *Not now. Don't think. Just put on your Sunday-go-to-meeting smile.*

Staring into the eyes of the figure on the recliner, I asked, "Could I get a drink of water?" My voice came out thin and scratchy so I cleared my throat to try again. "I could use a drink, please."

Walking over to the wet bar, the hand that induced me to sleep turned on the faucet and half-filled a short glass. Ski mask still in place, Green-eyes lifted the tumbler to my lips. The first sip tasted like heaven, the second was just as good, and the third bathed my throat with coolness.

"Thank you." My voice took on a hard edge, trying to mask the generous portion of fear surging through me. "Where am I?"

"In a basement." The reply sounded as cold as ice.

"What do you want with me?"

"Nothing . . . nothing at all," the decidedly female voice said. "I would prefer that you were in Great Falls, Montana doing whatever it is pastor's wives do, instead of snooping into business that is no concern of yours."

"The only thing I've been snooping into is the murder of a dear friend, and I have been accused of having a strong motive to kill him, so I would say that it *is* my business. I really think you can quit playing this cloak-and-dagger bit, Volvo Lady, or should I call you Cindy Gilmore? Maybe it's just plain old Rella Blanchard— Cinderella Blanchard to be specific. Catchy use of your first name," I said, letting derision take over the fear.

Pulling the ski mask off, Rella eyed me coldly. "Brilliant detective work, but it's a bit too late. In about two hours you'll be dead, my brother Craig will be the suspected murderer, and I will be on my way back to Israel with no one the wiser."

"You're working with Craig?"

"Working *with* Craig? I guess your deductive reasoning isn't all that good after all. Craig doesn't even know I'm alive, and you, Jamie Storm, are just a means to an end. It's amazing really. Here we are in my dear little brother's family room, and he doesn't even know I exist. Family room. That's a laugh. Craig has no family, and he never will if I have anything to say about it."

"But you were meeting him at Grindstone's tonight," I said. "You knew he liked to fish in Geist Reservoir."

"So I lied. Sue me. And as for knowing about fishing, I always, always know what Craig is doing."

Terror marched up and down my spine like ants on their way to a picnic. This woman was insane, and while I had counseled disgruntled wives, a few suicide attempters, and lovesick teens, I had never come face-to-face with pure insanity. My only chance was to keep Rella talking.

Replacing my harsh bravado with the soothing, even tones I used in counseling, I tried a new approach. "You said two hours. Why not now?"

"What?"

"You said I would be dead in two hours. Why prolong the inevitable? Why not kill me now?" I said it as if I were asking Abigail Thornbush why the bake sale was planned for a Tuesday evening instead of a Saturday morning. Non-threatening, just wanting a simple answer to a simple question. I looked straight into Rella's eyes.

"I have to wait for your killer."

"Who's my killer? If it's not you, and you're not working with Craig, then who is it? And how can you be so sure Craig won't come home?" Friendly, trying to help.

"Don't worry about Craig. He'll be occupied . . . until I'm ready for him to come home. Well, not by me personally, but trust me. He'll be occupied. Too many events at the school tonight for him to come home."

I wanted to scream as I listened to the cold, clearly unbalanced mind talking with pseudo-rational thought. Hoping the light didn't illuminate the fear reflected on my bruised face, I kept asking questions. Questions that didn't really matter once I was dead, but might keep Rella off balance.

"Who did you say was going to kill me?"

"I didn't say. I just said it wouldn't be me." With a sarcastic grin, she added, "It isn't part of my mission statement to kill you. Get it? Mission statement?"

"I know what a mission statement is. I have one myself." *Or did have. I've kind of forgotten it in the daily humdrum of life—to look for and rescue the dying. Now the dying is me, and I may never have a chance to rescue anyone again. Forgive me, Lord.* "But I'm more interested in yours since it happens to involve *my* life. Do you mind telling me what it is?"

Rella looked at her watch. "What's the difference? You'll be dead soon, and I hear dead men can't talk. I imagine the same is true for dead women." Rella smiled at her lame attempt at humor.

"My mission statement is simple," she said. "I adopted it at the age of seven. Adopted, now that's funny. I adopted a mission statement, but I was never adopted. I could have been, but no, I wouldn't leave Craig, and no one wanted a little boy who couldn't talk. He *did* talk though. It's just that no one heard him but me. He talked to a stupid bird that old lady Leeds gave him. He wouldn't talk to *me*, his sister, who turned down a life with a real family to stay with him, but he talked to a *parakeet*. Well, Petey's dead, and

I enjoyed wringing his little neck, a *fait accompli* via my mission statement—to make Craig's life as miserable as he made mine."

Insanity flickered in Rella's eyes. Her words dripped bitterness.

My fear ratcheted up a notch, but I forced myself to stay calm. I lowered my voice to barely a whisper, softening each word as I spoke. "He was four years old, Rella. Four, and he had just lost his parents. Surely you can understand that he wasn't responsible for you not being adopted."

"And I was seven—big deal. I lost my parents too. It wasn't a picnic for me either. Two weeks after I turned down a family who wanted me, he went off with the Haskells without so much as a backward glance. He left me alone like I was zero, zilch, nobody. You can't possibly know what it's like—not having family."

"No, I can't."

"Even the other orphans had *some* family. An aunt or uncle who made an occasional visit, brothers or sisters who were orphaned, too, or grandparents who couldn't take care of them, but came by to take them on outings. I watched as one-by-one children were adopted or put in foster homes. New kids came in and went out. I stayed. I wouldn't leave Craig, and then he left me without a moment's hesitation. Do you know what it's like to not have anyone?"

I ignored the question.

"It's the worst thing, the worst thing you can imagine."

"What about God?" Shifting gears, I tried to keep her off balance.

"God? How dare you talk to me about God. You know nothing about God." Rella's nose flared, her breathing heavy, and her eyes glistened with hate. "Oh, my parents took me to Sunday school. They even taught me to say bedtime prayers, and I believed every last word they spoke until the day God took them out of my life. No God would be that cruel. I hate Him. He took away everything in my life. He doesn't exist. There is no Redeemer, no mender of broken lives—just a sick, bedtime story that parents make up to keep their children in line. My daughter will not hear any of that drivel in my house."

"You have a daughter?"

"None of your business."

"I thought you said you were all alone."

"My daughter is nine. I was alone until several years ago. I will never be alone again, and she will never hear God's name spoken aloud."

Yeah, as if that won't happen in Israel. Out loud I said, "How can you hate Him if He doesn't exist?"

Fury etched livid-red spots on Rella's cheeks. Barely controlling her strained voice, she said through clenched teeth, "This is not about God. We will not talk about this. My question to you is a simple one. Do you know what it's like to not have anyone?"

I let my head drop to my chest before shaking it slowly. "No, I'm sorry, I don't."

"Sorry? You don't know the meaning of sorry. I decided on the day Craig rode away that he would never have family either. If I couldn't have him, no one could. And I've kept that promise. Every move I've made has been so that I could achieve my mission statement. My college education, my overseas work, my teaching at Highland, my national speaking engagements, all to put myself in positions to rid Craig of family and friends and leave him as lonely as he left me."

"That's a big job." I kept my voice even, sympathetic, though icy chills raced through my body. I was face-to-face with a crazy killer.

Rella's fury abated, and her voice took on a singsong tone. "But it's getting old now. I can't keep up the passion. I have more important things in my life now. So this is my grand finale. You will be killed in Craig's house. I will frame him with indisputable evidence. He will be sent to prison for life, and I can relax. I can let go. I don't have to ever come back once he's safely locked away in prison."

"So let go now. Why keep punishing Craig? Haven't you destroyed his life enough?"

"Nothing will ever make up for the years I spent alone. Nothing. But I can't keep coming back. I'm married now. I have a husband and a beautiful daughter."

"You have a family?" *Keep her talking.*

"I have a wonderful family. My husband knows nothing of my past, doesn't know I have a brother. My daughter will be given everything a family can give a little girl except siblings. I will never have more children. I won't give anyone the chance to betray her like Craig betrayed me."

"Haven't you already betrayed her by ruining her uncle's life? She will never get to know that part of her extended family."

The rage was back in an instant. "Shut up!" Rella yelled. She jumped up from the couch, and with three quick strides, she stood in front of me. She slapped my face with all the force she could muster, which was considerable, and screamed again. "Shut up, shut up, shut up!"

My head reeled back from the vicious slap. Tears stung my eyes. I blinked rapidly, trying to keep them from falling. "So *you* killed the Haskells, Dacia Stewart, Angela and her unborn child, a defenseless dog sitter named Kelly, Dr. Rice, and then his friend and mine—Tim Manter. And you're going to kill me too. Quite a legacy to leave your daughter."

"You think you're so smart. You're not smart at all. I didn't kill Ms. Stewart, although I must admit, it needed to be done." A crazy lilt punctuated her words.

"You must be proud," I said, earning another slap.

"This isn't about pride. It's about loneliness—something you won't ever understand. None of the rest of the murders can be traced back to me. The Haskells' deaths were ruled a hit-and-run—forgotten long ago. Angela and her baby died of the Hanta-virus, Dr. Rice of anthrax poisoning. My time attending classes at the university in Israel on biological warfare was well spent. Every-thing I used was completely untraceable. I *am* sorry about Kelly. I wanted to kill the Stewarts. Craig spent much too much time with them. Kelly and the dogs just got in the way. It accomplished my purpose. Craig walked out of their lives and never renewed his friendship with them."

"Tell me about Tim."

"Tim—unfortunate, but clearly Craig's fault. I thought he'd learned his lesson. That's what he went to see Dr. Rice about, you know. About everyone he loved dying. I thought he would be a hermit the rest of his life, but no, Tim came into his life and gave him some wild notion that the two of them could find Dacia's murderer on their own. I waited just long enough for Craig to really like Tim—for them to become good friends—before I ordered the hit. A simple bullet to the brain, and Craig was left alone one more time." Her face contorted into a smug grin as she related this last bit of information.

For the first time in my life I felt hatred for another human being. I loathed the sight of this disturbed, bitter woman who had taken Tim's life. *God help me to know what to say, what to do. I just want this woman dead. She's evil, pure evil.* Aloud I said, "I know this is probably out of the question, but could I please use the bathroom? If I die, it would be nice not to soil myself in the process."

Looking at the clock on the wall, Rella answered, "Sure. Why not? Your executioner should be here in a few minutes. But before you go, would you like to hear one little bit of ironic news?"

"Please."

"You've been working with Shawn Norman on this? Ambassador to Israel and . . ." She took a long pause for dramatic effect. "My husband." The high-pitched laugh resonated with madness.

I sucked in air. "His wife's in Israel."

"No, no she's not. She's standing in front of you."

"Your service told me you were on a teaching sabbatical. Shawn said he had to hurry home to his wife. That she stayed behind because of work."

"My service tells people what I tell them to say, not necessarily what I do. I have my home phone routed to my cell, so Shawn thinks I'm home. We talk every day."

I was stunned by this news. How could a completely insane woman fool so many people?

"Seriously, I need to go to the bathroom," I reminded her.

Walking over to the couch, Rella reached down between two of the leather cushions and pulled out a small, black pistol. "This is the very gun used to eliminate your precious Tim from Craig's life. If you do anything stupid, I will use it on you before you have a chance to meet the man who is so looking forward to killing you."

"Who would that be?"

Rella took a long time to untie and untape me, attempting to keep the pistol pointed at my head while using her left hand to undo the bungee cords and untwist the duct tape.

"I thought you would have figured it out by now. Phillip House. He's the one who killed Dacia Stewart in the park, you know. I followed her there, hoping to find an opportunity to slip a homemade bomb under her car. It was a project that one of your Highland High classmates made for the science fair. Lisa Ivy. Of course, she left off the fuse and detonator or she would have been expelled, but I thought it was pretty good for a teenager."

"Could we get back to Dacia?" My feet dangled free, and the bungee cord settled on the floor in snakelike fashion. Only my wrists remained taped.

"Dacia had a camera with her. She ran to a spot in the woods where she could see the parking lot. I followed her, hanging back so she wouldn't spot me, but I wanted to make sure she was going to be far enough away that I would have time to set the bomb. I saw House following her as well. He didn't see me hiding in the bushes because the undergrowth was so thick at Mounds. I thought maybe they were having an affair until I saw the crowbar in his hand. I waited and watched. It took him a matter of seconds to get behind her and bash her head in. I couldn't believe my luck. He dragged her further into the park. I quit following, but I knew she was dead."

"How nice for you." My sarcasm was in full swing. Fear was replaced by disgust.

Rella ignored me and continued. "Later, after he had gotten so important in politics, I sent him a little note with the facts of Dacia's death. I asked for forty thousand dollars a year plus a thousand dollar a year cost-of-living raise to keep quiet. I had him deposit it in my Israeli bank account, and it completely financed my mission in life. Every year on Mother's Day, so I can remember why I'm doing what I'm doing. My family has no idea that the company I work for has not sent me on so many speaking engagements.

"Tonight, when he kills you, the slate will be clean. He can walk away from his past, and I can walk away from mine. And Craig can rot in prison with no hope of parole. No more blackmail money. No more trips to the US. Just me and my family living out our lives in peace."

My gut twisted as I listened to the chilling words of Rella Blanchard. The last of the tape had come off my wrists, and as I slid off the barstool my legs nearly buckled under me. I felt wobbly as I took the first few steps toward the bathroom. My legs tingled. They were almost asleep again.

Please, God, let the bathroom have a window.

Rella walked with me to the bathroom door, keeping the pistol in the middle of my back as a reminder not to try anything stupid.

Once in the bathroom, I closed the door and looked around. Pulling down the toilet seat and cover, I stepped up and looked through the window. The window was way too narrow to climb through, and there was no other option.

Okay, God, next time I'll be more specific.

I looked around to see if it would do any good to scream for help but saw no one nearby. Stepping down, I flushed the unused toilet to mask the sound of opening the vanity. Turning on both the cold and warm water to full blast, I pulled the lid off a can of bathroom disinfectant. I knew I'd have to be ready to spray immediately and duck or dodge to the right or left at the same time. Hopefully, if Rella pulled the trigger the bullet would miss.

Splashing water on my face to clear the rest of the cobwebs away, I dried my face and hands on the hand towel. I took a deep breath, placed my finger on the spray nozzle, and swung the can behind my back.

Opening the door with my left hand, I saw Rella standing calmly in front of me with the gun trained at my head. Without a second's hesitation, I pulled the can from behind my back and sprayed Rella's eyes. Twisting to the left, I swept my arm down, knocking the .22 out of Rella's hand. She screamed with pain and rage. The gun dropped as she clawed at her eyes to relieve the stinging pain. I grabbed the nearest object I could find—a clay flowerpot with some sort of greenery in it—and slammed it down hard on Rella's back. She crumpled to the floor.

I ran to the end table where I'd seen a landline. Snatching the receiver off the cradle, I dialed 911. Without waiting for an answer, I tossed the receiver down beside the phone and ran up the stairway. Looking both ways, I could see an exterior door through the kitchen. I sprinted for it, as much as you can sprint with one shoe on. I heard Rella coming up the stairs, screaming my name.

I reached out to grab the door knob just as I saw his face peering in the window. Phillip House. I stumbled back and fell when the door swung open without effort. The veins in his neck pulsed, his eyes glittered with hate, and he grabbed me by the hair and yanked me to my feet. Spittle flew out of his mouth as he pulled my face inches from his.

"I warned you once. Now you're finished."

Pulling my knee up with blinding speed and gut-wrenching terror, I connected with his groin. He yelped in agony and let go of my hair, doubling over. He fell to the floor, clutching himself. I jumped over his writhing body to the landing and scampered down the steps to the fenced backyard.

Racing for the gate, I lost my footing and tumbled forward. Clambering back up, I tripped on the too-long skirt. The heel from my remaining shoe tore completely through the cotton material, ripping a hole in it. I scraped the useless shoe off my foot, pulled the skirt off, and tossed it out of the way. I ran for the gate, but saw it was useless. Rella beat me to it and stood guarding it, arms extended forward, gun cocked and pointed at my head. Rella wouldn't dare fire the gun outside, but escape seemed impossible.

I swung my head around wildly, looking for another exit. Instead of an exit, I saw House gimping his way toward me, his face red with rage, his eyes bulging nearly out of their sockets.

Of the thirty-six plans, flight is the best. A little Japanese proverb I had learned in an origami course I took with six other ladies from church, Abigail Thornbush being one of them. Abigail was actually quite good at it, which would have been fine if she could have kept her thoughts to herself, but she was Abigail, after all.

"Why, Jamie, this is art, not paper crumpling. Everyone makes a swan. Honey, why don't you use your imagination? Look at my butterfly, dear. Or what about Jo-Ellen's grasshopper? It takes a little extra work, but I think you'd be happier in the long run if you gave it your all. You know, God gave you abilities, and if you don't use them, you lose them."

In the midst of this desperate situation, I thought of Abigail. That couldn't be good. Flight definitely seemed like the right course of action, but how?

God help me!

With an ear-splitting shriek, gauged to throw my abductors off balance, I propelled myself forward, shoulder down, ramming House's mid-section hard. A giant whoosh escaped his lips. He fell backward onto the ground. I felt a sudden jab of pain in my right shoulder as I somersaulted past his body. No time to worry about the cracking sound.

I jumped up and kept running, not looking back. I flew up the stairs and back into the house. The front door seemed miles away. Desperation urged me forward. Pain ricocheted through my body, but I kept moving.

Trying to open the door with my right hand proved useless. Precious seconds wasted. I heard and felt the thunk of something heavy hitting the back of my head. An extended *nooo* came to mind before I fell.

CHAPTER THIRTY-FIVE

Blackness swirled around me, and my head throbbed with pain. I forced myself to lie still, hoping they would leave. I strained my ears for the sound of sirens. I prayed the 911 operator could pinpoint the location of the call I'd made. I had no way of knowing how much time had elapsed. I didn't think I'd passed out, but I wanted them to think so. I heard voices above me.

"Knock her out," Rella ordered.

"She's already out," House answered. "We gotta get out of here before someone calls the police."

"She already did."

"What?"

"Don't worry. I took care of it. Told them my kids were playing with the phone. They aren't coming," Rella said.

I felt the last remnant of hope slip away.

"Help get her to the car."

I forced my body to relax—to go "spaghetti arms" as Jake would say. He'd been hyperactive as a young boy. Our family pediatrician had suggested medication, but David and I wanted to use that as a last resort. So the doctor suggested that when Jake's behavior got out-of-hand to teach him to go limp all over. It would have a calming effect on his muscles and slow him down.

We made a game of it. We called it "spaghetti arms," and Jake loved it. The minute we said the words, he would slump to the ground like he'd been shot. Not a muscle would twitch until we begged him not to be dead anymore. Hopefully, my act was as convincing as Jake's. I didn't want to make this easy.

"Get her feet," House ordered.

I nearly screamed when House put his hands under my armpits and lifted. The pain in my collarbone was excruciating. They picked me up like a sack of grain and stutter-stepped me out to the garage where they shoved me into the trunk again. My mind kept screaming, "spaghetti arms." If I showed any pain, they appeared not to notice.

"Tie her up," Rella ordered.

"We don't have time. Let's just go. She's out like a light. I hit her hard. She'll be out for a long time."

"Sorry, I don't have your confidence. Give me your tie."

I heard the muffled sounds of the tie sliding out of his shirt collar.

Rella reached into the trunk and wrenched my arms backward. I bit the inside of my cheeks to keep from crying out. Every twist of the tie sent a new shot of agony to my collarbone. My concentration on remaining limp was heightened each time the pain gained intensity. I would not give into these thugs. At least not this second in time—maybe in the next—but not this one.

I don't know how long it actually took Rella to bind my hands, but it seemed like a lifetime. The trunk finally slammed shut and I prayed, "Thank you." I let the pent-up tears roll down my face. And for the next few minutes, I let myself cry.

The good part about pure agony is that it keeps you alert. There were no lingering effects of the drug Rella had used in my system, and thoughts of escape raced through my head. Some were stupid, some were unrealistic, but I kept thinking anyway. I noticed some freedom of movement, although painful and awkward with my hands tied behind my back. I didn't want to make any big movements that would alert Rella and House that I was awake. My best chance of escape was if they still believed I was unconscious.

I prayed that the Cliffhangers had started searching for me.

The car moved at a pretty good clip. According to my shoulder pain, the shock absorbers needed to be replaced. Being directionally challenged in the best of circumstances, I didn't even try to figure out which way the car was turning or how many turns it made. I used all of my energy not to scream when the car bounced over bumps. To take my mind off the pain, I steered my thoughts back to escape.

First off, I had to figure out a couple of tactical problems. I was tied up, in a dark trunk, in serious pain, and I had no idea where I was going. An hour, maybe two, passed, but I still didn't have a serious plan in place. I felt the car slow as it turned onto a bumpier road. The tires made crunching sounds. Gravel. My heart sank. There would be little hope of rescue now. I felt the car crunch off the rough gravel and onto pavement again. Each bump magnified the pain, but at least it kept me awake and aware. For that I was thankful.

God, if you want me to live, show me the way and give me the strength. If you're ready for me to come home, be with David and the boys. Protect and provide for them. Ease their grief and let them know how much I love them.

I could feel the spunk drain out of me the longer I stayed in the trunk. I was way past tears as I prayed, resigned now to the inevitable. I would watch for any possible chance to escape, and I would fight tooth and nail for my life, but reality told me I wouldn't make it.

My heart was ready to meet God, but I regretted that I'd never hold a grandchild, wouldn't get to know my youngest boys' life mates, wouldn't be able to snuggle in David's arms one last time. I'd had a good life on the whole, with the only major regret being not living it more fully, and of getting comfortable with my everyday existence and forgetting to change the world. A smile tugged at the corners of my mouth as I again remembered how certain David and I were that our love would conquer the world.

I have fought the good fight, I have finished the race, and I have kept the faith. The thought scuttled across my mind from somewhere deep inside. And with it came a bit of adrenaline. Maybe not much, but enough to get me moving. I groped around the floor of the trunk to feel something sharp enough to use as a weapon. I winced as the pain rolled merrily across the ridge of my shoulder. The pain made me mad. More determined. No time to give into fear. There was a fight to finish, a race to win, and faith to keep.

I crab-rolled inch-by-inch to every corner of the trunk. My hands fumbled onto a flat object with bristles on one end and a flat, sharper metal edge on the other end—an ice scraper. Maybe with a little effort, I could cut the tie that bound my hands.

Maneuvering the handle so the metal scraper was touching the tie, I seesawed the scraper back and forth, pressing down as sharp pain shot through my broken collarbone. I almost became numb to the pain with the rhythmic motion. Finally, I was rewarded with a snap of material as the tie ripped apart. Sapped of energy from the effort of freeing my hands, I lay still for a moment. Gently, painfully, I rubbed my arms. As the numbness in my arms decreased, my confidence in an escape increased.

Taking stock, I numbered my advantages. I was conscious, my hands were free, I had an ice scraper, my eyes had adjusted to the dark, and I had an immense desire to see my family again.

And that wasn't all. I had prayer, the element of surprise, and my head. Mom always said the Waymires were a hardheaded folk. *Think. Think. Use your head as a weapon.* My right arm and hand weren't of much use with a broken collarbone, but I still had my left arm. My legs were cramped, but otherwise unhurt. I could run like crazy if I had to.

Now to take stock of my disadvantages. No one, other than House and Rella, knew where I was, so there wasn't much hope of the Cliffhanger cavalry arriving on time. I had a broken collarbone; I was outnumbered two to one; I didn't have a sensible weapon; and I had no idea when the car would stop. My abductors had the advantage since I was lying in the trunk. Plus they had a burning desire not to get caught and nothing to lose by killing me. What's one more body in a long list of bodies?

Not the best odds, but not the worst either. I wasn't dead yet.

I don't know how much longer it was before the car started to slow down. I had no idea if I was still in Indiana, or if they'd crossed the state line. I felt the vehicle roll to a stop and wondered if this would be my chance of escape. My pulse quickened. I could hear my heartbeat. The smell of gasoline reduced my anxiety level. This was probably just a refueling stop, but I stayed alert and ready to bolt.

A wave of fatigue rolled through my bones like the tide rushing onto the beach. The car was in motion again, so I closed my eyes. I'd read somewhere that rest was as good a weapon as a gun or a knife. I didn't know about that, but I knew I needed to sleep if I was going to be able to have a chance of survival. I let myself relax and drift off.

CHAPTER THIRTY-SIX

Sunday

awoke with a start. Something was wrong. The car was no longer moving. I scuttled as far back into the trunk as possible and strained my ears for voices but heard none. Odd. Even with the engine and road noise, I'd heard the two of them talking. Their words had been muffled so I couldn't hear the actual words of the conversation, but I knew they were talking. Now? Nothing.

With pain and difficulty, I forced my arms behind me. Time to put my escape plan into action. I braced my back against the rear of the trunk, and pulled my knees tight to my chest. I was as ready as I was going to be.

Slam your foot into his nose like he's a punching bag. No mercy. Hit hard. Hit fast. Make him bleed. Make his eyes water. Fight the good fight. Steady your back against the rear of the trunk. My mind swirled with the mantra, repeating it over and over again.

The trunk opened, and my eyes immediately responded to the light. Although not bright, it was better than total darkness. I tried to look through my eyelashes without obvious squinting. I could see House standing outside the trunk. No Rella in my line of sight. House aimed a pistol—two-handed—at my chest. I didn't move a muscle.

"Get out."

I stayed still. My heart hammered against my ribs.

"I said get out . . . *now!*"

I didn't reply, didn't move. *Please God, help.*

"I am *not* going to mess up this trunk with you. Now get out." The barked words were impatient, angry, and full of hate.

I didn't move, didn't breathe. Sweat trickled down my neck.

Exasperation, frustration, and impatience caused Philip House to make his first mistake. He set the revolver on the fender and leaned as far as he could into the trunk. He reached for a handful of my hair, prepared to drag me out if I wouldn't come willingly.

Thunk. The sound of my feet meeting his nose was a sickening crunch of bone and cartilage. Blood exploded out of his face. He reeled back screaming. I lunged forward, and with my good arm grabbed the gun off the fender. House staggered and fell to his knees.

I glanced at the surroundings, keeping the gun pointed at House. My arm was shaking, but I don't think House noticed with all the blood in his eyes. As far as I could tell, we were in a wooded area with no human population. There was a Forest Service Porta-Potty about a hundred yards away. I guessed Rella was taking care of business.

I slithered out of the trunk, gun held firmly in hand, my right arm now virtually useless. House was on his knees, holding a white hankie up to his face, swaying back and forth. His second mistake. He should have recovered quicker. Running the three steps to his position, I raised the gun, and holding the barrel brought the butt down on the back of his head with every bit of force I had. He slumped to the ground, his bloody nose forgotten.

I backed to the car, keeping my eyes on the Porta-Potty and House. I was breathing hard and wanted to throw up. I looked in the front driver's door window for keys. None. Rella must have taken them with her to the privy.

For half a second, I considered the possibility of ambushing Rella when she came out of the bathroom. Dumb idea. I'd gotten lucky with House, but Rella was the seasoned killer of the two. House had only killed one person. Rella had killed many— in a variety of ways, all brilliant. All with the express purpose of keeping Craig lonely. Rella was insane, and insanity was far more dangerous than anything I'd run up against. No, flight was still the best option and I didn't have time to waste.

I dropped to the ground and snaked my way into the woods. It was early morning, I guessed. House must have stopped here off the beaten path for Rella to use the facilities. Or maybe this was where he was going to kill me, and the bathroom was just an added bonus. The sun hadn't come up yet, but I was careful to stay in the underbrush. I couldn't risk making noise. Rella would be out of the bathroom in seconds. Watching the ground for twigs, leaves, and other noisemakers, I crept slowly between brush and trees.

I heard the Porta-Potty door slam shut. An angry roar broke the stillness. Rella had found the empty trunk and the unconscious House.

Hunkering down behind a tall pine, I held my breath.

Expletives flew thick and fast in the air. The trunk slammed shut.

Something dropped on my neck. A pine beetle? Spider? I couldn't risk brushing it off. It inched its way slowly into my hair.

Muffled sounds emanated from the direction of the car.

I slowly brought the gun level to my chest, my arm resting on my knee for support. The index finger of my left hand touched the trigger. Not sure I could hit anything, I waited, prepared to do what I needed to do.

Silence.

It was unfortunate that it was my right collarbone that was broken. The gun was too heavy to hold with my disabled right hand. I doubted I would hit the broad side of a barn with my left, but hopefully, Rella wouldn't figure that out. I inspected the gun. It was not the gun Rella had poked in my face earlier tonight—not the one she'd used on Tim. *Must not be a .22 caliber.*

Zeb, the gun expert in our family, had schooled me on every type of rifle, shotgun, and pistol there was. I hadn't been particularly interested in guns. I'd listened, though, because I was interested in everything my kids loved. I'd learned all sorts of interesting tidbits that added together didn't mean much, but on various occasions, I was able to surprise people with my trivia knowledge. For instance, I knew a .22 caliber was lightweight and deadly close up, but didn't have the heft or thick barrel this gun had. I might be holding a .44 or .38 caliber.

I wasn't sure and didn't care. I didn't want to have to use the gun, but I would do what it took to finish well. It would be important to David and the boys to know I fought to the finish.

I heard an engine roar to life. Hope returned.

Maybe Rella thought I would take the open road to escape. That would be stupid. No, she must be taking House to the hospital or at least to civilization.

I waited as the sound of the engine whine diminished to nothingness.

Time to act. I stood up slowly and brushed off whatever was making a home in my hair, not wanting to know. I was sticky wet from earth crawling, so I removed my blouse and slip. I almost laughed. If Abigail could only see me now, what advice she would have. No shoes, no slip, no shirt—just undies, a tank top, and a revolver. What all the best-dressed minister's wives were wearing this year.

Creeping slowly through the foliage as if eggshells covered the forest floor, I retraced my path. The privy came into view, and I noticed the gaping door. Except for a dull splotch of red where House fell, nothing. Drag marks stretched from the blood to where the passenger door would have been if the car had stayed put. I was thankful Rella had taken the time to save House.

I had no idea how far away I was from any help. Giving the unused execution site a cursory look, I started walking. Rella's tire tracks should lead to a main road.

My throat ached for water. The ride in the trunk and the fight with House had expended a lot of my energy and sweat. Hoping to hear a creek, I stopped to listen for the sound of running water. I heard none. I kept walking.

The logging road I was on turned onto a wider country road. Wherever this was, I had to hand it to House. It looked like a great place to leave a body. Totally deserted, totally away from civilization. I shoved sweat-soaked bangs away from my forehead and kept walking. The lush vegetation suggested water, but I didn't see any. The rains must have fallen heavily in April to produce such thick green plants.

"Well, Sister Thornbush, how would you get out of this mess?" I said out loud.

"*I wouldn't be in this mess, dearie. I wouldn't be chasing all over the country trying to find some murderer. No sir, I would be home praying, or baking dinner for some sick soul, or cleaning the Lord's house. I wouldn't be gallivanting all over the world looking to do God's job. He says vengeance is His, you know.*"

I could actually hear the disapproval familiar to Abigail's tongue.

I licked my dry lips and thought perhaps Abigail had a point. I was in way over my head. But certainly there was more to the pastor's wife's life than staying at home, praying, baking, and cleaning. Not that those things were bad. They weren't, but I had a brain too. Surely it couldn't be wrong to use it?

Caught up in the imaginary conversation with Thornbush, I almost missed the sudden onslaught of footsteps behind me, but not quite. I jerked sideways, but dropped the gun.

The tree limb Rella swung at me smashed into the ground, jarring her arms. Not giving her time to recover, I kicked her in the side, knocking her back into a tree. All reasoning long gone, Rella screamed in rage and charged.

The impact knocked me off my feet, and Rella fell on top of me. We rolled over and over, each trying to gain the advantage. She put her hands around my throat and started to squeeze. Using my good left hand, I reached up and grabbed the little finger on the hand clawing my neck. I bent it back with all the strength I had left. No mercy, no grace. Fight the good fight. I heard a pop, followed by a scream.

Rella let go of my throat and grabbed her hand. Her pinkie was broken. I shoved her off and sat up. I grabbed her broken finger and twisted hard. She screamed again, trying to pull my hand away.

I held on. With my right hand I scrabbled in the dirt and foliage feeling for a rock. I found one. Forcing myself to withstand the pain, I picked it up, swung a wide arc with my arm, and smashed the rock into Rella's head. Her body went limp.

Adrenaline surged through me. I felt Rella's neck for a pulse. Beating. Good. Pulling off my tank top, I twisted Rella's arms behind her back and tied her wrists together. I snatched her shoes off her feet and put them on mine. A bit too big, but my feet were already bloody from walking, and at this point, I wasn't picky.

Black-eyed, broken, and scantily clad, I looked for the main road.

I walked out of the woods to find a convenience store less than two miles from where Rella lay bound and unconscious. It was 4:00 a.m. on Sunday morning. The car I had spent many an unhappy hour in was parked in front of the store. I approached slowly. Looking in the window I saw no sign of House.

The convenience store clerk looked like she was seeing a ghost. No, not a ghost, just a pastor's wife in bra and panties.

"I just called an ambulance an hour ago for a gentleman who looked in bad shape. You look worse. Can I help you?"

"I need a phone and some clothes. No ambulance. That guy you sent to the hospital tried to kill me."

The clerk took off her smock and handed it to me. "I really don't have any other clothes here. Sorry. You can use the store phone."

I called Scott. The police van took less than two hours to arrive. The remaining bunch of Cliffhangers rode in the vehicle. Looking at my friends, I broke down and cried. Rachel held me. Tough old Billy gave me his jacket, and Todd gently picked me up in both arms and carried me out to the van.

I finally caught my breath and looked at Shawn. Taking a deep breath, I tried to find healing words as I told him about his insane wife.

EPILOGUE

I t didn't take a grand jury long to indict Rella on several counts of murder, while House faced one murder charge and one of attempted murder. Billy covered the story and received a huge promotion.

Rachel stayed in Anderson with her mom. Craig asked her out, and they are now dating. Shawn resigned as ambassador to Israel and brought his little girl back to Indiana so she can visit her mom at the Indiana State Prison. He accepts who Rella is and what she has done, but he still loves her. He will not forsake her. Todd continues to farm. Scott is still doing the cop thing.

For about fifteen minutes I was an instant sensation, but declined interviews with all the major networks. Headlines read: Pastor's Wife Solves 30-Year-Old Murder and Jamie Storm Stops Serial Killer With a Prayer. I flew home as planned. It has taken David some time to accept the fact that he wasn't there to protect me and still isn't used to the fact that we are now millionaires.

The boys tease me, calling me Ramboette, but they recount the story to their friends every chance they get. Their pride warms my heart.

The Stewarts wrote a note of thanks for helping them find closure . . . and justice.

And me? I signed up at a gym and started working out after my collarbone healed. I can run a mile and a half now. I'm not winning any speed records, but I feel a hint of personal pride after each run. David and I settled uneasily into our old routine. I need time to sort out my feelings and put my life back into perspective.

◆◆◆◆◆

October

The timer ticked away noisily, reminding me that I had fifteen minutes before the macaroni, sausage, and cheese casserole would be finished. The rest of the meal—fudge brownies, fresh-cut veggies, orange fluff salad, and a loaf of garlic bread—was already boxed up in the fridge. Tom and Sue Wilkenson would be bringing their baby home from the hospital today, and I was first on the list to deliver a meal. It would give me a good chance to welcome little Natasha into the world . . . and get out of the house.

My life had slowed down to a crawl after my adventures with the Cliffhangers, and I was bored. So all activities, church-related or not, were welcome. The timer seemed to be ticking—patience . . . patience . . . patience. I stuck my tongue out at it. It didn't change its cadence. I was restless, eager to get going, so if the timer wasn't going to cooperate, I would just ignore it. I wiped down the counters again, straightened the junk drawer, and nearly leaped out of my skin when the doorbell rang.

The timer still had ten minutes left of merciless ticking. I tossed the dishrag over the faucet and went to the front door. I burst out laughing. Hats in hands, badges prominently displayed, officers McCready and Johnson stood on the porch trying, without success, to look all business. In reality they looked like two overgrown children, trying to wheedle their way out of punishment.

"What can I do for you guys?"

"The captain wondered if you might want to come down to the station," McCready said.

"Come down to the station?" Was this some kind of joke?

"It's nothing serious, ma'am," Johnson said, quick to allay any fears on my part.

"Go on."

"The Great Falls Police Department is opening a new division. The captain wants to talk to you about being a part of it."

I felt my pulse quicken and my interest level ratchet up a notch. "What do I know about police work?"

"I don't think he cares about what you know, it's about what you do."

"What do I do?"

"According to newspaper accounts and all the major networks, you crack old, hard-to-solve cases. He wants to talk to you about the corner of our basement that holds case files full of unsolved murders. Cold cases. Cases we don't have enough resources to work on."

I stood there motionless. My insides jumped around like live wires. This sounded too good to be true. Like the dream of a lifetime. A job, solving mysteries?

"Where do I sign?" I said. My voice sounded giddy with excitement.

"The problem is, the department doesn't have the budget to pay more than part-time," McCready said.

"Money, schmoney," I said in my most adult-like voice.

McCready and Johnson visibly relaxed.

"Give me five seconds." I raced to the kitchen, turned off the oven, kissed the timer, pumped my fist in the air a couple of times, then sedately walked back into the entryway, grabbed my Bears jacket off the hook, and smiled.

"Let's go meet the boss, boys."

ACKNOWLEDGMENTS

I love the alone time writing affords me, however, there are many people to thank who have contributed immensely.

Thanks to Jeannine Marjerrison—Mom—who passed her love of reading down to me and took us kids to the library without fail every other week. To the writers of those books who took a little girl to unbelievable worlds.

To the Plains Public Library that provided the small community with the best variety of books possible. My insatiable love for words was filled by you.

To Ron Rude, teacher, mentor, and encourager who gave all the students he taught a chance to be more than they believed they could be.

To Karen Alexander who spends her days teaching at-risk kids how to read, the most important job in the world, and who never lost faith in my writing. You are a pretty good beta reader also.

To Jeanne Cook and Norma Beishir for writing advice, to Phil Walrod for allowing me to write at work, to Kelly and Gordon for being perfect, to Doris, my favorite sister and beta reader, to Neil, Jerry, Tuck, Jimmy, and Brian who I love dearly, and to all the other encouragers who said I could write. Thank you.

To the staff at Deep River Books for the chance to see a dream realized. And to editor Barbara Scott. You are the best.

To the J.O.Y. group—what would I do without you? And for the study *Greater* for encouraging me to keep digging ditches.

And to God for doing what You do best—saving lives, creating beauty, gifting humans with your love—and for Your immense grace.

To my family who puts up with me day in and day out. I love you John. Thanks for doing all the work while I have fun. Muncher, Randa-Kay, Kinlee, Nebraska, Ethon, Cheryl, McKayla, Levi, Janice, Shaylin, and Xander—I love you. You guys make colors brighter, sun shinier, and life more livable.

ABOUT THE AUTHOR

 Carole Morden was raised in a log cabin that her uncles and her dad built in 1936, in the Cabinet range of the Rocky Mountains of Montana. The town of Plains was five miles from the cabin, and she looked forward to the family's two weekly trips into town—one on Sunday for church, the other on Monday to go to the library.

Carole is now a pastor's wife, living in St. Louis, Missouri. She has worked as a retail manager, administrative assistant, engraver, tree farm worker, disc jockey, and hair salon manager—all of which created active backdrops for her imagination. Carole and her pastor husband, John, have three sons and five grandchildren. She loves spending time with family, reading, and writing.

Connect with Carole:

facebook.com/JamieStormNovels

carolemorden@gmail.com